SONS OF THE SADDLE

William MacLeod Raine, hailed in his later years by reviewers and contemporaries alike to be the "greatest living practitioner" of the genre and the "dean of Westerns," was born in London, England in 1871. Upon the death of his mother, Raine emigrated with his father to Arkansas in the United States where he was raised. He attended Sarcey College in Arkansas and received his Bachelor's degree from Oberlin College in 1894. After graduation, Raine traveled throughout the American West, taking odd jobs on ranches. He was troubled in his early years by a lung ailment that was eventually diagnosed as tuberculosis. He moved to Denver, Colorado in hopes that his health would improve, and worked as a reporter and editorial writer for a number of newspapers. He began writing Western short stories for the magazine market. His first Western novel was *Wyoming* (Dillingham, 1908), that proved so popular with readers that it was serialized in the first issues of Street & Smith's Western Story Magazine when that publication was launched in 1919. During World War I, Raine's Western fiction was so popular among British readers that 500,000 copies of his books were distributed among British troops. By his own admission, Raine concentrated on character in his Westerns. "I'm not very strong on plot. Some of my writing friends say you have to have the plot all laid out before you start. I don't see it that way. If you have it all laid out, your characters can't develop naturally as the story unfolds. Sometimes there's someone you start out as a minor character. By the time you're through, he's the major character of the book. I like to preside over it all, but to let the book do its own growing." It would appear that because of this focus on character Raine's stories have stood the test of time better than those of some of his contemporaries. It was his intimate knowledge of the American West that provides verisimilitude to all of his stories, whether in a large sense such as the booming industries of the West or the cruelties of nature—a flood in *Ironheart* (1923), blizzards in *Ridgway of Montana* (1909) and *The Yukon Trail* (1917), a fire in *Gunsight Pass* (1921). It is perhaps Raine's love of the West of his youth, the place and the people where there existed the "fine free feeling of man as an individual," glimmering in the pages of his books that will warrant the attention of readers always.

SONS OF THE SADDLE

William MacLeod Raine

GUNSMOKE

First published in the UK by Hodder and Stoughton

This hardback edition 2012
by AudioGO Ltd
by arrangement with
Golden West Literary Agency

ISBN 978 1 445 88697 8

British Library Cataloguing in Publication Data available.

Printed and bound in Great Britain by
MPG Books Group Limited

1. Karen Meets Number 43211

THE light of opalescent dawn was streaming across the silvery sage. In this early morning atmosphere the bleakness of the desert lay under a veil of mist thinning before the sun. Against a background of castle buttes Karen glimpsed green splashes of palo verde and prickly pear. The girl drew a deep breath of delight. She loved this wonderful effect of space and light, the cloud skeins in a sky of Arizona blue drawn out as by some invisible hand.

Karen was keenly alive to natural beauty. The wind in the pines, sunlight sparkling on the waves of a breeze-swept lake, set emotions strumming. When the world was too urgent or when the pressure of little people disturbed, she could always find peace in open spaces. That was why she had spent the night at the Bar B B.

The roadster ran up the brown road ribbon to a little hilltop and passed a man on foot. He did not try to thumb a ride, but moved to one side without looking back to see who was coming. Karen wanted to offer him a lift, but she knew it was not wise ever to pick up a hitch-hiker.

The car ran down the incline, took another rise, and dipped again. The wheel dragged to the left.

Karen got out, glanced at the flat, and said 'Damn!' She did not stand around and look helpless but set to work at once. From beneath the seat she dragged out tools and coveralls. Into the latter she wriggled swiftly, then got down in the dust and set the jack. In spite of her slenderness she was muscular. She raised the car, then loosened the lugs and took off the wheel. It was a dirty job. Dust and grease covered her brown forearms. The gloves she wore were entirely ruined.

She rolled the wheel to the rear and brought back in place of it the spare. This she found it difficult to fit into the right position, for the jack had slipped and lowered the axle. While she was working at it the pedestrian topped the hill and drew nearer. He was carrying his coat. Karen saw that he was a tall man, wide at the shoulders and narrow at the hips. By his walk she judged that hard muscles packed the framework of the body.

'Please, I can't seem to manage this,' she said, smiling at him. 'If you wouldn't mind helping me——'

To her smile he responded not at all. His grim face did not lighten. But he moved forward and appraised the job.

'Got to block the car,' he said. 'Bring me some of those flat rocks.'

5

He built a support under the axle, reset the jack more securely, and again raised the car. His brown, unscarred hands moved with no lost effort. The wrists were supple, and the flesh of the arms rippled as smoothly as steel pistons.

But the arresting quality of the man lay in his face. The bone structure was strong, the expression harsh and bitter. Karen guessed his age as twenty-eight or thirty, but it was plain he had gone through years of hell.

He replaced the wheel and tightened the lugs, after which he put the tools under the seat.

'Awf'lly good of you to help me,' Karen said. 'I don't know whether I could have done it alone . . . If you are going to Barranca I can give you a lift.'

'Much obliged,' he said curtly, and followed her into the roadster.

Karen drove fast, with the confident assurance of the younger generation. The valley through which the car passed was bounded by red mesas freakishly eroded to fantastic shapes. Cholla and greasewood fled to the rear. A grove of saguaros, old and desicated, stood out on a rocky hillside. A gray mass of color, agitated like a sea wave, moved out of a wash toward a corral fenced with brush and mesquite roots, in which were long shallow feed troughs and flat-roofed sheds. Behind the flock of sheep were a Mexican boy and his dog.

'We need rain,' Karen said at last, to make conversation.

'Yes,' he agreed.

Karen grinned. That line had dried up promptly. Her good Samaritan evidently was not garrulous.

Presently she tried again. 'The road is full of chuck holes. They don't take care of it because money has been appropriated for a paved one.'

Since this called for no answer, he made none. There was distinct discourtesy, she thought, in his taciturn refusal to join in the amenity of casual talk. But it might be diffidence. She gave him the benefit of the doubt.

'My name is Karen Gilbert.'

His strong lean head swung round sharply. She knew the cold, gray eyes were appraising her, with no friendliness. The name had struck some chord of memory in him.

'Perhaps you know my uncle—Lyn Gilbert of the Bar B B,' she added.

He said, with curt hostility, 'I knew him, once.'

Many men had known Lyn Gilbert to their sorrow. Always he had been a hard man, with no pity in his bowels. Nesters had homesteaded water holes his cattle used, and he had harried them from their homes by various means inside and outside of the law. If necessary, his riders had torn down

6

their fences, trampled crops, fired houses. In the end the invaders had to go. There were whispered rumors that the one or two who were too stubborn to leave had found graves in dry gulches under piles of rubble.

Was this man one of his victims? The edge of Karen's curiosity was keen. Her feeling toward her unfriendly passenger was resentment, but back of it was an interest few strangers had aroused in her. It was the combination of bitterness and strength in him that fascinated her. In spite of his comparative youth he had gone a long way in life and found it not good, yet if she read aright the grimness of the deep-set eyes, so rigorously restraining an imprisoned fire, there was in him a quality so vital that nothing less than death could defeat it. What manner of man was he? What experiences had given him a disillusion saved from despair only by the stark fighting force in him?

'Since introductions are going,' he said, 'I've been known for eight years as Number 43211, kindness of Lyn Gilbert and his foreman Curt Ford.'

The girl was startled. His challenge hit her like a blow in the face. 'I—I'm sorry,' she murmured, aware of the inadequacy of her words.

'Tell Lyn I'm back,' he went on, and his mouth might have been a steel trap. 'Gordon Stone, back with two years off for good behavior.' There was a sardonic jeer in the voice at the explanation so out of harmony with the obvious banked violence in him.

'Was it trouble over homesteading land?' Karen asked.

'Any talking about it I do will be to Lyn and his gang,' he answered bleakly.

They were passing the suburbs of the town and in front of them they could see the brick office buildings and the stores of the main streets.

'Where can I drop you?' Karen said.

'Anywhere.'

'I'll stop in front of the Kenworthy Hotel.'

He stepped out of the car. 'Thanks for the buggy ride,' he said, his face drained of expression. 'I'll be thanking Lyn later for the one he gave me.'

As Karen put in the clutch she saw the released convict turn and walk into the hotel. She had intended to go straight home. A golf appointment at ten was on her schedule, and after that a luncheon at the country club. Before either of these she had to bathe, dress, and make arrangements for a dinner she was giving at the house next day.

But this man was very much in her thoughts. She knew she could not get him out of her mind until she found out more about him. Since she was by nature impulsive, she

7

moved to direct action. From the leading retail street she crossed to the financial one. In front of the Gilbert Building she parked, went inside, and left the elevator at the third floor.

The office which she entered was occupied by a middle-aged spinsterish woman busily engaged with a typewriter and by a small, slim man of about thirty. The man had a soft, pretty face with a chin just a trifle too indefinite. The features were small. Something about them suggested that he was sly and secretive. His rather fishy eyes lit up at sight of Karen, and he came forward with a smile a little too unguentary.

'A great pleasure, I'm sure, Miss Gilbert,' he said, and stroked his neat black mustache. 'Your presence brightens the —er—busy marts of commerce.'

'Is my uncle in?' Karen asked bluntly.

She was aware that Edgar Firkins admired her, and it always gave her an uncomfortable feeling to meet him. Since she was a little spoiled by reason of her good looks and her social position, she expected deference from young men and would have been disappointed if she did not get it. But she classified her uncle's secretary as a kind of human spider. She did not want him crawling around where she would have to step on or over him.

Firkins gave his hands a dry wash while he considered her question. He was constitutionally incapable of being direct. If driven to an affirmative he did not say yes, but wrapped his answer in verbiage. He moved about his business surrounded by an air of conspiracy.

'You—er—wished to see your uncle, Miss Gilbert?'

'I asked if he is in.'

'My impression is that—well, unless he stepped out——'

Karen walked to the inner door, knocked on it, and walked into a private office.

An immense man slumped in a large easy chair looked up at her with no sign of recognition. He had a curious resemblance to a rhinoceros. It was not only that his skin was leathery and hung in folds heavily wrinkled, that his gross body huddled into a shapeless mass. The eyes were small and beady, set in a face expressionless as an adobe wall.

'I just got in from your ranch,' Karen said. 'On the way I picked up a hiker.'

'You'll never learn sense,' he mentioned in a high falsetto. The squeaky voice coming from such a mountain of flesh was startling, it was so completely unexpected.

'He fixed a flat for me.' Karen brushed aside any discussion of her imprudence to make way for more important matters. 'He's just out of the penitentiary—been there for eight years.'

'Dear me! You pick such interesting friends, my love,' he mocked.

'Not one of yours,' she flashed back. 'He says you put him there, and incidentally he means to thank you personally for your kindness.'

The little tawny eyes fastened on her did not move. 'I've sent several scalawags to the pen in my time,' Gilbert said. 'For what was this guy convicted?'

'He didn't say,' she answered.

'Just confined his conversation to pleasant social topics— tennis, the next club dance, that sort of thing?'

'He didn't do any talking.'

'Outside of telling you he wanted to meet and thank me.' On the heel of his sneer he flung out a shrill question. 'Who is he? Did you find out?'

'Gordon Stone.'

Karen could not have said that the expression on her uncle's face changed, but a flicker of wariness seemed to film his eyes. The news might not be a shock, but it was a warning.

'So that killer is out—and back here?'

'Is he a killer? I'm not surprised. He looks . . . explosive.'

'He'll not explode long. I'll see to that.' His large, blank-wall face broke into a distorted, cruel grin.

Looking down at him, the girl felt a *scunner* run through her, to use a word she had picked up from her Scotch mother. There was a devil of destruction in him. Whoever stood in his way he would blot out of existence if necessary. It was not only that he had no moral sense. His callousness was combined with a terrible audacity that feared neither God nor man.

Her thoughts included not only this criminal Stone returned to life from a living death. She was herself within the orbit of Lyn Gilbert's plotting, a pawn to be used in his schemes regardless of her wishes or her happiness. She had not given up. She meant to fight. But there were appalling moments when she wondered whether she would be able to escape even in this free America. He was her guardian, and controlled the property left by her father. It made no difference that she was of age and had asked for an accounting, that she was independent of spirit and wanted to manage her own holdings. What she owned he held securely in his hands, even kept her ignorant of the value of the estate.

There were no illusions between them, no pretense of an affection that did not exist. Only his power over her held them together. Often rebellion churned in her, but always she recognized its futility. Of course she could walk out and leave her ranch and stock to him. It was an alternative she did not consider. She meant to stand up for her rights.

'Why did you send this man to prison?' Karen asked.

'You've mentioned the reason, my dear. He was explosive, to the point of danger—and a fool to boot.'

'I wouldn't say he is a fool,' the girl demurred. 'You mean he was in your way and wouldn't stand aside.'

He shrugged his massive, rounded shoulders. 'He was tried by a jury and convicted.'

'Of what?'

'Of murder.'

No doubt that was true. Her uncle did not tell lies likely to be discovered promptly. Given sufficient provocation, Gordon Stone looked capable of killing. There was in the man an urgent and compelling fire.

'Tell me about it,' she said. 'Who is this Stone? What did he mean when he said you sent him to the penitentiary? Whom did he kill? And why?'

'He's a nephew of old John Fleming. Always was a wild and turbulent devil. He killed and robbed a man named Brock after they had quarreled about a woman. He had been annoying me for quite some time before that, so I made it my business to see the law rounded him up.'

'You think he is here to make trouble?'

'Not if he knows what's good for him.'

'Perhaps he has come back to help his uncle,' she suggested, not without malice. Her uncle and Fleming had been enemies for half a lifetime.

'In which case I daresay he would have yore good wishes, my dear,' he grinned malevolently. 'But it's not that way. John cast him off when he went bad. If Stone wants grief he'll get plenty of it, but he'll have to play his hand without the old man.'

'Unless they make up.'

'I'll see they don't.'

'About this killing,' Karen continued. 'Was it a duel—a fair fight?'

'No. The evidence showed Stone lay back of some boulders by the roadside and shot his rival. Brock was carrying the payroll for the Little Bessie mine. The killer took that with him.'

Karen was disappointed. Her passenger had not seemed like a cold-blooded murderer. To shoot a man in the height of passion, both armed, was one thing; to lie in wait from ambush quite another.

'Circumstantial evidence?' she asked.

'An open and shut case against him. He made threats. The

10

killing was done with his gun. He was seen close to the spot, and they found some of the loot in his roll.'

Slender and erect, Karen stood frowning down at him, considering the facts. It would have been impossible to find any sign of kinship between his inert stolidity and her gracious vitality. The warm glow that beat through the olive skin of the girl, together with the light in the deep gray eyes, gave the lovely face extraordinary vividness. She looked as fine and spirited as a thoroughbred colt.

Suddenly she was sick of the whole business. They were a pretty pair, spewed up from the depth of hell, both her uncle and the convict.

She turned and walked out of the office.

2. Gordon Stone Picks Up Information

WALKING down Jefferson Street, Gordon Stone saw that there had been changes in Barranca during the years he had been shut up in prison. The dirt road had been replaced by pavement. The hitch racks and the false fronts of pioneer days were gone. Substantial brick store and office buildings lined the street, though some of the old frame ones remained.

He saw strange faces, as well as some he knew. Pete Milan sat at a cobbler's bench in the same little shop, no doubt still telling stories of his days in Cuba with Teddy's Rough Riders.

Stone opened the door and walked in. ' 'Lo, Pete,' he said.

The shoemaker stared at him, hammer in hand, 'Holy smoke, it's Gord Stone!' he exclaimed after a long inspection. 'You've sure changed.' Almost instantly he added: 'Glad to see you back. Shake, Gord.'

Milan's homely, puckered face registered pleasure. It was his opinion that young Stone had been given a raw deal, though he had been careful not to say so too publicly. Nor was he at all sure that it was a safe thing for the released convict to return to this part of the country. There was still trouble on the range, and it would be easy for him to be dragged into it if he were not careful.

The appearance of the man puzzled Milan. The Gordon Stone he had known had been a stringy, awkward youth, gay and happy-go-lucky, not differing essentially from fifty other cowpunchers of the neighborhood, but the years had transformed him into one compactly built and well muscled, with a lean, bitter face from which gray eyes looked out with steadfast assurance. Self-discipline had hammered him hard as steel. Road work had done the same for his body.

'Gonna be with us for a while?' the shoemaker asked.

'Yes.'

'Fine. You'll find things changed.'

11

'How?'

'Oh, I dunno.' Milan rubbed his bristly chin in search of an answer. 'Lyn Gilbert is top dog now. On the range, I mean. Some of his neighbors are still fighting him—Dave Landers, for instance, and yore uncle, old John Fleming—but he's got 'em whopped and they know it.'

Stone lifted a pair of resoled shoes from a chair and sat down.

'I'm listenin', Pete,' he said.

It was a long story, and its roots reached back into the days when Gilbert had homesteaded in the Kettle Hill country and started his herd with a few scrub longhorns. The fecundity of his cows had been amazing. The three or four small brands he had bought increased so fast that cowmen in the vicinity were moved to urgent protest. If Gilbert had not been a smooth, and at the same time a very tough, customer he would undoubtedly have been rubbed out. But he survived, and as his herds grew, became important in the region. The shoe was on the other foot now, and he led the cattlemen against the nesters taking up the water holes, and against the rustlers who lived in pockets of the mountains and raided the range.

Honest settlers of the Kettle Hills, even when in temporary alliance with him, resented the ruthlessness of the man. He was known to have shot down suspected cow thieves and looked for the evidence later. Back of him he had a turbulent, fighting bunch led by his foreman Curt Ford. None of this was news to Stone. He had been brought up so close to the Bar B B that the insolence and arrogance of its riders had fretted him as they had all outsiders with whom they had come in contact. He had shown fight, and in liquidating him they had wrecked his life.

Since Gordon had been out of the picture, Milan explained, the fight of the Bar B B had been less against the small hill men and more a campaign to destroy the cattlemen whose stock ranged the country needed by the increasing herds of Lyn Gilbert. The Kettle Hills had been settled at a time when there was free grass for all. The nearest land office was seventy-five miles distant, and the cowmen had been casual in acquiring ownership. There were flaws in some of their titles, and through dummies Gilbert had brought suits contesting ownership. The pressure of the Bar B B cattle, always dangerously imminent, steadily increased. As a result, several small ranchmen had thrown up their hands and sold out to Gilbert for a song.

'How about my uncle?' Stone asked.

'He's slipped bad since you left, Gord. The old man ain't got the fight in him he usta have. 'Course he thinks he has,

12

and he's so doggoned stubborn he'll never quit, but right now he's hemmed in so he doesn't know which way to turn. Lyn pulled his wires and took the government grazing permit above his place from Fleming. There's been a heap of trouble between them last year or two.'

'What kind of trouble?'

'Several kinds. Over grazing lands, for one thing. The old man claims Curt Ford has killed some of his cows and run off others. They had guns out onct, and one of the J F boys was wounded.'

'Dave Landers is in it too, you say.'

'They got him worried, all right. He's patched up some kind of truce with them, but it won't last. It will be Dave's turn after they get Fleming. The Kettle Hill stockmen haven't got a chance against Lyn. He runs the politics of the county, names and elects judges, picks the sheriff. What he says goes in this neck of the woods.'

'And if a fool is obstinate enough he can always be dry-gulched or shipped off to the penitentiary,' Stone said with cold bitterness.

Milan lowered his voice. 'Sh-sh! Not so loud. It pays to be careful what you say in this town. As regards the drygulch-ing, I wouldn't know about that.'

'Sounds like Russia, with Gilbert the czar . . . Have you seen Jack Turnbull lately?'

'It's been quite a spell. Jack's lying low just now. He got into trouble and wounded Buck Hayes in a fight. Buck is one of the Bar B B riders, so the sheriff is lookin' for Jack. By the way, Jack was workin' for yore uncle when he had the dif-ficulty. If you want to see him I wouldn't wonder but what they could tip you off where he's at down at Pratt's feed store. He hangs out there. At least he did.'

Stone rose. 'Much obliged, Pete. I'll be driftin'.'

'Watch yore step, son. You ain't exactly a favorite son with some of our citizens.' Milan hesitated, then went on with what he had thought of saying. 'You don't aim to get into any jam with the Bar B B crowd again, do you, Gord?' he asked, his face puckered into an anxious frown. 'Not buttin' in or anything, I'll say this. Don't let Lyn get a notion you're startin' in to buck him. He's our leading citizen now and re-spectable as the devil, but——'

'——but he'd just as soon have me bumped off as bat an eye if he could get away with it.'

'I didn't say any such thing,' Milan denied promptly. 'All I know is what I hear, an' probably half of that ain't so. Lyn subscribes to the churches and his name is at the head of every charity list. What I mean is, don't monkey with the buzz saw. Then you won't get hurt.'

13

'Has Curt Ford joined the church along with his boss?' Stone drawled.

'Curt is a rough character and always will be,' the shoemaker admitted. 'He'll fight at the drop of the hat.'

'But he has a heart of gold,' the other added, with a lift of the upper lip. 'I'll remember that, Pete.'

Milan's troubled gaze followed him down the street. This strong, grim man had come back to fight. He had no doubt of that, any more than he had that he was doomed to defeat. The combination against him was unbeatable. Gilbert had the support, not only of his hired warriors at the Bar B B, but also of the political ring of which he was boss. He could play it either way. Inside the law or outside it he could smash anybody who challenged his supremacy.

3. 'I'll Fix Yore Clock Later'

At Pratt's feed store several oldtimers were gathered for gossip. They sat back against an adobe wall in tilted chairs and discussed current events. Just now they were swapping yarns about the early days. They had reached an age when memories of the past were dear to them.

A man leaned against the door jamb and glanced scornfully over these survivors of frontier times. He was a large, thickbodied man with arrogant shoulders, flinty, shallow eyes, and brindle hair beginning to turn gray. The vest over the flannel shirt was open and the corduroy trousers disappeared at the bottom into cowboy boots. The harsh face, the open throat, the big hands were all brown as coffee.

'Listen to 'em, Buck,' he jeered. 'You'll learn all about how this country was when Copper Hill was a hole in the ground.'

Buck was a tall, thin slat of a man in overalls and Stetson hat. He had no eyebrows. An ugly scar from a knife slash disfigured the right cheek. His splenetic laughter applauded the big man. He knew his companion had no occasion to annoy these harmless old men, other than the compulsion of his disposition to be unpleasant and insulting whenever he could.

'Hope we're not boring you, Mr. Ford,' tartly retorted a little man with a face like a wrinkled winter pippin. 'Because if we are we'll get off the earth for you.'

A cackle of uncertain mirth followed this thrust. All of those present knew that Curt Ford was no safe object of derision.

'That'll be enough from you, Pinckney,' the big man ordered harshly.

Jasper Pinckney flushed. He was close to eighty, but in his time he fought Apaches and held his own in the rough and

14

tumble of the early days. Without shame he could not silently submit to this bully.

'I don't have to ask you when I can speak,' he said, 'I'm still wearin' man-sized boots.'

Ford strode up to the little man. His fingers closed and tightened on the scrawny shoulder close to the throat. The pain of that iron grip drove the blood from Pinckney's face.

A step sounded on the porch. Sharply a crisp voice said, 'Stop that, you scoundrel.'

The bully whirled. He was facing a lean-loined man who weighed about one hundred and seventy-five pounds. His eyes narrowed to shining slits of triumphant light. The fellow whoever he was, had delivered himself into his hands.

'You've bought cards, have you?' he asked, elated.

'I'm in,' the stranger answered.

A vague memory stirred in Ford. Where before had he seen that lean, strong-jawed face?

His teeth showed in a savage grin. 'You'll be out soon, fellow.'

One of the old men cried in startled recognition, 'Great guns, it's Gordon Stone!'

'By God, it is!' yelped Ford. 'The jailbird back with us again.'

He lashed out with his right, the weight of his heavy body back of the blow. Stone sidestepped, let the fist pass over his shoulder, and countered with a short, hard uppercut under the chin.

The old men scurried out of the way like startled hens, but they watched the fight eagerly from a safe distance. Ford was a notorious bruiser, recognized as the most formidable in the county. Moreover, he weighed thirty pounds more than his opponent. They were all for Stone, but felt sure he was in for a beating. That he had taken lessons of an ex-prize-fighter in prison and become an expert boxer they did not know. One purpose dominated his life, and to accomplish it he had to be strong in every way. Both brain and body he had kept fit.

Ford was a sledge-hammer slugger, with no rules except to hit the other fellow hard and often. He rushed, his arms going like flails. Stone backed, protecting himself, and landed three straight lefts to the face. Again Ford plunged at him, intending to close and wrestle him to the ground where he could beat the lighter man by sheer strength. Stone dropped him with a right to the jaw.

The foreman clambered to his feet and dived once more at his evasive foe. Hard fists played a tattoo on his bruised and bleeding face. Still he crowded forward. Stone gave ground— too far. His foot missed the floor and he went backward from the porch.

15

Ford gave a yell and leaped down, intending to land with boots on the stomach of his enemy. The ex-convict rolled aside, just in time, and was on his feet before the Bar B B man could seize him.

'Come on and fight, you prison scut!' roared Ford furiously. 'Stand up and take it.'

Stone did not answer in words. He feinted for the face with the left and sank a heavy right into the belly, then threw himself at the other, his shoulder striking against the chest of his antagonist. Ford stumbled back, tripped on the lowest porch step, and crashed down heavily. His head struck one of the posts. He lay motionless as a log.

'By golly, he did it!' one of the oldtimers shrieked joyously. 'Licked the everlastin' daylights outa him. Got Ford lying there cold. What you know about that, boys!'

'Look out, Gordon!' Pinckney shrieked. 'Fellow's gonna gun you.'

Gordon Stone turned swiftly. The man called Buck had his gun out and stood crouched, ready for action.

'So you come back from the pen and pick a fight soon as you reach town,' he said, the words dripping out venomously. 'You're through, fellow. It ain't safe to leave you alive.'

There was murder in his yellow eyes. A second time Pinckney's thin voice was raised in a shriek. 'Don't do it, Buck.'

'I'm unarmed,' Stone said, and dropped on his knees beside Ford.

From Buck's throat came the yell of the wild beast ready for the kill. 'That's right, fellow. Beg yore head off for the mercy you ain't a-going to git.'

Stone's trembling fingers found what they were seeking, the butt of the revolver projecting from its holster under Ford's arm. As the weapon came into sight Buck fired, startled into the knowledge that he had been trapped by the apparent terror of this stranger. He shot a second time, swiftly, wildly, then dropped the gun with an oath to clutch at his wrist. The .38 held by Stone had blazed at him once. That was enough.

'Push that gun my way with yore foot,' Stone ordered.

'You wouldn't kill me when I'm helpless,' Buck whined.

The face of the ex-convict was a blank map. 'Do as you're told.'

'I didn't really aim for to shoot you,' the Bar B B rider pleaded. 'I was only foolin' to scare you.'

With the slightest wrist movement Stone tilted the barrel of the revolver up. He said nothing.

'Don't!' cried Buck. 'I'll do like you say.'

With his foot he pushed the revolver on the ground toward his foe.

'Turn yore back.'

Begging desperately for his life, Buck did as he was told. Stone patted his body to make sure he had no other weapon.

'Get out of here,' he said quietly. 'On the jump.'

With an awkward lope, holding his wounded wrist, Buck fled up the street.

'Who is that man?' Stone asked.

'Name's Buck Hayes. One of Lyn Gilbert's Bar B B men. Got quite a rep as a gun-fighter.' Pinckney broke into a cackle of excited laughter. 'Gosh all hemlock, Gordon, you musta spent all yore time in—up where you been—learning how to tame bad men. You done mopped up two of the toughest hombres in this corner of the state.'

'Temporarily,' suggested somebody in the gathering crowd.

'That's right,' assented Pinckney. 'You better light a shuck outa here, young man. While the going's good, as they say.

'Why?' asked Stone, eyes like granite. 'I find this fellow Ford manhandling you, and when I protest he attacks me. I defend myself. The other ruffian tries to kill me. In self-defense I use Ford's gun, taking care not to kill the man. Why must I leave?'

'It's sure enough true, what you say,' agreed Pinckney. 'Still and all, I'd hit the trail.'

'I'm asking you why.'

There was a moment of awkward silence.

'Don't ask questions, mister,' a voice replied. 'Do like Mr. Pinckney says. Get out.'

A man with a doctor's bag pushed through the crowd. He was a plump, bustling little fellow.

'What's the matter with this man—shot?' he asked, stooping beside Ford.

'He got the tarnation stuffing whopped out of him,' one of the oldtimers explained gleefully. 'I reckon he hit his head when he was knocked down.'

The eyelids of the unconscious man flickered, then presently opened. Flashes of lightning obscured his vision, alternating with stabs of darkness.

'Where—what the hell——'

Remembrance pressed through the pain in the back of Ford's head.

'You've been hurt,' the doctor said. 'Don't exert yourself.'

The foreman swore. 'Hurt nothing.' He scrambled awkwardly up and leaned heavily against a porch post. Even then, the facts still not clear in his mind, the man's vanity flung out an excuse. 'He hit me with brass knucks.'

'Nothing of the kind,' Pinckney denied promptly. 'You jumped him, and he whipped you good with his fists.'

'That's a lie.' Ford put his hand to the back of his head and saw that it was covered with blood. 'I'll mosey along to the office with you, doc.' Bleakly his cold, shallow eyes rested on Stone. 'I'll fix yore clock later, you damn convict.'

'I'll try to be there when you do,' Stone said quietly, his voice low and clear.

Public comment was stilled until Ford was out of range. Then it broke out in excited clamor.

'If that don't beat the Dutch. I never saw the like of it . . . Cleaned up on both of those bully-puss warriors, by jinks . . . He's got to light a shuck, Stone has, right damn now, or else . . . Wisht we had a few more citizens would stand up to these hired rowdies.'

Stone drew Pinckney to one side.

'I'm lookin' for Jack Turnbull. Fellow told me I might get news of him at the feed store here. Can you find out for me where he is?'

'Might,' the wrinkled little man admitted. 'I'll ask Shattuck here. He's kin to Jack.'

Pinckney consulted another of the chair-warmers. They whispered together for a couple of minutes, then called to Stone to join them.

'I reckon you know Jack's in trouble,' Shattuck said. 'The sheriff has orders to arrest him for shootin' up this same Buck Hayes about a month ago.'

'I heard that,' Stone nodded.

'If you was anyone else I wouldn't tell where Jack is holed up, but today's rumpus cinches it that you're not kowtowing to Gilbert.'

'That was settled nearly nine years ago when he and his crowd framed me for murder,' the young man answered coldly.

'Well, Jack is staying in the old cabin at Three Pines back of Landers Ranch. When you show up on the mesa, give a yell, then get off yore horse and get on again. He'll know you're a friend.'

'Much obliged.'

'You ain't asked for any advice, so I'll give some anyhow. Soon as you see Jack you and he beat it outa this country together. Go some place far away for yore health.'

Stone had nothing to say to that.

4. Karen Asks Questions

AFTER dinner Karen was in the living-room writing a letter. She had decorated and furnished the room herself, made it an expression of her personality. The large alcove window of leaded panes was filled with potted plants. From two wall brackets ivies drooped. A rosebush burst with blooms. The Bokhara rugs, the upholstery of the comfortable chairs, the warm tone of the harmonious room, lent accent to the vivid charm of the girl.

Her uncle seldom sat down in it, so that she was surprised when he came in and settled himself heavily in the largest chair. She did not look round. If he had anything to say to her he would let her know.

He did not speak. His big frame slumped down. Not the least motion disturbed its relaxed ease. Lyn Gilbert's mind was busy with the problem of Gordon Stone. The returned convict had served notice of war and had struck the first blow. That he had scored an initial success was of no importance. Was his presence a bluff? Or had the man cards up his sleeve that made him dangerous? What did he know that could spell trouble? Even as a boy young Stone had been a menace. It was because Gilbert recognized the force of his indomitable stubbornness that he had got rid of him. Would it be better to rub him out now, finally, before the fellow got into action? There could be no profit for the owner of the Bar B B in having the matter of the Brock killing stirred up again. There might be decided loss.

The logic of his callous reasoning drove him to the inevitable decision. He would destroy the man and play safe.

From Gilbert's two hundred and eighty pounds of bulk came a squeaky falsetto. 'Well, your friend has started playin' hell already.'

Karen stopped writing, half turned her head, and asked, 'What friend?'

'The name is Gordon Stone,' her uncle said.

'Did he *say* he was my friend?'

'I haven't talked with him—yet. I'm giving him the benefit of the doubt.'

The girl turned in her chair, putting her arms on the back of it. 'What has he been doing?'

'Fixing it so he'll go back to the penitentiary—or the graveyard.'

'If it's one of them I don't think it will be the penitentiary,' Karen said thoughtfully. 'D'you mind giving me a bill of particulars?'

'He met Curt Ford and Buck Hayes down at Pratt's store and attacked them. Hayes he shot. Ford he beat up terribly.'

'You mean he—killed Buck Hayes.'

'Fortunately, no. Shot him in the arm.'

'Well, he picked on two sweet and gentle apostles of light,' Karen contributed blandly. 'Any particular reason for this maniacal outbreak?'

'I suppose he came back intending to get even with Curt, who was a witness against him at his trial and afterward married the girl he had been courting.'

'Oh, it's the dramatic finale of a romantic episode. The plot thickens. You know, I wouldn't have picked Glenna Ford for the heroine of so thrilling a melodrama. She's pretty, in a placid way. But hasn't she a good deal of—avoirdupois?'

'She's a fat cow,' Gilbert put it bluntly. 'But she was not bulky when Curt married her. She was slim as you are . . . And don't make the mistake of thinking this little affair is over. If Stone wants war, he can have plenty of it. And right damn now.'

He hoisted his massive frame out of the big chair and shuffled toward the door. There he stopped to tell her he was going to the ranch and would not get back that night.

After he had gone Karen sat at the desk, no longer writing. Her mind was occupied with thoughts of this stranger who had come back from prison. There was no reason why she should take an interest in him. He had repelled her casual friendliness, even before he knew she was the niece of Lyn Gilbert. Evidently he had learned nothing from the punishment he had endured, but was again ready to embark on evil ways. Yet, when she recalled his lean, clean build, the direct, searching eyes, the unconquered look of him, it was impossible for her to dismiss him as a criminal and an assassin. The appearance of a man could not so belie him.

She returned to her writing, but in a few minutes pushed away the pen. Her uncle had said the trouble was at Pratt's feed store. Old Jasper Pinckney, the grandfather of her friend Rhoda, spent a good deal of his time there. Impulsively she decided to find out from him just what had occurred.

Her uncle had taken the car. There was not in those days a two-car family in Barranca. She walked to the little house in the suburbs where the oldtimer and his wife lived.

They were sitting in the living-room before an open fire. It was spring, but the evenings were cool. Both of them wore slippers. Jasper was without a coat, as in the old days when he had been a cattleman.

Mrs. Pinckney was a round, chirpy little person who emanated good will. She fussed around her guest until the girl was comfortably seated. They talked for a few minutes about the weather and Rhoda and whatever else came to mind. Then, abruptly, Karen began to tell them about the man who had changed the wheel of her car and ridden to town with her. When she named him, Jasper let out an exclamation, 'Gosh all hemlock!'

'You know him?' Karen asked.

He said he did.

'There was trouble down at Pratt's feed store today. Were you there when it took place?' the girl continued.

'Sure was, and I wouldn't of missed it for a hay farm.'

'Will you tell me just what took place?'

Jasper told her.

'Then this Gordon Stone wasn't to blame at all,' she commented, more pleased at what she had heard than she would have thought possible.

'He ought to be give a medal,' the old man said in his high voice. 'Any man who would knock down the ears of those two bully-puss scoundrels had orter have a vote of thanks from the town.'

'But Stone is a bad man, isn't he? I've been told he was sent to prison for cold-blooded murder and robbery.'

'No such a thing,' Jasper denied. 'I mean he's no bad man. Never was. A mite wild. That's all.'

Mrs. Pinckney offered a mild correction. 'I liked him. Most everybody did. He was one of those high-spirited boys who laughed a lot and made fun. But I must say, Jas, he was more than a mite wild. That boy was a case.'

'But he was convicted of murder and sent to prison,' Karen insisted. She wanted information.

'What of it?' Jasper exploded. 'There were those who wanted him out of the way. Quite a few of us never were satisfied he killed Harrison Brock.'

'But the evidence——'

'——sure made it look bad for Gordon. He was sewed up in a sack so he couldn't twist out anyway.'

'Well, then——'

Jasper leaned forward and tapped her knee. His excited voice broke. 'Point is, it was too durned neat. Somebody sewed that sack up—maybe.'

'You mean—my uncle?'

'I ain't sayin' who I mean,' the old man answered doggedly. 'But Gord Stone isn't a fool. If he'd taken the Little Bessie payroll he wouldn't of left a lot of the money in his roll, would he?'

'It wasn't all found there, then?'

'No. I don't recollect how much. About a fifth of it, I'd say.'

There was something that did not ring true about this, Karen thought. Why would Stone leave some of the money there and not all of it? She raised the question aloud.

'Gordon claimed it was a plant,' explained Pinckney. 'Looks thataway to me too. The fellow who stole the money kept the bulk of it and used the rest to fix the guilt on the boy.'

'The rest of the money never was found?'

'No.'

'Was nobody except Stone ever suspected?'

'Well—suspicion ain't evidence,' the old cattleman said warily.

It was quite evident he did not intend to name anybody.

21

'What worries me is that Gordon is heading for trouble again sure as God made little apples,' he said. 'If I knew anyone who had any influence with him I'd sure want them to tell him to light out of here before it is too late.'

Karen was of that opinion too, much more urgently than her scant acquaintance with the man justified. She told herself that if he was innocent she did not want him to fall a victim of her uncle's plotting a second time. In her bosom there was a warm glow of joy, for she now had no doubt that he was not guilty. Evidence was not necessary. She had looked into his face and knew.

He must be saved in spite of himself. But how? As she walked home, moving lightly and swiftly with the buoyancy of perfect health, her mind was full of the problem. Old Jasper had told her Stone was looking for Jack Turnbull, who was lying low back of the Landers Ranch. She wondered if it would be possible to reach him through Jack, and if so what she could say that would have any weight with him. It was written in his salient jaw, in the cool steadiness of his level eyes, that he was a determined man not to be moved from any course upon which he had set himself. She had no arguments new to him, nor was she of any importance in his scheme of life.

Restlessly she paced her room, snatched into a stress of emotion quite unaccountable. He had set the seal on his own destruction. Her uncle and his allies would wipe him out. Was he mad, not to know that he could not drag in the dust the vanity of Buck Hayes and Curt Ford?

Curt Ford! The thought of him sent her mind off at another tangent. He had been a witness against the young man at his trial. Later he had married Glenna—after Harrison Brock had been killed and Gordon Stone was in the penitentiary. She stopped abruptly, eyes shining, lissom body rigid. His two rivals for the hand of Glenna destroyed at one blow. How damnably pat! What a fortunate coincidence for Ford, unless . . .

She stepped to the telephone and rang a number.

'That you, Hal?' The girl's voice was low.

The answer came, 'Yes.'

'Karen Gilbert speaking. Are you willing to compromise your reputation for me?'

'Any place, any time,' he replied. 'Because of course yours will be compromised too, and you'll have to marry me.'

'Don't be too sure about that. Hal, I want to go into the country and uncle has the car. Can you take me? I'd rather nobody would know, because we'll be out practically all night.'

'Can I take you? Girl, I'll crank my flivver and be round before you can say Jack Robinson twice backwards.'

Karen hung up. For a moment she stood in hesitation. This was probably a crazy business, with no rhyme nor reason in it. There was still time to draw back.

She brushed doubt aside. No, she would carry on.

5. Gilbert Whispers

GLENNA FORD opened the door to Gilbert's knock. She was a pretty woman who had let herself go and seemed to be bursting out of her clothes. Her blonde hair was unkempt.

'I'm glad you've come, Mr. Gilbert,' she said. 'Curt fell from a horse and got kicked.'

'Where is he?' the ranch owner asked.

'Upstairs—lying down. He got a nasty cut. It's a mercy he wasn't killed. I always told him that roan stallion——'

'I'll go see him.' The big man brushed past her and waddled up to the second story.

Glenna followed. She called to her husband. 'Mr. Gilbert to see you, Curt.'

The foreman lay on the bed. He had not taken the trouble to remove his muddy boots. Sulkily he looked across at his boss.

'I hear the roan stallion kicked you, so I came to commiserate,' Gilbert said, a titter of derision in his falsetto voice.

'Get out of here,' Ford ordered his wife.

'I thought maybe——'

'Did you hear me?' he roared. 'Get out!'

She scuttled away without a word.

Gilbert shut the door. 'I hear Stone showed you and Hayes up proper,' he jeered. 'All Barranca is talkin' about it.'

The foreman ripped out a furious oath. 'I slipped and hit my head. If any liar says anything else——'

'Too bad another story seems to have got around. If anyone asks me I'll tell him how it was.'

'No need to tell 'em a thing. My gun will do what talking is necessary.'

The Bar B B owner observed Ford's damaged face with malicious interest. A bandage was tied around the head, but the cut and bruised cheeks, the swollen lips, and the discolored eyes were in evidence. He sat down ponderously close to the bed, where he could enjoy the spectacle.

'He certainly worked you over good, Curt.' Gilbert's fat belly shook with mirth which did not show on his leathery face. 'While you were slipping he must have been right busy.'

'I can beat that jailbird any day of the week,' boasted the man on the bed angrily.

23

'Any day but Wednesday,' corrected the other. 'That doesn't seem to be your lucky day. My, you look a sight! Probably you stumbled on a ripsaw when you slipped.'

'Don't worry about how I look. Take a squint at him when he's on the slab after I've poured bullets into him.'

'If, as, and when.'

'What's eatin' you, Lyn?' Ford slammed a big fist down on the bedspread. 'I'm on to yore sly fox ways. You've got something on yore chest. Unload it—or get out.'

'Loaded to the hocks with hospitality,' Gilbert murmured. 'Here I've driven thirty miles to sympathize with you, because you slipped, and you're handing me my hat.'

'You heard me,' the foreman told his boss.

Gilbert leaned forward, his little eyes gimleted on Ford. He asked a question softly, spacing his words. 'Whyfor d'you reckon Stone came back?'

'You tell me,' snarled Ford. 'You're smart as fresh paint and know everything. Why did he come?'

'He sent me a message before he reached Barranca. What he came for was to square accounts with his old friend Curt Ford.'

'Sent a message how?'

'By my niece. He fixed a tire for her and she gave him a lift to town.'

'How could he square accounts? Bump me off—that what he means?'

'I don't think so, but you never can tell. My guess is he's hoping to land you in the pen.'

'How could he do that?' the foreman demanded impatiently.

'He couldn't unless——'

'Not a chance. What can he know now that he didn't know eight years ago when he was fighting to save his neck? You're always figuring out something in that wise head of yours, and half the time there's nothing to it.'

'But sometimes I figure out a way to send another guy to the pen instead of you,' Gilbert said, almost in a murmur.

'Just what was this message he sent you?'

'He said he'd come back to thank you personally for sending him by perjury to prison. I'll bet he enjoyed making a small payment on account today in public.'

Ford cursed, savagely. His employer watched him, ready to feed the man's rage if necessary, to bolster the fear he had awakened.

'What d'you want me to do?' asked the foreman sulkily.

'Not a thing. Why should I care what you do?'

'Don't pull that on me. You've got something in yore nut. What is it?'

Gilbert rose, tiptoed to the door, and opened it suddenly. He left it ajar, so that he could see into the hall.

'What's the big idea?' growled his host.

'Only that I've known women with a large bump of curiosity.'

'Not Glenna, in regard to my business.' Ford showed his teeth in an evil grin. 'I knocked that out of her long ago. Well, shoot yore stuff.'

'I was only thinking that if I were you I'd get the jump on him,' the owner of the Bar B B whispered. 'He's dangerous.'

'To me or to you?' jeered the foreman.

'To you. I'm not in it.'

'Are you trying to fool yoreself or me, Lyn? Who robbed him of the little ranch his dad left him? Who pulled the wires that sent him to the pen? What you want, as usual, is for another guy to do yore dirty work.'

The ranch owner shook his head reproachfully. 'You're too suspicious, Curt. I come out all the way to the Bar B B to help you, because we've stood together all these years, and you can't allow me a decent human motive.'

'What d'you mean we've stood together? Sure, I've pulled off some raw deals for you—while you were making about a million dollars and I wasn't making a red cent.'

'You blow your money, Curt. I save mine. But no need going into that. We're giving this convict too much weight, very likely. As you say, he hasn't a thing on you, unless he happens to find out this and that and put them together. Maybe he'll be satisfied to drop the whole thing now that he has knocked you out and got everybody convinced he's a better fighter than you. Well, I'll be drifting back to town.'

Gilbert picked his hat from the bed and rose.

'Sit down,' snapped the majordomo.

'Better stick around the ranch for a couple of weeks till your face is healed up, so folks won't laugh at you. I'll check up on Stone and give you warning to duck if it looks like he's going to jump you again.'

'Sit down, you old devil!' shouted Ford. 'I ain't scared of any man alive, and you know it, let alone this scalawag from prison. I'm gonna settle his hash—and soon.'

The big body of Gilbert lost shape as he sat down. 'If you're hell-bent on that, Curt, you want to figure out just how you're going to do it,' he said, his voice so low it barely reached the other. 'You don't want any comeback. It's got to be sure and secret, or sure and open so you can call it self-defense.'

'I don't aim to give him first crack at me, if that's what you mean,' blurted out the man lying on the bed.

25

'No. He's got to be tricked. We'll find a way. I've already thought of something.'

Giblert leaned forward and whispered into his foreman's ear.

6. Hoofs Drum in the Night

KAREN waited on the porch for Hal Ferguson, and when he drove up walked out to the gate to meet him. The young man helped her into the roadster and took the seat beside her.

'Where away, lady fair?' he asked.

'To the Landers Ranch.'

If Ferguson was surprised he did not show it. He was a freckle-faced, homely lad, with a gay and friendly manner. One of his many good points, as Karen saw him, was that he did not always want to be making love. Quick to take his cue, he could fit into any mood. It was a reasonable guess that the charms of a good many girls had found lodgment in his eyes, but none permanently in his heart.

He did not ask her why she wanted to go to the Scissors Ranch. In good time, when she wanted to tell him, he would find out. Without a word he let in the clutch and started.

It was pleasant to drive through the velvet night, the wind of travel stinging them. Karen leaned back, silently, until they had covered eight or ten miles.

'You'll likely think I'm doing a crazy thing, Hal,' she said at last.

He turned, to smile at her. 'I like people who can do crazy things,' he answered. His voice was steady, light, cheerful.

The girl's fingers gave his muscular forearm a little pressure. 'You are the only man I know that I could have asked to bring me,' she said gratefully. 'You're an understanding sort of hairpin.'

'Thanks for them kind words.'

She told him of her meeting with Stone and of her talks with her uncle and with Jasper Pinckney. Only once he interrupted.

'I remember when he was tried. Though I was only a kid I managed to sneak into the courthouse the day the jury brought in its verdict. Of course I didn't for a moment suppose he was innocent, but I liked the way the fellow took it. The sentence was for first-degree murder—death. Later the governor commuted it. Stone stood there, chin up, and never batted an eye. He was going to his death unafraid. You could hear a sort of sob run through the room.'

She nodded. 'Yes, he would be like that. There's something invincible in him, as though somehow he could snatch victory out of defeat. What I'm afraid of, Hal, is that he doesn't

26

know what he's up against. Before he had been back here two hours, he had made enemies of two of the most dangerous men I have ever known. Add to them my uncle, with his sly, unscrupulous cruelty and the great power he wields, and you have a combination not to be beaten. I want to tell him what he has to fight.'

His keen, sky-blue eyes rested on the girl. He did not know any other like her. Karen did everything with high spirit, seemed to throb with life like a meadow-lark in song. Her dark beauty was tempered like a Damascus blade. A fine girl, but with the worldly wisdom to appraise a scoundrel and keep her own counsel.

'I didn't know you were on to Lyn Gilbert,' he said. 'First time you ever gave me a hint of it.'

'He's my uncle,' she said simply. 'But I found him out years ago. I'm one of the pawns in his game, you know. I'm not going to let him destroy this man if I can help it.'

'How can you help it?'

'I can warn him, at least.' She added, with a flare of passionate resentment: 'They've done enough to him. Mrs. Pinckley says he was a nice, gay boy, full of laughter and jokes. I don't believe he could even smile now, except in bitterness. He's a hard, grim man, with lips like a steel trap, all the joy in life frozen out of him.'

His boyish face lit up. He could almost feel the heat running through her lithe brown body, and he loved her for the generosity that flamed up in her so gallantly.

'So you're enlisted for the length of the war,' he said.

The laughter which bubbled from her soft throat was at herself. 'He won't have a thing to do with me. You'll see. He'll be very rude and practically tell me to mind my own business.'

They left the main road and followed a country one that wound into the hills. Presently they came to a fork.

'Right or left?' he asked.

'I'm not sure. One of them must lead to the Scissors Ranch. We don't want that one. Let's try the right.'

The moon was a thin, crescent silver, outlined without substance. Numberless stars filled the sky, but the light in them died down before it reached the earth. Out of the denser shadows cholla and mesquite stood vaguely as they passed. The road was definitely reaching for the uplands now, either taking the grades directly or circling the hills. Ahead of them the shadows of the higher slopes darkened the land. The road had narrowed to a single track, upon which the chaparral encroached so closely that greasewood and Spanish bayonet slashed at the wheels.

'We'll be down to a cow trail soon,' Karen suggested. 'Yes.'

27

The driver stopped, letting the engine idle. 'Think we're headed right?'

'Listen.'

The girl sat rigid, every sense alert. To them came the drumming of hoofs, the faint murmur of voices. Hal switched off the engine and the lights. Evidently some kind of trail intercepted the road thirty or forty yards in front of them.

A rider emerged from the mesquite and drew up on the road. A second and a third joined them. They discussed which way to go. There was a slight difference of opinion. One of them laughed.

Karen felt something sinister in this sudden emergence of night riders out of the darkness. From where had they come? On what nefarious errand were they going? The blood pumped faster through her veins. Blurred though objects were in the night, one of the group would pick up the car presently if his horse shifted its position. She did not think of it at the time, but she recalled later that the slight breeze filled her nostrils with the aromatic scent of sage. Hal's fingers found her wrist and tightened on it. She did not know whether it was her pulse or his that beat so wildly.

From the group of riders a sudden cry rang. An outstretched arm pointed toward the car. The horsemen vanished, melted into the brush.

Instantly young Ferguson shouted a 'Hello!' He did not want these men to think they were enemies. 'We've lost our way,' he added.

Somebody well back in the chaparral answered, 'Who are you?'

'Hal Ferguson and Miss Gilbert.'

Horses moved in the mesquite, breaking a way through the brush. A voice warned, 'Don't make a mistake, or we'll drill holes through you.'

Karen spoke, to reassure them. 'There are only two of us. Mr. Ferguson isn't armed.'

A sorrel horse crashed past clumps of prickly pear to the road. Swiftly its rider took in the two in the car and called to his companions.

'All right, boys.'

'We're looking for the Landers Ranch,' Karen said.

'Then you've missed the road. You should have taken the other fork back about a mile.'

'We weren't sure. Where does this one go?'

The girl asked the question casually, but the man addressed took his time to answer. He was a heavy-set, squat puncher known as Cheyenne. He rode for her uncle.

'Takes to an old cow camp,' he said. 'One not used any more.'

28

'I don't understand why you spoke of shooting holes in us,' Karen said sharply. 'Is that what my uncle pays you for?'

The challenge took the men aback. One of them laughed a little, embarrassed.

'Sho, Miss Gilbert, don't get us wrong,' he said. 'We don't go around harming young ladies, let alone you.'

'But other innocent travelers are fair game,' she suggested.

Cheyenne explained. 'We're on the lookout for a pair of outlaws—killers. So we didn't want any funny business. When you spoke of course we knew it was all right.'

'Who are these bad men?'

'One of 'em is a convict just back from the state pen. Fellow called Stone. The other shot up one of our boys.'

'And the sheriff has sworn you in as deputies to arrest them?'

'Well—you might put it thataway.'

'You don't think they'll murder us if we meet them?'

'Not unless they've got the jumps and are goosey. I'd holler right out and tell them who you are.'

'Perhaps you'd ride back with us as far as the fork,' Karen said. 'I'd feel safer.'

'All right. We're in some hurry, but—— Well, let's get going, Miss Gilbert.'

Hal found an open place in the brush and turned the car.

'You're not afraid of Stone and Jack Turnbull, are you?' he asked the girl.

'Of course not. I'm trying to delay these fellows. They must have heard that Jack and this man Stone are lying hidden at the cabin back of the Landers Ranch. We met them as they were on their way to attack. My uncle and his foreman Ford probably arranged it tonight.'

'May be so. But I don't get the point, Karen. Soon as they leave us they'll head right back.'

'Yes, but not down the road. They were crossing it. I should think the idea was to get at the cabin from the rear unexpectedly.'

'Look here, girl. You have some crazy plan in your nut. What is it?'

'We're going to wait a little, so they will have time to get out of hearing. Then we'll run down the road and get to the cabin before they do.'

'No,' he protested. 'If there's going to be trouble I'm not going to drive you into the thick of it. I dare say you're guessing wild about what these fellows mean to do. But say you're right. That means fighting around the cabin, which is no place for you.'

Cheyenne drew up beside the car. 'All right, Miss Gilbert.

Here's the fork. If I was you I'd head for home. It's late. Time you get to the Scissors everybody will be in bed.'

'I expect you are correct about that,' Karen said. 'Thanks for seeing us this far. 'Night.'

Ferguson started toward town. The car had gone about a quarter of a mile when Karen spoke.

'Here's a good place to turn, Hal.'

'We're going to Barranca,' he told her.

'Maybe you are. I'm not.' She turned the engine switch off. The car slowed to a halt. 'Nothing doing,' Hal said. 'Sorry, Karen, but your idea is out.'

'So am I,' she retorted, and swiftly opened the door and stepped to the road. 'Good night, Hal. Thanks for the ride.'

'You can't do that!' he cried.

Karen started back down the road. The young man watched her for a few moments, then turned the car. He ran alongside her.

'Get in,' he snapped.

She looked up and smiled pleasantly. 'Oh, are you going my way?'

'Seems I am, though I think you're crazy.'

'We started out to save those boys, didn't we, Hal?'

'All right. All right. You're bossing the show. I'll take a shot at it, since I'm dealing with such a stubborn little devil. Hop in, young fellow. This way to the war.'

She rejoined him. He kept the car at low speed, to make as little noise as possible. When they came to a hill he shut off the motor and coasted down.

'Suppose they are on the road,' he said. 'What do we do?'

'Keep going. They'll have to get off it. Knowing who I am, they won't dare shoot. It will be the same way when we get to the cabin. There won't be any war.'

At the foot of the hill Hal turned on the engine switch again. He had been running without lights, but with the brush hemming in the narrow road so closely he no longer found it feasible to do this. In any case, they must be beyond the horsemen by this time. He speeded up a little, taking the jolts of the chuck holes as best he could.

A valley opened before them, a pool of darkness into which the trail dropped rather sharply. It occurred to Ferguson that if the road pinched out on them they might wander all night without finding the little cabin they were seeking. And it was apparent that they might easily lose the thin, traveled track, since they were on a slope of rubble not hemmed in by the chaparral. Wagon or car wheels would leave few marks in the ground-up disintegrated granite.

Halfway down the incline he stopped, to sweep with his eyes the blur of night in front of them. A breeze beat faintly

30

out of the west and brought with it the murmur of pines on the ridge to the right.

'Country seems filled with absentees,' he said. 'Lady, can you tell me where your friend the convict is holed up? Or do we just cruise around till we don't find him?'

'Haven't the least idea, but it can't be far.' She stopped, her gaze caught at attention. 'Isn't that a light?'

He followed her pointing finger. 'Nothing else but,' he agreed. 'We're on our way.'

The car crunched down through the gravel.

'Whoever is there can hear us for a half a mile,' Karen mentioned. 'Hope they are not what Cheyenne calls goosey. Too bad if they shoot first and ask questions later.'

Hal grinned across at the girl. 'If you've got any last words——'

Out of the night a voice hailed them. 'Who's there?'

'Friends,' Hal called back; and Karen mentioned their names.

'Get out and stand in front of the car lights,' the voice said curtly.

They slid out and showed themselves.

7. In a Jam

OUT of the shadows Gordon Stone moved.

'Miss Gilbert came to warn you,' Ferguson answered.

'Of what?'

The voice of the convict was sharp as a pistol shot.

'Maybe she'd better tell you herself,' Hal said quietly.

Stone looked at Karen, waiting for her to explain. She discovered that she had nothing to say. All she could tell him was what he knew already. He had powerful enemies in her uncle and Ford. Upon his return he had lost no time in challenging them both and in profoundly humiliating one. For surplusage he had added another foe to the list, a man whispered to be a sly and treacherous killer. But this was no news to him, any more than it would be news that they were plotting to destroy him.

'We came to let you know you are in danger,' she said lamely.

His sardonic smile mocked her. 'Did you hire a detective to find that out?' he drawled.

'My uncle says if you want war you can have plenty of it.'

'And sent you to tell me so?'

'No. He doesn't know I'm here. When he's ready to strike he won't warn you.'

'I've had that notion myself. I see you know yore fine old relative. And, by the way, just why did you come, outside

31

of wanting to let me in on this secret of old Lyn's kind intentions toward me?'

Another man stepped into the fan-shaped shaft of light made by the car. He was a young, broad-shouldered man in shiny leather chaps and gray flannel shirt. His warm smile was a certificate of friendliness.

'Go easy, Gord,' he suggested. 'Miss Karen came outa the goodness of her heart. She doesn't need any letter of introduction from the President to tell me that. I'm kinda in this, since the willing lads of the Bar B B are lookin' for me too. I say thanks, and plenty of 'em.'

Karen nodded at Turnbull. 'You always were a gentleman, Jack.'

'That's fine,' Stone said coolly. 'Now it's understood to begin with that I'm no gentleman I don't have to make a good impression.'

'You don't even have to be decent to a girl who faced danger to try to help you,' Hal said, flushing angrily.

Stone lifted his eyebrows. 'Danger?' he repeated.

'That's the word I used. We were stopped coming here by three men who told us not to move unless we wanted to be shot into rag dolls.'

'Where?' snapped Stone. 'When?'

'Back there on the road less than half an hour ago.'

'What three men?' asked Turnbull.

'They were Bar B B riders. One of them was the man called Cheyenne.'

The hunted men looked at each other.

'They must have found out we're here,' the cowboy said. 'I wonder how.'

Gordon Stone stabbed a question at Karen. 'How did *you* find out we were staying at this cabin?'

'One of your friends thought you might be here. He knew I didn't mean to harm you.'

With four quick strides Stone stepped to the car and shut off the lights.

'These men let you come through?' he questioned.

'No. We pretended to head for town, then slipped back without lights.'

'Lucky for us you did,' Turnbull acknowledged. 'If we hadn't been warned, they would likely have trapped us.'

'We'll have to move fast, Jack—up the cañon, I reckon,' Stone decided. 'If you'll rope and saddle our mounts, I'll roll up our war sacks.'

'What about—our friends?' the other fugitive inquired, nodding toward Karen.

'We'll see them to the Scissors Ranch. They'll be all right there.'

The man's coldness, his failure to respond to the generosity that had brought her and Hal here, stirred the anger of the girl. 'Why bother about us?' she flung at him, a cool lash of sarcasm in her voice, fires gleaming in her fine eyes. 'We won't trouble you, thanks just the same.'

Stone paid no attention to what she had said. 'That road up the hill leads to the Landers place,' he said to Ferguson. 'Take the car up it far as the cottonwoods. If you hear firing, make for the ranch. If you don't, wait till we show up, providing it's not more than twenty minutes. I'll give an owl's hoot, to let you know who we are.'

The hot color glowing beneath her olive skin, Karen looked at this man's harsh face, so drained of expression, so empty of emotion. She resented the hard indifference with which he ignored her, the finality of judgment that made decisions for her with or without her consent. Yet she had no choice but to obey, since there was probably wisdom in what he planned.

Abruptly she turned and walked to the car. Turnbull followed her.

He said, with some embarrassment: 'If we don't see you again soon, Miss Karen, I want you to know we're mighty grateful to you and Hal.'

She lifted her eyebrows. 'Did your friend ask you to speak for him too?'

Jack lowered his voice. 'Gord has had a right bad break, ma'am. After all he's been through he hasn't got used to the idea yet that the world is full of mighty kind people. He's been shut up in a grave for eight years, his mind poisoned with thoughts of revenge and full of hate. We—we got to make allowances.'

'You're a good friend, Jack,' the girl said, and gave him her hand impulsively.

'We rode the range together and slept under the same blanket,' the cowboy said simply. 'I know him. He's the salt of the earth.'

'Only the salt has lost its savor,' she added.

'Give him time and he'll beat back all right. He's got to learn to forget.'

'And to forgive.'

'That's easy to say, Miss Karen, but I don't reckon I would forgive in his place. Anyhow, it doesn't look like he'll get a chance, the way things are workin' out. We didn't choose to be outlaws. It has been forced on us unjustly.'

'I know,' Karen said gently. 'I was annoyed at him, but it's all over with now. I hope you both have golden luck, Jack. Remember that lots of us are on your side.'

He left, to wrangle the horses. Hal drove the car up the

33

road that led to the Scissors Ranch. They traveled slowly, since they went without lights. It was a wagon-road of a sort, one upon which to bring supplies to the outlying camp, but it was unlikely a car had been over it before. Big rocks jolted the wheels and saplings tore at the radiator and the fenders. The grade was so steep that it had to be taken in low.

Darkness hemmed them in like a heavy fog. What lay ahead of them was a blur of shadows. Once Hal got off the road and had to back onto it again.

'Swell for the car,' the boy said cheerfully.

Karen peered into the gloom. 'Trees just ahead, to the left,' she told her companion.

They were the cottonwoods Stone had mentioned, at the mouth of a ravine cutting down to the hill. Hal turned on his dim lights and left the trail-road to park in an open space among the trees. They had not been there five minutes when a sound brought them both to sharp attention. It came from above. Horsemen were riding along the ridge.

Both of them realized at once that this must be a support party for the attackers. Evidently the outlaws in the cabin were to be taken on two sides.

'We've got to go back and let our friends know,' Karen said.

He assented, without words, by starting the engine and swinging the car round. The automobile plunged down the rocky road, lights on full. Back of them they heard a shout. The blast of a gun reached them above the noise of the rattling car.

Hal drove as fast as he could with reasonable safety. Faint yells pursued them. The bumping of the car was so violent that Karen clung to the seat to keep from being thrown out. A tire blew out. They kept going.

'We're down!' Hal cried.

He jumped to the ground. Karen was already flying forward to meet the two shadowy horsemen advancing toward them.

'They've cut us off from the Scissors Ranch!' she cried. 'They're coming down the road now, some of them.'

Jack Turnbull laughed, grimly. 'They're pushing our backs to the wall, looks like.'

'Where do we go from here?' Hal asked. 'We can't let them start shooting, if that's what they mean to do, while Karen is here.'

'That's what they mean to do,' the cowpuncher said. 'The Bar B B wouldn't be interested in taking us prisoners.'

'Let's get in the cabin,' Karen suggested. 'Soon as they find I'm here, they can't attack it.'

'How will they find you are there?' Hal wanted to know. 'In time to do any good?'

'They wouldn't,' Stone said harshly. 'Soon as they show up, they'll start blasting at it, no questions asked. No, it's the cañon for us. All four.'

'We blew a tire,' Hal explained.

'You couldn't take a car up there anyhow,' Turnbull said. 'It's one of those climbs where you hang on by yore eyebrows . . . Let's go.'

Stone brought his horse up to Karen. She looked at him, half minded to say that she could walk as well as he.

'Get on,' he ordered.

'You're the one they are after, not I,' she told him.

He did not argue the matter. There was no time for that. He picked her up and flung her astride the saddle, with no regard whatever for her indignation or for the stretch of silk-clad shapely leg exposed to view.

'We'll be on our way,' he ordered curtly.

On his bay gelding Turnbull led the party. Karen followed. She was furious, but her anger did not blot out the anxiety which flooded her. They must get away . . . at once . . . before they were trapped by the enemy.

Already pounding horses were debouching into the valley. They could hear calls and answering shouts. The party which had come down from the direction of the Scissors Ranch had apparently formed a junction with the group led by Cheyenne.

'Looks like they've done lit out!' an excited voice cried.

'Must be headin' for the cañon,' another guessed. 'No other way for them to get clear of us.'

Stone said, to those with him, 'Ride like the heel flies were after you.'

'And what about you and Hal?' Karen asked.

'Do as you are told,' he snarled at her. To young Ferguson he gave instructions: 'Stick close to them as you can. I'll hold these fellows back for a while.'

'If I had a gun,' the young man began.

'Can't you understand plain English?' Stone snapped. 'I said for you to light out after yore friends. I'll be along later.'

Hal turned into the cañon. He could hear the hoofs of the two horses in front of him striking the rocks on the trail. The grade was stiff and rough. Sometimes the path dropped into the dry bed of a mountain stream filled with boulders.

Presently a blur seemed to come out of the darkness to meet him. It resolved itself into Karen and her horse. She had stopped and turned in the saddle, waiting for him.

'That you, Hal?' she cried softly, and a moment later flung at him the question urgent in her mind. 'What does he mean to do?'

35

'He's going to try to stand them off till we get a start.'

'But he can't. They are seven or eight to one. He must be crazy.'

'Maybe he'll slip away before they locate him.'

As if in derision of Hal's suggestion there came the sound of a shot, and almost before the echoes had died away the drumming of several guns in action.

Karen's heart hammered like that of a bird imprisoned in the hand. 'They have him trapped. He'll be shot. What can we do?'

Turnbull's voice came to them, a moment before he could be made out in the darkness.

'What's the matter? Why don't you keep coming?' he asked.

Anxiety trembled in Karen's answering words. 'You must have heard the shooting. They're . . . killing him.'

Another blast of gunfire roared up the cañon. Turnbull swung from the saddle.

'He's down in the rocks where they can't see him. I reckon he's okay, but I'll drift down and have a look-see. Take my bronc, Ferguson. Keep going till you reach the mesa above. There's a clump of live-oaks to the left. Pass through them. You'll come to a cattle trail that runs due west. In about a half mile it will dip down into an arroyo. Wait for us there.'

'Make him get away from those rocks and come up the cañon,' the girl urged. 'If he doesn't he'll be murdered.'

'Sure,' agreed Turnbull cheerfully. 'We'll beat it right up here. Don't you worry. Remember yore job is to keep right up the gulch. Be seeing you down at the arroyo soon.'

He vanished in the shadowy gloom of the gorge below.

All her life Karen had known stories of range warfare. Living as she did in the heart of a cattle country, she knew that the cow business always had been accompanied by lawlessness. This had been inevitable during frontier days from the nature of the occupation. A man's stock roamed the hills unguarded. Title of ownership could be changed by the simple process of touching up a brand with a running iron. A bunch of stock could be driven into some mountain fastness and slipped into a trail herd headed north. Legal right for a ranchman lay in his holster. If he were strong enough he held his own; if not, his property passed into the hands of more savage and ruthless fighters. But that had been in the early days. Law and order had come into the mesquite, except that stretch of it where her uncle still ruled by force and chicanery. Whispers of his evil deeds had come to her, but never before had Karen been brought into actual contact with the execution of them. The shock of it appalled her. To hear about trouble on the range was as distant as news of war in Manchuria. To think of the strong, virile body of Gordon Stone lying lax and lifeless was close as breathing.

'We can't go away and let them be killed,' she protested.

'Stone and Turnbull are running this show,' Hal answered. 'We've been given our orders. I'm not going to gum up the works by doing anything different. There's nothing I could do anyhow, since I'm not armed. We'll get going, Karen.'

Reluctantly she gave way, turning the head of her mount up the cañon.

8. Cheyenne Makes a Deal

JACK TURNBULL found the footing in the steep cañon treacherous. His high-heeled boots had not been built for rapid descent among rubble and rocks. But he was in a hurry, for he was more anxious about Gordon Stone than he had admitted to Karen. Three or four times a shot boomed out in the silence and came reverberating up the gulch. So far as this was news at all, it was good news. His enemies had not made an end of the many they were attacking.

Clouds scudded across the sky and blotted out the moon and most of the stars. There might be rain, but he thought it unlikely. There was no feel of it in the air.

A strong draft of wind told Jack that he was near the mouth of the cañon. He took shelter behind a boulder and called softly to his friend. No answer reached him. That might be because Stone had not heard, or it might be because he dared not risk letting the Bar B B men know his whereabouts. Cautiously Turnbull slipped forward, every sense keyed to alertness.

He was startled by the roar of a gun fired within fifty feet of him. After a few moments he called a second time. No reply came to him, but a scatter of pebbles fell close to him. Stone was warning him not to advertise their location.

On hands and knees the cowboy crept toward his friend. In a sibilant whisper he announced himself, just as he was edging around a boulder. His heart jumped. He had come face to face with another crawling man.

'Doctor Livingstone, I presume,' Stone murmured with a grim smile.

'You're not hurt?' Jack said quickly.

'I'm not. One of them yelped like he might be awhile ago. Where did you leave Miss Gilbert and Ferguson?'

'Halfway up the cañon. We're to meet them back of the live-oaks. She sent me down to bring you out of this.'

'Kind of her. But she's right at that. Time we were getting

37

scarce. They're moving nearer. About ready to rush the fort, I'd guess.'

A voice lifted across the darkness to them. 'Fellows, we're deputy sheriffs. One of us you've shot. That's hell enough for one night. We aim to dig you outa there. Better surrender while there's time.'

The muscular fingers of Stone pressed into the flesh of his companion's forearm. It was a silent suggestion not to betray their place of concealment. The warning was not necessary, for Turnbull was of the same opinion as his friend, that if they were captured neither of them would reach town alive. They would be killed, officially, while resisting arrest.

'We know you're there,' the voice continued. 'We're giving you a minute to come out with yore hands up.'

The allowed time passed. Those hidden in the rocks could hear men below arguing. Some of them apparently had no wish to charge the position. After all, they were only hired hands. Forty dollars a month, plus food and a bunkhouse, did not cover jobs as dangerous as this. It was one thing to drygulch a victim for a good cash bonus, but quite another to push to a finish a fight against desperate men protected by cover.

Swept away by the wind, the clouds no longer obscured the moon and stars. It was too light for the besieged to make a run for safety.

'We'll dig deeper into the rocks,' Stone said.

Crouching low, they moved back among the larger boulders.

Out of the murmur of voices one broke angrily. Jack recognized it as that of Cheyenne. 'By God, I'll go get 'em if I go alone.' Shortly after that the talk died down.

'They're on their way—some of 'em,' Stone whispered. 'Keep an eye over there to the left. I'll watch here. Don't shoot unless you are driven to it. They may make a bluff and quit without finding us.'

'Not Cheyenne,' Jack answered. 'He's a fighting fool.'

They waited, for what seemed a long time. Again clouds blotted out the moon and all but an occasional vagrant star. Out of the night, from below, bullets whistled past them two or three times. The trapped men guessed that these shots were fired to cover the stealthy approach of a storming party.

Somebody stumbled, fell, his weapon clattering against rocks as he went down. Instantly the darkness was alive with the sound of moving men. A blur of them took vague shape, then broke into units that scattered among the boulders. To Stone came a dribble of slipping rubble, faint and indefinite, made by feet moving with utmost caution. The report of the stalker's advance was intermittent. There were long moments

38

of silence, then again the stir of activity, closer to him than before. Stone made no least noise, but every nerve was taut, every muscle ready.

Slowly and warily a head came around the edge of the rock wall behind which the hunted men were crouched. A pair of bright eyes mirrored, for an instant, consternation. A hand carrying a .45 jerked upward. But the advantage of the surprise was with Stone. The barrel of his revolver crashed down on the head, and a heavy-set body lurched to the ground.

Jack joined his friend. 'Cheyenne,' he whispered.

Stone helped himself to his foe's weapon and made sure he carried no other. He dragged the squat figure of the cow-puncher back of the rock.

They had no rope with which to tie their captive. It occurred to Turnbull that they were like the hunter in the story who had caught a bear and called for help to turn it loose.

'What you aim to do with this bird?' he asked.

'Trade him to his friends. We give him back to them in exchange for a free pass out of the cañon.'

Cheyenne showed signs of returning consciousness. His heavy body stirred and his lids fluttered. Presently he opened his eyes and looked into a murky world filled with shooting stars. The fireworks died down and his vision cleared. He took his time to speak.

'You pistol-whipped me,' he charged.

'Right guess first time,' Stone told him curtly. 'You're in a jam.'

'You're in the jam, fellow. I got seven friends mav'rickin' around within call. If I give a yell——'

'You'll be buying a through ticket to hell. I'll bump you off the way I would any other wolf.'

Cheyenne was a tough and fearless scoundrel, a bull-necked, strong-jawed ruffian who did not fear any man alive. His hard eyes clashed with those of the man whose gun covered him. He read in them a cold, relentless quality that quelled insurgent impulses. The ex-convict was steel-strong. He would do exactly what he had threatened to do.

'Then there would be three of us traveling there together,' Cheyenne said coolly.

'With you leading the way.'

'You win,' Cheyenne said. 'I keep my trap shut and wait till the boys drift in and blow you off the map.'

'There's only one trouble about that—from your view-point,' Stone told him, drawling his words so that they seemed to drip out, icily cold. 'You wouldn't be here to enjoy the explosion. We put you out of business the instant your friends find us.'

Cheyenne chewed tobacco with a manner of hardy indifference. 'I'm damned if I do and I'm damned if I don't. I might as well yell.'

'There's an out for you if you want to take it. We're willing to swap your life for ours. Better make up your mind in a hurry. Any minute it may be too late. D'you want to be a dead lion or a live wolf?'

The Bar B B puncher's mind worked swiftly. Hard and stubborn though he was, he faced facts with realistic reasoning. These men would kill him if he stood out. They had nothing to gain by letting him go, if it came to a finish fight. What was the sense in playing a losing hand when he could toss it into the discard? It was not good enough. Fighting was Cheyenne's game. He was paid to do it, and he enjoyed earning his wages. But he had no intention of sacrificing himself for fifty dollars a month and food.

He grinned wryly. 'I've heard that the guy who fights and runs away will live to fight another day. What's the lay-out, Mr. Stone?'

'Quite simple. You and yore friends go down the cañon, Jack and I go up it.'

'Everybody happy,' added Turnbull.

The wall-eyed gaze of Cheyenne rested on Jack. 'Except Yorky, who is lying down below with one of yore bullets in his belly.'

'Not one of Jack's,' corrected Stone. 'He just got here. Now listen, fellow. You're to step out in front of this boulder and yell to the rest of the pack. Jack and I will keep you covered with our guns. The easiest way I know for you to commit suicide would be for you to try to run or to doublecross us in what you tell them. Get that fixed in yore mind.'

'I've got it. And I'll say this. When I make a bargain I don't rue back on it.'

'Fine. Don't yield to the temptation to make an exception of this time, because you never would again. You'll explain to the other wolves that you've been trapped and that the only way out for you is a trade. Your life for ours. They are to hotfoot it down the cañon and wait there till you arrive.'

'A swell out for you,' Cheyenne said, and eyed his captor with hardy defiance. 'But where do I get off? After the boys beat it down the cañon, you can pour lead into me and make a getaway. I say nix on that.'

'I'm setting the terms,' Stone said, his voice low and icy.

'Don't be a fool, Cheyenne,' Jack broke in. 'What good would it do us to gun you after we had promised to let you go? We'd be hunted down like coyotes. You know that. Besides, we've got nothing against you individually. You're just a poor sap pulling chestnuts outa the fire for Lyn Gilbert and

40

Curt Ford. Ask them for me why they don't do their own dirty work.'

'Hell, I'll play with you,' Cheyenne snarled. 'You've got the deadwood on me this time. Let's go.'

He rose unsteadily to his feet and walked out in front of the boulder. The other two kept their weapons trained on him.

'Say yore piece,' ordered Stone.

The squat puncher raised his heavy voice in a yell that could have been heard even at the mouth of the cañon.

'Listen, fellows. Cheyenne talkin'. These so-and-sos have took me prisoner. They aim to bump me off if we don't let 'em go. We couldn't dig them out anyhow without losing two-three men. For tonight this man hunt has bogged down. Can you hear me, Bill?'

'I can hear you,' a voice answered.

'And you, Webb?'

'Yep.'

'All you boys move on down to the mouth of the cañon and wait for me there. These scalawags have promised to turn me loose. If they don't, you know what to do about it later.'

'We sure do!' someone yelled.

The defenders could hear their enemies trooping down the trail. Stone waited until the sound of their footsteps had died away.

'We'll be going,' he said.

'Going where?' demanded Cheyenne. 'Are you aimin' to throw down on me?'

'No. But you're traveling up the cañon with us a few hundred yards,' Stone told him. 'I don't intend to have yore friends surging back up here until we're in the clear.'

The Bar B B puncher looked at him angrily. 'All right, Sure Shot. You're calling the turn now. But don't forget about that other day I mentioned awhile ago. You'll be hearin' from me. By yore own say-so, you shot Yorky.'

'Who was trying to murder me.'

'Who was a deputy sheriff sent to arrest you,' amended Cheyenne.

Turnbull had a word to say about that. 'You could get away with a cock-and-bull story like that if we didn't have witnesses. One of them, young Ferguson, a first-class young fellow not mixed up in this row; the other, Miss Karen, a niece of Lyn Gilbert.'

They climbed the steep path, Cheyenne in the van. Jack had tied a handkerchief around the man's wounded head, but he felt as if heavy hammers were pounding inside of it.

After a time Stone told the prisoner that he could go.

Cheyenne looked at him out of stony eyes. 'Don't forget that other day,' he warned.

An hour later Turnbull and Stone passed through the live-oaks into the arroyo back of the grove. Karen had been waiting anxiously, her heart heavy with dread. Every leaden minute had increased her distress. She had come to save them, but instead they had stayed in the cañon to face death that she might escape. If anything happened to them, if they were killed, she did not see how she could ever laugh and be gay again. Hal Ferguson had tried to comfort her with cheerful talk. Stone and Turnbull were hardy outdoor men, able to take care of themselves as well as anybody in the state. The night was dark. They would avail themselves of the cover of brush and rocks. Soon they would be here in person to laugh at her fears. But nothing he could say really helped, for she knew he was tortured with fears himself.

At sight of the hunted men Karen gave a cry of joy. She begged Jack to tell her they were both all right, that neither of them had been hurt.

'We're fine as silk,' Turnbull said. 'It's the other fellows that are the worse for wear. One got shot and another one pistol-whipped.'

'You—killed one?'

'Wounded. I don't know how badly. . . . We're going to head for the Dailey Ranch. Mike will run you back to town in his car.'

'And where will you go?'

'We'll keep that information strictly under our own hats,' Stone said brusquely. 'Everybody in the county seems to know where we've been staying. I reckon we won't make that mistake again.'

Karen flushed. Her eyes were bright with anger, but she made no answer other than a look of proud scorn.

'He doesn't mean you, Miss Karen,' explained Turnbull quickly. 'It was lucky someone knew where we were, or you couldn't have found us and we would have been trapped in the cabin.'

'You needn't apologize for him, Jack,' the girl answered quietly. 'Of course he means me. I'm Lyn Gilbert's niece, so of course I would betray you if I could. He's used to people who do that sort of thing. He couldn't understand someone like—like Hal, for instance, who would let them cut off his hand before he would tell.'

Stone looked at her darkly. 'You're not in this. Lyn Gilbert is yore uncle, and we're at war with him. I suppose it makes you feel important to butt in. Maybe it gives you a thrill. Well, if you've got to drum up excitement over something that's not your business, throw in with him and get it on his side. I don't want any of that scoundrel's kin lined up with me.'

Her bosom rose and fell fast. 'Do you think I want to line

42

up with you, just because I took the trouble to see you weren't murdered?' she asked contemptuously. 'The men I know are clean and decent. They recognize the same qualities in others.' Abruptly she turned to Ferguson. 'Let's get out of here, Hal.'

Jack Turnbull said gently: 'We'll have to ride double, Miss Karen. It's not more than four-five miles, but over pretty rough country. If you'd rather ride with me than Gord——'

'I would,' she interrupted instantly. 'Thank you.'

At first they were too busy picking a way along the arroyo for conversation, but the cowboy had it on his mind to justify his friend and took the earliest chance to do so. They were riding across a red hill shoulder under a battalion of stars and the footing for the mounts was good.

'I'd hate to have you get Gord wrong, Miss Karen,' he said. 'I wouldn't blame you if you did, because he certainly hasn't been pleasant to you.'

'I never met a man as rude, as suspicious, and as ungrateful,' she said promptly, with emphasis.

'I don't reckon he's really ungrateful—not down in the bottom of his heart.' Jack fumbled for the words to express his friend's state of mind. 'I don't want to hurt your feelings, but he was an innocent boy framed for a murder he didn't do by your uncle and Curt Ford because he was in their way. I can't prove it, but I know it's so. They sent him into a living grave and kept him there until the life was squeezed dry in him. It's not surprising he came back bitter of heart, hating the enemies who had ruined him and the friends who had turned their backs when he was in trouble. Before he's been in Barranca an hour he has to start fighting against the same old gang to keep from being wiped out. You know your own self they must have made up their minds to destroy him. Tonight proves it.'

'Wouldn't it prove, too, if he had any sense, that I'm not one of his enemies? Do you suppose I enjoy setting myself up as a mark for scandalous talk by spending a night in the hills with a lot of men?'

'It was certainly fine of you to come,' Turnbull said in a low grave voice. 'I'll never forget what you did tonight—and I don't think Gord will either.'

'He must be grateful,' she answered, derision trembling in her voice. 'For thanks I get a savage slap in the face.'

'I know, Miss Karen,' the cowboy admitted. 'No defense for that. All I can say is his nature has been warped badly. But give him time and he'll come round.'

Anger flamed up in her. 'I'll give him all the time there is from now to eternity. I hope I never see him again. I'm not used to being treated like something the cat dragged in from

43

the alley. I'm supposed to be somebody in Barranca, and I don't like being put in my place by a convict.'

A rocky descent dropped sharply before them. Turnbull gave the horse its head while the animal picked its way. Conversation ceased for the time.

The young man could understand the girl's resentment. She had no doubt been spoiled by too much attention, and the rude cavalier manner of Stone was a new experience to her. She probably felt humiliated and hurt, with very good reason. Of course it would not do her any harm. All her life she had been willful and imperious, going her own way and making others fit into her plans. Some day she would have to learn, and it might as well be now, that the world was not entirely her football.

None the less Turnbull felt that her faults were for the most part only skin deep and not flaws of character. She was a brave, gallant young soul full of generosities and imprudences. He had always liked her impetuous democracy. Perhaps he liked it none the less because it was cased in a body so gracious in its loveliness, because she was unconsciously so provocative and exciting. It gave him a thrill to feel her warm, breathing person so close, to know the pressure of her encircling arm when the trail grew rough.

At the ranch they roused old Tom Dillon from sleep and borrowed his dilapidated flivver. While Karen and Tom were waiting to get started, the girl chatted with the other young men, but ignored Stone completely.

'Look out for yourself, Jack,' she called to Turnbull as they started.

'Sure will, Miss Karen,' the cowboy answered.

The car went bumping into the night.

9. Lyn Gilbert Cracks the Whip

KAREN was not yet up when Lyn Gilbert rose from the breakfast table. He gave orders to the maid that his niece was to be at the office at eleven o'clock.

It was half an hour after the appointed time when Karen reached the Gilbert Building. Firkins met her with his usual oily welcome.

She brushed that aside as quickly as she could. 'My uncle wants to see me,' she said. 'Is he in?'

'He's just a little—er—annoyed, Miss Gilbert. A few minutes ago he called the house to remind you. His impression is that the time set was eleven. Of course, naturally, young ladies —er—don't have a business man's sense of promptness, so——'

'Tell him I'm here,' she ordered.

44

Gilbert looked at her when she entered without moving a muscle of his huddled body. 'You're half an hour late,' he squeaked.

'Yes, I couldn't get here earlier,' Karen answered carelessly. 'I got up late. Wasn't in till after three.'

She knew why he had sent for her, and though she was more disturbed than she pretended, thought it just as well to take the bull by the horns.

'Five minutes to four,' he piped up. 'What were you doing all night?'

'Don't you know?' she asked.

'Yes, I know. That's why I told you to come here.' He slammed a ham-like fist on the desk. 'You've been consorting with my enemies, with murderers and outlaws. You prevented Sheriff Scott from arresting two ruffians wanted by the law. Don't deny it, miss. I'm not a fool.'

'I'm not going to deny it, except to say that Jack Turnbull is no murderer and I don't believe the other man is either.'

'You don't know anything about it. Turnbull tried to kill one of my men a few weeks ago. The other scoundrel is a convicted murderer and last night he just missed killing poor Yorky, who will be in the hospital for months. But I didn't send for you to discuss my business. I'm telling you that you are through meddling. I won't have it. And I won't have you running around the country at night with bad men and getting the name of a loose woman.'

Karen felt the blood burning beneath her dusky skin. 'Is it necessary to insult me?' she asked.

'Apparently it is,' he sneered. 'You insult yourself when you do such things. You've conceived some kind of foolish infatuation for this convict Stone. There's no sense of fitness or decency in you. Well, you are my brother's daughter and I'm going to protect you till you are married. You're going out to live at the Bar B B, where you can be watched and prevented from making a fool of yourself.'

'I'm not,' she flung out. 'You can't make me.'

'Can't I?' His motionless body had all the pent-up savage force of the rhinoceros he resembled. 'I'll show you about that, missy. I'm your guardian. You'll live where I say, and by God! you'll do what I tell you to do.'

'No,' she rebelled.

'I'm going to get you married. You've thrown away your good name and disgraced me. The sooner you have a husband the better.'

'When I want a husband I'll marry,' Karen answered stormily.

'When I want you to have a husband you'll marry,' he corrected in his high falsetto. 'You've had too free a hand. I

45

ought to have taken you in hand earlier. But better late than never. You're going to learn to obey. Till you do you'll stay at the ranch.'

'A prisoner.'

'Call it that if you like. You won't be given a chance to play the idiot any more. I'm going to crack the whip.'

'Will you have me flogged when I'm not good?' she demanded, scornfully furious.

'It may come to that.'

'I'm not going to your ranch,' Karen told him defiantly. 'I have one of my own. I'll go there, and I'll get a lawyer to protect my rights.'

'Your husband can do that.'

'Have you picked one for me yet?' she cried, her voice trembling with anger.

'I have one in mind.' A finger moved and he pressed a button. His secretary came into the room. 'Firkins, have you ever thought of getting married?' he inquired.

The little man gave a deprecatory 'tee-hee' of assumed embarrassment. He smirked at Karen.

'I wouldn't say that I have never—er—dreamed——'

'Yes or no,' cut in his employer.

'Well—er—yes.'

'How would you like to marry Miss Gilbert?'

The eyes of Firkins goggled. The man was struck aghast. This was wish-fulfillment with a vengeance, beyond any possible expectation, if Lyn Gilbert meant what he seemed to be saying. But cautious approach was his habit.

'If Miss Gilbert were willing, I won't deny that an affirmative answer on my part——'

The big man slammed the desk again with a fist. 'Good God, man! Can you or can't you say yes?' he screamed in his thin, high voice.

'It doesn't matter what he says,' Karen interrupted contemptuously. 'I wouldn't marry your flunky if he was the last man on earth.'

'I'm offering slightly damaged goods, Firkins,' explained Gilbert offensively. 'The young lady has been out all night with a pack of disreputable ruffians playing hide and seek in the hills. But you won't mind that, will you? You're not quite Caesar, and after you're married you can keep her under lock and key.'

Firkins glanced at Karen apprehensively. He guessed that volcanic emotions churned in that slim, straight figure so rigid with anger.

. 'I'm sure—er—that however indiscreet Miss Gilbert may have been she has done nothing—er—essentially reprehensible,' he murmured.

His defense of her infuriated the girl. 'I'll be obliged if you will not discuss me, sir,' she exploded, 'since my conduct cannot ever possibly in any way concern you in the least.'

'She's a good deal of a vixen, Firkins,' Gilbert said imperturbably. 'You'll have to be rough with her. Read Shakespeare's "Taming of the Shrew" and you'll get the idea.'

'I'll not stay here and listen to this,' Karen announced, and moved toward the door.

But with an agility surprising for such a mountain of a man her uncle was out of his chair and at the door before her.

'Not quite yet, my dear,' he said softly, blocking the way. 'I'll let you know when this conference is closed. Go back and sit down.'

Karen trembled with rage. 'You had better let me go,' she told her uncle in a low voice.

'As your guardian I intend to prevent you from following dissolute ways.' There was a faint glimmer of an ironic grin on his wooden face. 'Since you can't be trusted to rule yourself I'll take the job in hand, missy. I've phoned to Nelly to pack a suitcase for you. Curt Ford has sent a car to take you to the ranch. You'll be supervised there, just as other erring girls are in institutions. When your conduct shows promise of amendment we'll have another little talk.'

'You can't do this to me!' Karen cried. 'This is a free country—America. You can't put me in prison as if you were a sultan. I'll call for help. I won't stand it.'

Imperiously she tried to look him down, but his little eyes did not lower.

'It's too late to be sorry now,' he piped. 'You've gone too far. I'm sending you to the ranch so that you may have plenty of time to think of the error of your course. You'll stay there until I feel sure you mean to behave better.'

'I'd rather rot there than marry this man, if that's what you intend,' she burst out violently.

'After last night's performance you won't have much choice in husbands,' he snickered. 'Girls can't flaunt their amours so flagrantly. Now Firkins here is kind, gentle, and altogether quite a ladies' man. In the circumstances you might do worse. But that will wait. You'll have a quiet time alone, far from your town friends, to reflect on the widsom of obedience. Then we'll talk of Firkins, perhaps, or of some other man suitable to me as your husband.'

'I'm not going to the ranch,' she reiterated.

A knock sounded on the door. Curt Ford walked into the room, his harsh, brown face badly scarred and bruised.

'So you came yourself,' Gilbert said malevolently. 'I reckoned the doctor wouldn't let you up so soon, for fear you might slip again.'

The flinty shallow eyes glared at him. 'One of these days, Lyn, you'll talk too much,' the foreman growled.

'You know what your job is, Curt,' the ranch owner said, ignoring the resentment of the other. 'Take this girl to the ranch, make sure she doesn't leave. Don't give her a chance to slip away, day or night. If she makes you any trouble try bread and water for two-three days.'

'I won't go with you,' Karen interposed, a little wildly. For already she was aware that willy-nilly she would have to go. She did not quite see how her uncle was going to contrive to force her, but she knew he would.

Lyn Gilbert waved the other two men out of the room. His small, tawny eyes fixed themselves steadily on her.

'Get this, girl, I never start anything I can't finish. Either you're going to the ranch or you're going to a reform school.' He spoke slowly, spacing his words to give each one full weight.

'Reform school,' she echoed. 'What do you mean? Have you gone crazy?'

'Last night you played into my hands. You raced all over the country like a wild hellion with a gang of outlaws. If I say you're an incorrigible I can't control and ask Judge Latimer to send you to the reform school he'll do it. Don't make any mistake about that. If you don't go peaceably, without a word, to the ranch, you'll go under guard to the reform school.'

Karen was shaken. Fear rose up and choked her. He might or might not be telling the truth. In any case she would not let it be plastered in headlines all over the front page of the newspapers that her uncle had applied to have her sent to a girls' prison because of her wild conduct. She would die of shame. Never would she be able to look people in the face again. Every tabby cat in town would talk her over spitefully.

'You wouldn't do that to me, would you? I'm your brother's daughter.' She offered her plea in the certainty that it would be rejected.

'It's because you are my brother's daughter that I have to do my duty by you,' he said smugly.

'Would it be your duty to drag my name in the mud because I prevented your hired men from murdering two fugitives?'

'You've dragged *my* name in the mud by your outrageous conduct. Always you've done what you pleased—laughed at public opinion. Now you've got to pay for it.'

There was some sediment of truth in what he said. Having no mother, she had gone her own way, careless of comment. But she had always kept her self-respect. Her wildness had been of manner rather than of reality. It had been born of

48

the untamed, vital youth in her. Yet she knew that Lyn Gilbert could and would distort her imprudences to his end. She was whipped, for the time being, at least.

She stood before him, straight as a young aspen, a contemptuous pride in her dark face. Since she had to surrender, it would be defiantly. Her mind searched for barbed words to pierce his rhinoceros skin.

'You know that's a lie,' she said in a clear low voice. 'I have never been bad or done anything to make a decent man ashamed. But you thrive on lies, as you do on all kinds of injustice. This is the first time I ever told you what I think of you, but from now on it's war between us. You are an evil man. It hurts me to feel that you are kin to me. There isn't anything to which you wouldn't stoop. When honest men get in your way you drive them from their property. If they stand on their rights you . . . murder them. It is common talk. There is no good in you.'

He listened, unmoved, with a thin, satiric smile. 'You are a violent young hussy. Perhaps the reform school would be better than the ranch.'

Karen threw out a hand in a little gesture of despair. 'I don't know what I ever did to deserve having you for an uncle . . . I'll go to the ranch, since I must.'

'I thought you would decide it was better. It doesn't pay to oppose me, my dear. A great many people have found that out.'

She flung out her challenge urgently, unable to repress it. 'Count me one of them. I can't live and breathe the same air you do. I'm going my own way, and I'm going to fight for my rights.'

'Are you going to do yore fighting from the Bar B B?' he asked blandly, with a falsetto giggle.

'I'm going to see a lawyer, as soon as I can.'

'The more fool you,' he jeered. 'I'll give you a piece of advice. Behave yourself. Don't mix in business that's not yours. Cut out this high and mighty tone and trust me. Do that, and I'll treat you right. I don't aim to rob you. When you marry you'll get yore property, if you act like a niece ought to do.'

'No,' she flung out vehemently. 'I'm not your niece. I'm just one of the people you rob. I serve notice on you. As soon as I can I'm going to start a lawsuit.'

'That will be fine. Then you'll get nothing . . . Understand. You're going to the ranch of yore own free will. No compulsion.'

'I understand,' she said, her dark eyes drenched with hatred. 'If you're through with this talk, I'm ready to start.'

He shuffled into the outer office after her. For the benefit

49

of the stenographer he gave Karen pious advice. 'I hope you'll be a good girl and have a nice time at the ranch,' he said. 'Remember that discipline is good for the young. If there is anything you need—any books or magazines or clothes—let me know and I'll arrange to get them to you.'

Without answering she turned her back and walked out of the room.

10. Jack Turnbull Lays Down the Law

JACK TURNBULL moved to the edge of the butte's bald top and looked down through the fringe of pines to the roll of hills below. They were far up in the Silcote Range, in a country rarely traversed by riders, but their enemies knew these fastnesses as they did their own faces in a looking-glass. The morning was young, and the sun not yet over the notched skyline, yet the thin drift of smoke from the campfire, rising straight as a pillar, might tell the location of their hideout to watchers with glasses.

There were still lakes of mists in the hollows of the hills below. His gaze swept a wide stretch of wooded land waves and detected no stirring of life. None the less, danger might be lurking in some hidden pocket of the great bluff, creeping closer to take them unaware.

He strolled back to the campfire to renew an interrupted argument. Stone squatted on his heels, a frying-pan in his hand. One eye watched the coffee-pot to be ready for it when it boiled.

'I've kept my mouth shut too long, Gord, because of that none-of-yore-damned-business way of yours,' Jack said. 'Well, the silence stuff is all off. It's a hell of a lot of my business, since I'm in this jam with you. I'll talk turkey from now on. You've got to shake off the shadows you lived under in the pen. You got a rotten deal. Forget it. Wipe it off the slate. Make a new head start.'

His friend squinted round at him, ducking his head to keep the smoke out of his eyes. 'Where am I to make this new start—back in the penitentiary, after Gilbert has put me there a second time?'

'He aims to put you there or under the ground. Me too. Both of us are in bad. The *News-Times* will come out with a lot of stuff backing up the stories they have already run about us being desperate outlaws and killers. But everybody in Barranca knows Lyn has a strangle-holt on the *News-Times* because he owns the mortgage. This whole thing will be hashed out by the citizens, and a right smart percentage of them will be on our side if we give them a chance.'

Stone tossed the flapjacks and put the frying-pan back on

the rocks which encircled the wood coals. 'Make oration some more, Jack,' he drawled. 'How do we give them this chance?'

'First off, yore main purpose in life oughtn't to be revenge. I don't blame you for feeling that way, but it won't buy you a thing.'

'Have to differ with you about that,' dissented Stone. He moved the coffee-pot to a flat rock close to the fire and emptied the flapjacks into a tin plate. 'Chuckaway, fellow. Come and get it . . . For this reason. My one chance to beat Gilbert is to prove that I was framed by him and Curt Ford to save their own bacons. If I try to act like a good pious Christian I'm done for. That's a cinch.'

'I'm not denying you've got to get the goods on them. What I'm kicking about is yore attitude to other folks.' Jack poured himself a cup of black coffee and put three spoonfuls of sugar into it. 'Gilbert and Curt Ford are exceptions. The devil spewed them outa hell. But you act like most everybody is yore enemy. You carry a chip on yore shoulder all the time. Take the way you treated Miss Karen when she came out to the cabin to save our lives. You were plumb downright mean to her. It won't do. We can't make the grade unless we have the friendship of a lot of people. Lyn has built up a big front for himself, but in doing it he has made enemies a-plenty. Unless you're just a plain darn fool you'll try to get the backing of those who hate him. We've wounded three Bar B B men between us. Our only out is self-defense. If folks go sour on us it won't be worth a damn.'

Gordon Stone poured himself a second cup of coffee and stared down at it. 'You're right, Jack. I'm a darn fool and can't help it. When I was in trouble before nobody lifted a hand for me. They let me be railroaded through. I won't ask a thing of any of them.'

'There wasn't a thing any of them could do for you. Lyn fixed it not only so he had an open and shut case but so Barranca believed you guilty. What would you expect of the people? Even yore uncle, John Fleming, thought you killed Harrison Brock.'

'He'd known me all my life and thought I was an assassin,' Stone said bitterly.

'He's been sorry for it since, though he's too stubborn ever to say so,' Turnbull went on, putting a slice of bacon on a flapjack and doubling the latter to make a sandwich. 'We got to admit that you and I did a lot of hellin' around together those days. The crowd we ran with turned out a pretty bad bunch. Yore uncle had some excuse for quarrelin' with you.'

'How d'you know he's been sorry since?' Gordon demanded.

51

'He gave me a job later. I knew why, though he'd swear on a stack of Bibles that wasn't the reason. It was because I had been yore pal. Whenever I talked about you the old man got violent—went right up in the air. That was because he was worryin' for fear he hadn't done right. He hated to think he'd let Lyn Gilbert poison his mind and had thrown you down when you were fightin' for yore life.'

'So you say.'

Turnbull cocked a questioning eye at his friend. 'The old man is ready for to bury the hatchet, if you would make the first move.'

'I'll not make it,' the ex-convict replied harshly.

'I swear you're contrary as a pair of pigs, both of you. Once I used to figure you smart as a new whip, Gord, but yore fool prejudices certainly make you act dumb. You're up against Lyn Gilbert, who is pretty near the Czar of Russia in this neck of the woods. You'd give a leg to beat him, but you throw away what chance you have by turning your back on those who might be yore friends. Can you tie that?'

The cowpuncher flung up his hands in a gesture of disgust.

Gordon nodded gloomily. 'I know you're right, Jack. Give me the devil. I deserve it. Far as my uncle goes I'll have to stand pat. I won't go back with my tail between my legs. But I'll do my best with other folks. I'll dig up a smile like a politician and turn it on when you tip me the wink.'

'Good. We'll start out by writing a letter to the *Courier* that tells our side of this business. Hatfield heads the opposition to Gilbert. Maybe he will publish it. If he does, you can bet half the people in the county will wish us well even if they feel Lyn is too strong for them to come out and say so publicly.'

'Much good that will do us,' Stone said with a sardonic grin.

'No can tell. It might.' Jack looked across at his companion coolly. 'One of these days you and I may be on trial before Mr. Lyn Gilbert's court for murder. Two-three honest citizens are liable to slip on the jury. If public opinion is back of them they stand pat for acquittal . . . maybe.'

'You're right as usual, Jack. Trouble is, any letter we write will only tell what we *claim* to be true. I've got to turn over a rock and dig up facts if we're going to blow Gilbert and Ford off the map . . . If I could find out where Linc Conway is living. I've always had a hunch that little cuss knew plenty about the killing of Brock. He did some talking just before the trial, then shut up like a clam and claimed he didn't know a thing. My idea is that Gilbert got to him.'

'I've got another notion in my cocoanut too—that Linc lit out because he figured he knew too much to stay healthy

52

here. He's at Carbondale, Pete Milan says. You remember Pete, the little cobbler. Well, Pete met him there and had a chin about old times. That was four months ago.'

'I'll run down to Carbondale and look him up,' Stone decided. 'You'd better come along with me. We'll slip away unnoticed and let Gilbert's warriors hunt the hills for a pair of desperate outlaws who aren't there. What say?'

'I say bully. The sooner the quicker.'

'We'll get that letter off our chests first, then cut through Starlight Pass and strike the railroad at Tie Siding.'

'Suits me fine,' Jack agreed. 'It will be swell to sleep on a mattress instead of a Tucson bed [1] for a change.

Gordon agreed that it would.

11. 'Every Morning Starts a New Day'

AT CARBONDALE Stone discovered that Lincoln Conway was herding sheep for the Little & Bronson outfit. After some telephoning he learned the man he wanted could be found in charge of a bunch on Squaw Creek. The two friends rented a car and drove out to find him. It was a desolate desert country with few inhabitants. They stopped at one bleak adobe house to inquire directions of a Mexican. He could tell them where Squaw Creek was, but knew nothing of any sheep now grazing there.

They missed the way, and after many wasted miles were set right by a boy riding bareback from school. The sun was setting in a splash of brilliant colors behind the truncated buttes when the travelers saw a distant cloud of dust which might mean sheep. As they drew near, they noted a gray blot on the red landscape.

'Sheep,' Stone grunted.

A dog passed around the herd. A movement like the wave of a restless sea agitated the mass. It poured forward toward a corral entrance.

The herder watched them approach. He was a small man with a limp. The two men descended from the car and moved toward him.

'Hello, Linc, oldtimer!' Turnbull sang out.

The little man stared. 'Well, doggone my skin if it ain't that no-'count pilgrim Jack Turnbull! I ain't seen you since —hell, since about six years ago. What in heck you doing here?'

'How about my friend?' Jack asked. 'Doesn't he come into this reunion?'

The sheepherder looked at Stone. They could see the shock run through him as recognition dawned.

[1] Tucson bed is one where the sleeper lies on the bare ground.

'It's Gord Stone, ain't it?' he said at last.

'Right you are,' Turnbull answered. 'Same old Gord, large as life. We heard you were out here and ran out to see you.'

The brown face of Conway twisted into a wry grin. 'You don't see much. Take a man or a horse, when he gits stove up he ain't what he was. I got busted wide open by a fall, and now I'm fit for nothing but to wrangle Mary's little lamb. Me, Linc Conway, who usta be a top rider. Can you beat it? By golly, boys, sometimes I find me talkin' to myself. That's no josh about sheepherders going crazy.'

Jack slanted a swift look at Gordon. Conway was talking to cover his unease. The released convict was one man he did not enjoy meeting.

'A fellow has to take whatever job he can get these days,' Turnbull said casually. 'I'm ridin' the grub line myself. Got room tonight at the wagontail for a couple of cowhands?'

'Sure. Y'betcha! It . . . it'll be like old times.'

They helped him fasten the corral and gave him a lift back to the wagon. He was rather a forlorn little fellow, with a face insufficiently modeled, the scant eyebrows raised in a perpetual puzzled inquiry.

He slapped together a supper of beans, ham, coffee, and hot bread, supplemented with a can of tomatoes. They ate it sitting on their heels before the campfire. The talk was of old days, the years during which Conway had been a high-riding cowpuncher and not a lowly sheepherder.

'We'll have to get you back on a ranch soon as the Kettle Hill cattlemen have Lyn Gilbert whipped, and that won't be long now,' Jack said with casual confidence. 'You may be a bit stove up, Linc, but there's plenty of work beside riding you could do.'

'That's sure enough so,' assented the herder eagerly. 'Boys, this ain't livin' at all. I'd as lief turn my toes up to the daisies. If I could get back into the cow country, I could still make out to ride an easy-gaited bronc. On the roundup I could do the cooking, and I usta be a pretty good blacksmith.'

'Trouble is, everybody is holding off putting on any extra men until Gilbert is licked,' Stone contributed. 'We've got him on the run, but it may take a year or two yet to settle his hash. If we had something on him and Curt Ford, something that would discredit them, it would just about do the trick. But of course there's no use talking of that. Lyn is too slick to leave any evidence of his dirty work. For instance, I know that he and Curt railroaded me to prison, but there's no way in the world of proving it.'

The faded eyes of their host brightened. Excitement quickened his blood. But he was a cautious soul and did not want to make any mistake.

'I had a notion Lyn Gilbert was ridin' wide and handsome these days,' he said, his wrinkled hatchet face thrust forward for information. 'Three-four months ago I saw Pete Milan, and he told me Lyn was tops at Barranca. What's happened since?'

'The town is tired of his deviltry, and it aims to snow him under at the coming election.' Turnbull conveyed misinformation easily and carelessly. 'I would say he is not entirely licked yet, but he sure would be if there was any evidence tying him up to any of the lawlessness we all know he has pulled off. A year ago he was cock of the walk. But not now. Why, Gord here whaled the stuffing outa Curt Ford the other day—with no comeback except that when they tried to drygulch us later we laid out two-three of them. Both of us put pills in Buck Hayes, a Bar B B puncher named Yorky is in the hospital, and Cheyenne is packing a busted head. What does Lyn do about it? Nothing. We've got his goat. His day as big mogul is past.'

Conway hitched himself closer. 'Jumpin' horn toads! Tell me about the rookus with Ford.' If there was one man in the world he hated it was the foreman of the Bar B B.

The more talkative of the guests was nothing loath to oblige. He never thought of the affray at Pratt's feed store without pleasure.

'It wasn't important,' Stone cut in impatiently.

'I'll bet Ford wouldn't agree with you,' Jack grinned. He turned to the sheepherder. 'Why, Curt was jouncin' around old Jas Pinckney and Gord interfered. Curt went for him all spraddled out. Gentlemen, hush! Gord worked him over proper, and when the mill ended Mr. Ford was asleep on the ground. Everybody satisfied but Buck Hayes. He charged in to gun Gord, who wasn't armed. While Buck was braggin' what all he would do, our friend here grabbed Curt's gun and sent him yelpin' down the street with a bullet in his wrist. Barranca is still cheerin' about it.'

The herder stared at Stone open-eyed.

'Gosh!' he exclaimed. 'You must be some hell-a-miler. Curt has the rep of being the best skull-and-fist-fighter in this part of the country.'

'He can't fight for sour grapes,' Stone said contemptuously. 'Doesn't even know how to put up his fists.'

Conway was impressed. If these fellows were riding the top wave, if the tide had turned against Gilbert, he wanted to be in on the victory. There might be a job waiting for him in the cow country if he lined up with them. Their cocksure manner impressed him. Moreover, he had a little debt of his own to settle.

He yearned to speak, to tell what he knew. But if he did there were two risks. One was that Stone would punish him for what he had done, the other that Gilbert would snuff him out for what he was about to do.

Hesitantly, he made a suggestion. 'I might sorta trail along with you boys, if it worked out that-a-way. Fact is, I—I—' he stopped and cleared his throat—'I'm noways friendly to either Lyn or Curt. Both of them have done me dirt. I got in a kinda jam, an' they sure made me sweat blood. I reckon you got a legitimate kick comin' at the way I done, Gord, but my own life was at stake same as yours was. Naturally you'll be sore at me—still and all——'

His confession bogged down. Stone gave him a lift.

'Couldn't we let bygones be bygones, you and I?' Gordon said gently.

Conway's face muscles worked. 'I'm certainly willing to do that if you are. I aimed to come forward at yore trial, but Lyn and Curt got to workin' on me. They handed it to me straight. If I did, I was a gone goose. I'd never live to get on the stand.' The head of the little man drooped. 'Boys, I hate to tell this. Up till that day I wore man-size boots. I'd never been a hell-raiser or a gun-fighter, but I didn't have to be ashamed when I saw myself in the glass. Different from then on. Since I let those devils bluff me I've known I was a quitter and a weakling, one who wouldn't go through to a finish. I hope neither of you boys have to live the rest of yore life with a coward.'

He spoke quietly, despair in his voice. Turnbull kept his eyes on the fire. He did not want to look at this unhappy man, who for years had been ridden by a sense of guilt. The confession of the collapse of manhood made him uncomfortable.

Stone spoke, his voice quiet and comforting. 'Every mornin' starts a new day, Linc. You do wrong, and you're thrown down hard. If you are what you called yourself, a quitter, you don't get up again; but if you are a man you make a new beginning. I'm trying to do that right now. While I was in prison I fed myself with hate and thoughts of revenge. The world had treated me badly, and I was going to be against everybody—except Jack here, who stood by me through thick and thin. I found it wouldn't do, though I hated to admit it. Jack helped show me. So did some other people who went out of their way to do me a friendly turn.'

'Yes, but it's different with you.' The Adam's apple of the sheepherder moved up and down, a barometer of his emotion. 'You weren't in there by any fault of yore own. Me, I was just a plain . . . coward. No dodging it. Just an eternal fact that damns me.'

'No,' Stone denied firmly. 'We're none of us brave all the time. The test came for you at a bad moment, and you slipped. Life is giving you another chance now, just as it is me. Listen. Jack and I dressed this thing up to make it sound well to you. I'm going to tell you the truth. Lyn Gilbert is as strong as he ever was, except for the fact that we have challenged him and are still alive. Rumors are reaching us that others too are getting up on their feet to oppose him. If you go in with us you're joining a forlorn hope. We may all three be blotted out, but we'll go down fighting. You can stay here and hug your shame, or you can ride the river with us like a man.'

The eyes in the brown wrinkled face gleamed. 'Would you trust me, after the dirt I did you, Gordon?'

'To the limit, Linc. You've been through hell, and you'd never throw down on yourself again.'

'Then, by Godfrey, I'm with you. Tell me what you want done, and I'll do it.'

'Let's hear your story first,' Stone suggested. 'What is it you know about the Brock killing?'

'Not a thing about the killing itself. We were on the roundup, you remember. I had come in early from the branding to drag up some wood for the cook. After I had finished I went over to my roll to get some Bull Durham. We were camped in a bunch of cottonwoods. As I came forward, hidden by the trees, I saw a man putting a small canvas sack in your war bag. The man was Curt Ford. For some reason, I don't quite know why, I stayed hid behind a tree until he went to his horse and rode off. It kinda puzzled me, but I didn't get the hang of it till I learned about the payroll robbery. When Gilbert tried to fix it on you I knew it was a frameup. Instead of talkin' with yore lawyer I went to Curt and kicked—said I wouldn't stand for it. That night three men hustled me back into the mountains and kept me there till after you were convicted. They laid it on the line—Curt and his boss—that if I ever let out a bleat I would be rubbed out *pronto*.'

'So you kept quiet,' Turnbull said.

'I kept quiet, but I thought about it all the time. Couldn't sleep. Couldn't forget that Gordon was an innocent man serving a sentence in the penitentiary. Curt watched me, like a hawk. He was scared for fear I'd bust out and talk some day, and he figured I was better outa the way. Well, he gave me on my string of mounts a bay gelding he'd just picked up. Said it was a good, safe horse. I never was a bronco-buster and didn't figure to tackle outlaws. This bay was a notorious bucker, one of the kind that trampled on a rider after he was throwed. Curt fixed it so I mounted this brute in a bed of boulders. I got piled *pronto*. Broke a leg and had internal injuries. They took me to a hospital, where I stayed four months. 'Course I knew Curt had hoped I would get killed. He and Gilbert visited me at the hospital, to let me know if I opened my mouth I would never come out alive. I knew doggoned well they weren't going to leave it lay like that. Soon as they got me out in the hills I would be drygulched. So I slipped outa the hospital unexpected and lit out from Barranca for parts unknown. I've been living under cover ever since. That's the whole story.'

'Will you tell that story before a notary?' Stone asked.

Conway drew strength from the courage of the others. His jaw tightened. 'By gorry, yes!' he cried. 'I've waited for a chance to even the score with those devils and figured I never would get a break. Now it has come I'll go through with you all the way from hell to breakfast!'

'There's danger in this, Conway,' the ex-convict said.

'Any more than you boys will be facing?' the sheepherder asked.

'No, but Gilbert's killers will get you if they can, to wipe out your evidence.'

'Linc will have to lie low somewhere,' Jack suggested.

'Yes.' Stone gave that consideration. 'He'll be safer with us than anywhere else.'

'We're on the dodge, Linc,' Turnbull explained. 'Have to get on the jump when they crowd us.'

'Suits me,' the little man replied. 'Me, I need some excitement. Herding woolies is all same being dead. I'll trail along, boys.'

Next morning they took the train for Tie Siding. They carried with them the story of Lincoln Conway, sworn to before a notary of Carbondale.

Nine hours later the three men stole a ride on a local freight to Barranca. They slipped from the train in the yards and made a detour around the town in order to reach unobserved the residence of Hatfield of the *Courier*.

The editor came to the door in slippers and shirt-sleeves when they knocked. He was a plump, bald-headed young man who looked soft. Stone had heard he was a fighter. The first sight of him disappointed.

'My name is Gordon Stone,' the leader of the delegation said, and introduced his companions. 'We would like to have a talk with you.'

Hatfield hesitated. He did not intend to be a pawn in anybody's game. 'Come in,' he said briefly.

Before Stone could tell the purpose of their visit the editor made his position clear.

'I was glad to get your letter and to publish it, gentlemen,' he said. 'The *Courier* is here to give the news. You will understand that though we are politically against Mr. Gilbert we are not conducting a personal fight against him, nor are we taking sides in any feud connected with him.'

Gordon Stone liked his straightforward manner. He prepared to revise his earlier impression of the man.

'Fair enough,' he said. 'We've come to bring you a news story, but one with dynamite in it. Perhaps you won't want to publish it.'

'I'll know better about that when you've told me what it is,' the editor replied.

The appearance of Stone surprised him. He had expected the ex-convict to be strong, rough, and probably sinister, but he was looking at a face which immediately attracted him. The experiences of a warped life had refined it. There was power there, but it was not brutal. The steady eyes had a direct candor that won approval.

Without comment Gordon handed to the editor the signed statement of Conway. Hatfield read it twice, the first time swiftly to get its general meaning, the second time to ponder on it as he read.

'Very interesting,' he commented at last, 'and, as you say, full of dynamite.' He drummed on the table with his fingertips, reviewing the possibilities. 'If I publish this—and if it isn't true, or if Mr. Conway weakens and recants—I'll be blown out of Barranca.'

'Yes, but it is true,' Gordon said quietly. 'We're taking it to the district attorney in the morning.'

'How do I know you are?'

'You may have it delivered yourself. We're going through, Mr. Hatfield. I was sent to the penitentiary on false evidence framed up by Lyn Gilbert. That I have come back to prove. Before I am through with him Gilbert will be a discredited man.'

Hatfield asked searching questions, many of them. He called up the notary public at Carbondale and made sure he knew that Lincoln Conway in person had written and signed the paper. He sent a reporter up into the Kettle Hill country to make investigation of certain facts alleged by Conway. Not until he was thoroughly satisfied of the truth of the story, three days after the night visit of the three men, did he run the statement of the sheepherder in the *Courier*.

But he did not wait that long to tell the fugitives a bit of news that interested them. Just as they were leaving his house he mentioned it.

59

'I've been told reliably that Gilbert has sent his niece to the Bar B B ranch to live as a punishment for warning you of his intended attack on you. She wrote a letter to a young lady in town explaining the facts. He gave her a choice. She could go there or to the reform school.'

'To the reform school!' Stone echoed quickly. 'What had she done? Why, that's absurd.'

'He claimed she had spent the night in the hills with outlaws and bad men, that he could no longer be answerable for her moral character.'

Gordon's eyes grew hard and cold as chilled steel. His jaw tightened. He said nothing.

Jack Turnbull expressed himself in one biting epithet. 'The damned sidewinder!'

12. Gilbert Reads a Headline

THE court of public opinion, which was in session all warm and sunny days throughout the year, sat *en banc* at Pratt's feed store to consider the case of Gilbert vs. Stone and Turnbull. The oldtimers present had read the letter in the *Courier* signed by the two hunted men, and were unanimously but for the most part cautiously ready to cast their votes in favor of the fugitive pair.

Jasper Pinckney was the most outspoken of the ancients lined up in chairs against the adobe wall.

'Not a word in that letter ain't so, in my opinion,' he announced flatly. 'Gordon came back not lookin' for trouble, like he had a right to do. Curt Ford and that tinhorn desperado Buck Hayes jumped him. He cleaned 'em up proper, right here where we had ringside seats. Then Lyn's Bar B B warriors started in to put him and Jack Turnbull outa business. I got the story from Hal Ferguson, who was kinda drug into the fracas. He was one of these innocent bystanders, you understand. Hal doesn't like Gordon for sour grapes, but he says they certainly fought and licked this mess of scoundrels sent out to fill them full of holes.'

'Gilbert's story is that it was a posse of deputy sheriffs they attacked unexpected,' old Greeley Shattuck demurred.

'No such a thing!' Pinckney cried, with the thin violence of eighty years. 'Lyn's trying to save face. Every last one of the crowd was a Bar B B man. O' course Scott eats outa Gilbert's hand. He is Lyn's sheriff, not ours. He'll back any play his boss makes. Just the same those birds were killers out to get the boys. You can't turn an Injun into a white man by calling him George Washington or Abe Lincoln.'

'I wouldn't go far as you do, Jas,' one of his neighbors

protested uneasily. 'Lyn Gilbert is an old and respected citizen of this country and I don't reckon——'

Pickney snorted. 'An' I expect Curt Ford is another,' he jeered, his wrinkled, winter pippin face querulously full of challenge. 'Hell's bells! Those birds have had this county's goat for years. Couldn't one of us call our souls our own till Gordon Stone got back and stood up on his hind legs. I don't aim to crawl any more. Me, I killed buffaloes and fought Comanches before Lyn came out on a train and started branding other folks' calves.'

After a moment of awkward silence Shattuck answered. 'Sho, Jas, you're talkin' foolish. No sense in raking up a lot of old gossip. Mighty few of us were Sunday-School teachers those days.'

'It's true, ain't it?' snapped Pinckney. 'Common talk among the cattlemen, wasn't it?'

'There's a lot of loose talk that ain't so,' Shattuck replied. 'I never heard of anyone who saw Lyn running a brand on calves that weren't his.'

'Hump! A rustler doesn't call in his neighbors when he gits busy with a running iron. Lyn was a slick proposition. He always has been. So he got away with it.'

'You're going to talk yoreself into trouble, Jas,' another oldtimer told him sharply.

'Trouble for who?' he wanted to know. 'If enough folks say what they think there won't be trouble for anybody—except for those who override the law themselves and use it to hogtie those who stand on their rights.'

"That's so,' a big shambling man in overalls agreed. 'This here is a free country, and we got a title to speak our minds. If these boys are being hounded unjustly like they claim, Barranca had ought to know it.'

A few blocks distant in his office Lyn Gilbert was considering sourly the same matter. He had been for years on top of the world in which he moved, largely because nobody had forcefully challenged his domination. Outwardly he snorted at the possibility that an ex-convict would walk into his domain and upset his supremacy, but within him uneasy doubts disturbed his assurance. He had never been quite satisfied with the way the Brock murder affair had been left. There were one or two loose ends he ought to have tied up. For instance, Linc Conway knew too much. He had left the country and probably would never again be heard of in Barranca. But as long as he was alive he was a potential menace. Also, there was Cheyenne. He had plenty on Cheyenne, enough to send him to the penitentiary for the rest of his life, but the man had been sulky of late. He had resented it when Lyn had let his sarcastic tongue ride the cowpuncher for the failure of his night attack on Stone. If Cheyenne told what he knew it would be awkward.

Gilbert realized that times had changed. In the old days he could rub a man out if he got in the way too much. Now it was more difficult. There was a sentiment for law and order in the country. One had to work secretly or under cover of legality.

There was, Lyn knew, a strong feeling against him and his methods. With cynical realism he faced facts. He had no friends. His support was bought and paid for, or else it was based on fear. He won because of the smoothness and the audacity of his attack, but if the impression ever became general that he was not in an impregnable position his allies would scuttle away like rats from a sinking ship.

The vague unease in Gilbert crystallized three days later into sharp fear. He reached for the *Courier* at breakfast, according to his custom. His eyes ranged over the front page to pick up headlines, preliminary to a more careful reading, when a two-column story at the right drew his attention.

FORMER BAR B B PUNCHER
ACCUSES LON GILBERT OF
FRAMING GORDON STONE

No muscle of his slack body moved, but the double-column head struck at him like a blow in the face. This was the first open move against him his enemies had dared to make in many years. He was surprised and disturbed that Hatfield of the *Courier* had dared to print such a story. It meant that the opposition was gathering courage. Stone was beginning to rally a party around him. Some of the smaller cattlemen must be backing him. Somehow the fellow's reckless daring had caught their imagination. It was too bad he had not succeeded in blotting the man out in that night raid. If it had not been for Karen's interference Cheyenne's party would have got him. Of course it was not too late yet. He must put his mind on the job. These thoughts came in flashes as he read the story.

A sworn statement, signed by Lincoln Conway, formerly a Bar B B rider, will be filed at the office of the district attorney today. This will charge that Lyndon Gilbert and his foreman Curtis Ford fabricated some of the evidence upon which Gordon Stone was convicted of the murder of Brock and the robbery of the Little Bessie payroll.

According to the story of Conway, who is now living at Carbondale, he saw Ford hide some of the stolen money in

Stone's blankets at a roundup camp near Three Cotton-woods. It was the discovery of this money in the possession of Stone, together with the fact that the killing was apparently done with a bullet from the young man's .45, that clinched the case of circumstantial evidence. At the time of the trial nine years ago the defendant claimed stoutly that the weapon had been taken from his roll while he was on circle at the roundup.

The affidavit states that Conway was abducted and held a prisoner until after the conviction of Stone, and that subsequently he remained silent on account of fear of death due to threats made by Gilbert and Ford. Later Conway was seriously injured by a fall from an outlaw horse, which he says the foreman of the Bar B B induced him to ride in a bed of boulders by telling him the animal was safe and gentle.

While Conway was in the hospital recovering from the fall he was, he says, visited by Gilbert and Ford, who again threatened his life if he talked. As soon as he was released from the hospital Conway left this part of the country secretly. He did this, his statement sets forth, because he was afraid harm would befall him if he returned to the hills.

The reason he gives for making this belated deposition is the desire to relieve a troubled conscience.

Gilbert knew that the district attorney, Arthur Driscoll, would make no move without his sanction. The man owed too much to him. But the effect on public opinion would be very bad if Conway's affidavit was not challenged. He would have to run a story in the *News-Times* denying with fiery indignation the slanderous lies propagated by his enemies. He must file a suit for libel against the *Courier*, to be dropped later at a convenient time. Above all he had to get rid of Conway. Without the little man present in person to support them, the charges would fall to the ground as propaganda from the enemy.

One of his men had better drop in at Carbondale and take care of Conway. Mentally he ran through the available men he had in his pay. Ford—Hayes—Webb—Cheyenne. Curt Ford would not do. He was too well known at Carbondale and too closely connected with the case. Automatically he eliminated Buck Hayes. The fellow had not fully recovered from the wound in the wrist received during the fight at Pratt's store with Stone. Moreover, Gilbert suspected there was a soft streak in the man. If there was danger in it he would not go through to a fighting finish. Tom Webb had guts but no brains. He would be likely to boggle the business and

63

get caught. This left Cheyenne. The owner of the Bar B B considered the man carefully. He was cool, determined, wily, and remorseless. This was his kind of a job. Since Cheyenne was already in the Brock killing, he was the logical one to wipe out the little chap who threatened his safety. Why drag somebody else into the affair, thus increasing the number of those who knew too much?

Gilbert telephoned Ford at the ranch and told him to send Cheyenne to town. Before he had laid the receiver down his mind was busy contriving ways of building barricades against attack. Despite the heaviness of his lax body, he was a man of explosive energy. Lyn had no intention of taking this challenge lying down. He would stand and fight as long as he could hit. He called his attorney and instructed him to bring suit for libel against Hatfield and the *Courier* in the sum of one hundred thousand dollars. He dictated a *News-Times* editorial demanding that the authorities run down and capture or exterminate if necessary the band of outlaws nesting in the hills under the leadership of a murderer recently released from the penitentiary. Over the telephone he summoned to him his two chief lieutenants in Barranca, Sheriff Scott and District Attorney Driscoll, and with them he outlined a law-and-order campaign to influence public opinion and hold their ward workers in line.

An hour later the cowboy Cheyenne was shown into the inner office. He did not remove from his head the broad-rimmed Stetson set at a jaunty angle.

The beady little eyes of his boss took in the man, squat, broad-shouldered, bowlegged, in years reaching toward forty. A top rider, hard as nails physically and mentally.

'You sent for me,' Cheyenne said. He was no spendthrift of words. When the occasion was important he knew the value of silence. What conversation he made was usually directly to the point.

'Yes. Sit down, Cheyenne.'

The cowpuncher sat down. His saturnine, tanned face had as much expression as the side of a house. The shallow, flinty eyes rested steadily on his employer. He waited, chewing tobacco evenly, with no apparent haste or curiosity.

'Looks like there's a job for you,' continued Gilbert. 'That little runt Linc Conway has come to life. He's got a story in the *Courier* today claiming I helped frame Stone at his trial.'

'Chickens coming home to roost, eh?' Cheyenne jeered.

The big man hitched his chair forward till his gross body pushed against the desk. His voice had been low, but he let it fall almost to a whisper.

'Home to you, not me,' he countered.

64

The impassive gaze of Cheyenne took in the big man derisively. 'I didn't see my name in the story. I'm only a hired hand. Linc doesn't know a thing against me.'

Gilbert leaned across the desk. 'If the case is reopened and Curt is dragged into it, that brings you in too.' The words came in a squeaky murmur.

'Not on yore life, Lyn.' The squat rider shifted his quid placidly, no evidence of disturbance in his stony face. 'There's not a thing against me. I didn't kill Brock, and I can prove it by men who saw me on the Dunne trail ten miles away at the time.'

'I know that. Point I'm making is that if Curt is crowded to the wall and talks——'

'All he can do is put a rope round his own neck,' Cheyenne interrupted hardily. 'He can't touch me.'

'He can say you were waiting on the Dunne trail to get Brock if he came from town that way and that he divvied the loot with you.'

'Sure he can say it, but he can't prove it. I'm sitting pretty. For you can't talk without admitting you knew all about it too. No, sir. This is Curt's funeral, and far as Linc's charges go, yours too. I'm an innocent bystander.'

'Right after the holdup you spent a lot of money at the Golden Eagle gambling. Where'd you get that money? Someone is liable to ask that.'

'Wouldn't worry me. As you know, I got some dough from my father's estate a month before that time. So I blew it . . . And listen, Lyn, if I had some notion of holding up Brock there wasn't any talk of killing him. That wasn't necessary. Curt did it because he was jealous. If he gets in a jam it's his own fault.'

Gilbert shifted to another line of approach. 'Cheyenne, we've got to get rid of that man,' he whispered.

'You and Curt. Like I said, I'm not in it.' His gaze fastened with impudent effrontery on his employer. 'If all stories I've heard are true you're no amateur at drygulching.'

'Not so loud,' Gilbert urged. 'I don't trust Firkins a lick of the road. He's a double-crossing snooper . . . Cheyenne, Curt can't go to Carbondale. He's too well known there. That puts it up to you. Drift in kinda inconspicuous. Make inquiries, and when you've found Conway arrange it so he won't talk any more. It will be worth a hundred to you.'

The cowpuncher's grin was a sneer. 'A whole hundred iron men. Think of that! You're too generous, Lyn. If you throw yore dough around that reckless you'll go bust. Practically a fortune, and all I have to do to earn it is stick my head in a rope.'

'All right, Cheyenne,' sighed Gilbert. 'I don't aim to be

close. Say two hundred. You'll find Conway hanging around Carbondale somewhere. At least he was there two days ago. You want to be careful.'

Cheyenne rose. 'Nothing doing. Nice to have met you. I'll be driftin' back to the ranch.'

'Sit down,' Gilbert snapped. 'What's eatin' you? It's safe enough, and two hundred is a lot of money.'

'Easy for you to sit here and say its safe. Different with me. I'm the guy who might have to take the drop from the trap. I'll do it for a thousand and expenses.'

The puncher stated his terms with cool hardihood. The big man slumped opposite him was in a trap. If anybody did this killing it would have to be Cheyenne, since Gilbert could not employ anybody else without leaving himself in the power of the cowpuncher.

'Outrageous!' yelped Gilbert, in a voice still muffled. 'It's a holdup. Why, I could get Stone himself blotted out for five hundred, let alone a little no-account weakling like Conway.'

'They hang you just as high for rubbing out a little guy like Conway as they do for one like Stone,' mentioned Cheyenne evenly. 'But it's an open market, Lyn. Get some other warrior to do yore dirty work. Or do it yoreself.' The rider mocked his employer openly. 'There's an idea. Hop down to Carbondale and meet Mr. Conway in person.'

Gilbert paid no outward attention to the malicious persiflage of his employee. He stuck to the matter in hand.

'I'll go to five hundred. It's too much. But seeing it's you——'

'Seeing it's me, I'll split the difference. Seven-fifty. That's my last word. Take it or leave it.'

The owner of the Bar B B took it reluctantly, after many demurs, and with bitter complaints that he was being robbed.

Cheyenne heard him out, scarcely taking the trouble to hide his contempt. When Gilbert had finished he added a proviso.

'One half in advance, and one hundred expense money.'

Gilbert roared, in a falsetto whisper: 'A hundred dollars expense! Why, you can get a room for three dollars a week and good twenty-five-cent meals at a Chinese restaurant.'

'I'm representing a first-class outfit,' Cheyenne grinned. 'I wouldn't want to discredit the Bar B B.'

In the end his boss compromised on seventy-five.

The cowboy returned to the ranch, packed a telescope grip, and entrained for Carbondale that evening. Before leaving the Bar B B he staged publicly a quarrel with Curt Ford and was given his time. It might be necessary later to be able to prove he was on bad terms with Gilbert's outfit. The quarrel with the foreman was not entirely simulated. Cheyenne took pleasure in making a few vitriolic comments he had had bottled up in his system for some time. During the progress of the row Gilbert arrived in a car. He supported Ford, and was in turn bitterly 'cussed out' by the cowboy. Since this explosion had been his own idea, he was not as surprised as he pretended at the insubordination of Cheyenne.

13. Karen Frees Her Mind

TOM WEBB said, 'I'll git the mail for you,' and retrieved from the box the *Courier,* some advertising matter, and two letters for Ford.

They had ridden to fix a line fence that ran along the ridge back of the ranch. Now they were headed for the white house again. Karen was not allowed to go alone. The excuse for detailing one of the men to accompany her on her rides was that the outlaws in the hill might injure her. The explanation was not intended to convince. Whenever Curt Ford offered it he did so with a cynical sneer.

Webb passed the *Courier* to Karen. 'Might like to look at it when you get back,' he said. On the Bar B B he was known as the hairy ape because of the black growth which covered his arms, legs, body, and face. He was a primitive, simple soul who always let somebody else do his thinking for him.

After her bath Karen slipped into a dressing-gown, lay down on the bed, and read the *Courier.* Almost instantly one of the front-page headlines caught her eyes. With intense interest she raced through the story of Lincoln Conway's charges against her uncle and his foreman. Not for a moment did she doubt its truth, any more than she questioned the fact that it had been inspired by Gordon Stone. She knew it would have its effect. The criticism of Lyn Gilbert, never substantiated by sufficient evidence, would churn to the surface again, and this time it would have back of it a deposition sworn to under oath. If the man Conway stood to his guns his story would hurt the owner of the Bar B B a great deal.

From the corral there came to her a clamor of strident voices. Two men were in violent argument, while others watched them without taking part. One of the men was the foreman, his opponent the man called Cheyenne. Each was shouting vituperation at the other.

A car ran up the road and stopped between the corral and the house. Gilbert was in it. He listened to the quarrel, then lifted his high, squeaky voice in sharp command.

The two in verbal combat swung round toward Gilbert.

They moved in his direction, storming at each other as they advanced. Karen could not make out the words spoken, except some harsh and strident oaths. Apparently her uncle supported Ford. He turned on the other man, anger in his voice. Cheyenne retorted, shaking his fist at Gilbert. The foreman cut in again, with savage invective. Knowing him and Cheyenne, Karen wondered that no guns flashed. Both were known as men of swift and violent action. Instead, Cheyenne strode to the bunkhouse.

Gilbert eased himself out of the car and walked with his foreman to the house. Karen had already raised the window of her room to listen. She heard the men stamp up on the porch. They were just below her, but out of sight.

'The boys ate it up,' Ford was saying, with a jeering laugh. 'The story will be all over Barranca soon. Nobody will figure that Cheyenne is operatin' for this outfit.'

'Not so loud,' Gilbert cautioned. His voice was low. The girl caught the words ' . . . sounded like a fake.'

'Did you want us to gun each other?' Ford asked with bitter sarcasm.

'Shut your trap, Curt. Somebody might be listening.'

They walked into the house. Karen took off her shoes and slipped down the back stairs. She passed through the kitchen into the dining-room. Voices came from the small room adjoining it which was used as an office. The first was Ford's, obviously worried.

'If the damn little squirt backs up his affidavit we'll be in a fine jam.'

'*You* will,' corrected the squeak of his employer. 'Not I.'

'Don't you think you won't. Don't think it for a minute. Conway has got you in it, and by Moses, you'll be in it if I am.'

The listening girl heard her uncle urging the other man to keep his voice down, not to get so excited. She caught a word of reassurance: 'Cheyenne will fix it.'

After that they spoke in murmurs, too low to be heard. It must have been five minutes later that there came the scraping sound of a chair being pushed back.

'I'll drive up and see old John Fleming first,' Gilbert said. 'Got to fix it so he and his friends don't line up with his scalawag nephew.'

'The old man will likely do anything you ask of him,' the foreman said, with heavy sarcasm. 'You've sure been a friend to that oldtimer.'

Gilbert ignored the thrust. 'I'll talk with Karen and see if she's come to her senses yet. Tell Glenna to bring her down.'

Karen thought it time to be gone. She soft-footed it from

the dining-room into the kitchen and ran up the stairs. When Glenna knocked on the door of her room she was reading the newspaper.

Mrs. Ford was in a Mother Hubbard. 'Your uncle is here and wants to see you,' she said.

'How nice of him to remember I'm still alive, though buried,' Karen answered, turning a page of the magazine.

Glenna sat down in the easiest chair. She was inclined to puff a little when she climbed stairs. 'Better hurry, dearie,' she advised. 'He doesn't like to be kept waiting.'

The girl on the bed finished the paragraph. 'Doesn't he?' she asked carelessly.

Rising, she dressed leisurely, while Glenna admired her clothes.

'You certainly have got style,' the foreman's wife sighed. 'I usta be a classy dresser myself, but I never had your touch . . . Better not take so long, dearie. He has a sharp tongue when he's riled.'

Karen did not hasten. At sight of her Gilbert snapped his annoyance. 'Broke your neck coming, didn't you?'

'Do you want to see me—or don't you?' the girl asked coldly. 'If not, I'll go back to my room.'

'Sit down,' he ordered. 'And don't get sassy with me.'

'I'll stand,' she told him. 'Then I can get into the clean air quicker when you're through.'

'You don't do yourself any good talkin' that way,' her uncle reproved. 'I come up here in a friendly spirit, to find whether you're inclined to be anyways reasonable now you've thought your conduct over. And you start in by jumpin' down my throat.'

'I'll be entirely reasonable,' Karen said. 'Turn over my property to me and I'll let you alone—never speak to you again.'

'I'm your guardian, and you're under age. I aim to look after your property like the law requires me to do . . . Have you thought any more about getting married?'

'I've thought about not getting married,' his niece told him sharply.

'Edgar Firkins sends all kinds of love to you, my dear. I expect he would have written you a poem if he'd had time.'

She ignored that, eyes flashing angrily. 'How long do you expect to keep me here a prisoner?' she demanded.

'I wouldn't call you a prisoner. You go riding, don't you? Have the run of an eighteen-hundred-acre-range. If you mean when can you go back to town, why, that depends entirely on you. Soon as I'm convinced you aren't going to consort with my enemies—go trolloping around with bad men and outlaws—the welcome sign will be out for you at my house in Barranca.'

'I don't want to go back to your house—ever. But I'm not going to stay here, and I'm not going to make any promises. I read today's *Courier*. I believe that story, and I intend to break with you publicly.'

'So you're going to throw in with that villain Stone—get yourself talked of all over the country. Not if I can help it. You're my brother's daughter. You'll stay right here, and there will be a bolt on your door at night. I'll set bounds for your walks and rides. I'm not going to have a scandal in the Gilbert family, missy. From now on you'll follow a chalk line.'

'That's the way I want it!' Karen cried defiantly. 'You frightened me in your office, when you talked of reform school. I know now there is nothing to it. I'll fight. This is America. You couldn't do such a thing, not even with the help of your corrupt politicians. I have friends who'll support me. You'll see. So do your worst and see where you get. Handcuff me if you like.'

Gilbert did not want to drive her too far. What she had said was true. Just now, with public opinion in flux, he had no desire to weaken his power by an open fight in his own family.

'All I'm asking is for you not to mix in my business,' he said mildly. 'Is that too much?'

'All you want is to run me the way you've been doing everybody else in the county—and to make me marry some nitwit who will let you go on controlling my property. I won't have it. It isn't yours. It is mine. And I'm not yours to dispose of. I'll have you know that.'

The girl faced him, her slender body tall and erect, her eyes stormy.

He shook his head sadly. 'Temper, my dear. That is not the spirit in which to adjust your difficulties. You understand I didn't send you here as a punishment but to protect you from the impetuosity of youth.'

'I understand that you are a hypocrite!' she cried and walked out of the room.

Gilbert shrugged his heavy shoulders, hoisted himself from the chair, and shuffled out to the car. Ford joined him there.

'The young lady doesn't seem to think much of you, Lyn,' he jeered. 'Seems to be on to your curves.'

'Naturally you were listening,' his employer countered. 'You would be.'

'Her voice carries when she is annoyed,' Ford said. 'I reckon the boys heard when she called you a hypocrite. Oh, well, they probably had their own notions anyhow. You heading for the Fleming place?'

Gilbert put the clutch in and started without answering the question.

The foreman shouted advice after him: 'Because if you are you'd better go loaded for bear. You'll be welcome as loco in his pasture.'

14. 'Crooked as a Dog's Hind Leg'

GILBERT knew that Ford was right. Old John Fleming hated him with a bitter and passionate animosity. There was still enough explosive force in the owner of the J F Ranch to make this visit dangerous. But Gilbert was no coward. He had never courted peril or taken pleasure in it. There was nothing of high adventure in his cold blood. His preference was to attain his end by tortuous chicanery inside the law. Yet when it seemed wise he could take a risk boldly.

Fleming was an individualist, a cattleman of the frontier type. He had fought Comanches, drought, cattle diseases, bad markets, and rustlers with unflinching courage, and because of the force in him had survived. But he was now in a new age, one in which the virtues of the oldtimer were not important. His enemies now were the subtleties of political chicanery, combined with a sabotage none the less criminal because it operated under legal protection. Gilbert was back of these. He intended to take over the J F Ranch at the proper time to round out his holdings, and for years he had been nibbling at Fleming's range and at his solvency.

When Gilbert drove into the yard Fleming was sitting in a rocking chair on the porch reading a newspaper. As soon as he recognized his visitor he rose from the chair.

'Don't get out of that car!' he roared. 'I don't want you on my land.'

Gilbert answered mildly, in his shrill falsetto: 'I come to fix things up with you, John. No use us not being friends.'

The effrontery of this took Fleming aback. The man could talk about friendship, after he had filched from him the government grazing land, killed his cattle, wounded one of his riders, and ruined the life of his only nephew. John was no fool. He understood that the owner of the Bar B B had not come in the spirit of a good neighbor, had not given up his intention of ruining him. For some purpose not yet apparent he wanted a truce long enough to get something out of the man he was in process of destroying.

'You trying to tell me you got religion in yore old age?' Fleming scoffed. 'I don't believe it. You're spawn of the devil, spewed out of hell.'

71

'That's no way to talk, John,' remonstrated Gilbert amiably. 'Maybe we've both done things we shouldn't. Not many of us oldtimers left. We'd ought to patch up our differences.'

Fleming was tall and lean, and in spite of his years he still carried himself as straight as a ramrod. He wore the high-heeled boots, the broad-rimmed gray hat, the open vest of the cattleman. In his movements there was a swift energy untempered by the discretion of second thought. He had always been aggressive, impetuous, ready to fight at the drop of the hat. Even now he was capable of bursts of sudden strength, but age showed in the lax muscles at the throat, in the loose skin at the back of the hairy hands.

'I reckon you want a Lyn Gilbert compromise,' he said contemptuously. 'You take what you want; the other fellow gets off the earth.'

'Only what's fair, John.'

Fleming's hawklike eyes were bright with anger. 'By thunder, you're a hell of a man to talk about what's fair. You damn scoundrel, if you were dealing with yore own mother you'd cheat her out of her last nickel. No use being mealy-mouthed with me. I know you. Crooked as a dog's hind leg. You wouldn't enjoy making money if you weren't turning the screws on someone. What'd you want? Spit it out, and get off my land.'

The man in the car shook his head regretfully. 'You always did go off half cocked, John. Your temper has been a curse to you. I've long been ready to fix things up between us, but you wouldn't have it.'

From under heavy white eyebrows Fleming glared at his foe. 'Going to fix things up, are you?' he cried. 'That's fine. To begin with, all you'll have to do is turn the government grazing back to me, pay for the stock yore ruffians have run off and killed, move yore cattle off my range, fire the damn scoundrels you employ in town and on the ranch, and give back to my nephew the good name and the eight years you robbed him of by yore infernal lies.'

Gilbert showed no anger. 'You're excited, John. Be reasonable. If Gordon Stone went bad I'm not responsible for it. Why, you kicked him out yourself long before the Brock trouble came up.'

'So I did, like a hotheaded fool, and maybe drove him on to his evil ways.' Fleming raised the arm which held the *Courier* and shook it at his enemy. 'I read what Gordon said the other day, and this story of Lincoln Conway that has just reached me. It's all true. You framed that boy, you damned wolf. Don't sit there and tell me lies. I won't listen to them. Get that car started down the road, or by Gad! I'll shoot you

72

down like I ought to have done forty years ago when you were rustling my stock.'

'You've got me wrong,' Gilbert shrilled. 'You named yourself right, a hotheaded fool. I came to see you about your nephew. I've been mighty patient till now, but I'm about wore out with him. If you have any influence at all, tell him to get out of here. He can't terrorize me. I've had enough.' He made one of his rare gestures, the outward sweep of a hand. 'I'm going to defend myself and wipe him off the map. In self-protection, because no criminal alive can threaten me and get away with it.'

'If you're here when I get back I'm gonna fill you full of lead,' Fleming shouted. He turned and rushed into the house for a gun.

The Bar B B man's beady eyes swept the scene. He saw a man standing at the door of the bunkhouse, another close to the kitchen, and a third moving forward from the corral.

'When I come back next time it will be as boss of this outfit,' he snarled, and started the engine.

By the time Fleming appeared on the porch again he was a hundred yards down the road, traveling fast.

15. Glenna Meets an Old Love

CURT FORD sat at the desk in his office, a half-filled bottle of whiskey in front of him. He was not writing or reading. Nor was he thinking, except as thoughts happened jerkily. His mind was heavy and inert. Through long experience he knew the cow business from A to Z, but he was essentially a dull man.

The bottle was to help him pass the time while he waited for a report from Webb, and it would be much later in the evening before the Bar B B rider arrived with it. The Hairy Ape was doing a little night riding, assisted by three others. The enterprise was entirely outside the law, and though those engaged in it were all employees of Lyn Gilbert he had no part in it. Ford was master-minding the project. Since Gilbert had reported his reception at the Fleming ranch the foreman understood there was an open season on old John. The owner of the J F had declared himself, and could now be treated as a recognized enemy rather than as a victim who must be ruined with hypocritical reluctance.

Ford poured a third of a glass of whiskey into a tumbler. The glass was still in his hand when the door of the room opened. He took it for granted that the intruder was his wife Glenna. 'What d'you want now?' he growled, not turning his head.

The voice that answered sent a chill down his spine. It

dragged the words in a drawl cold as the wind of a northern blizzard.

'I dropped in to settle unfinished business.'

Ford pivoted and stared at Gordon Stone, his eyes bulging and his jaw fallen. It was incredible that the man could be here, where the lift of a voice would bring a dozen armed enemies running. Amazing, but true. That his foe had come to kill him the foreman did not for an instant doubt. What else could the fellow mean by unfinished business?

A gun belt hung from a nail on the wall not five feet away. It might as well have been in Barranca. Ford rejected the impulse to make a dash for it. He knew that though Stone had no weapon in sight there must be one within easy reach. Probably in a scabbard strapped to his left side.

Curt Ford was a hardy ruffian. He drove down the fear rising to his throat. The thing to do was play for time—watch his chance to take advantage of any break that might occur.

'Where did you come from?' he asked harshly.

'Doesn't matter. I'm here. Don't make a mistake. Put yore hands on the desk in front of you.'

The foreman hesitated. Once more he played with the thought of the holstered revolver hanging on the wall. Considered and repulsed the urge. The force in this man's grim arrogance quelled insurgent impulses. The deep-set eyes in the harsh face were like half-scabbarded steel. If Ford made a false move the strong brown hands would get into action instantly.

But he had to save face, had to make a bluff. 'All I have to do is give a yell and twenty men will come on the jump,' he growled.

'You'd get a fine funeral probably,' the visitor said.

That was exactly the trouble. Stone had put a finger on the difficulty. Before the Bar B B men arrived their foreman would be no longer living and his killer would be vanishing in the darkness.

Reluctantly, the hands of Ford slid forward on the desk. By an effort he could keep his brutal face from betraying his terror. His voice he could hold steady by sheer will power. But his heart felt as if it were packed in heavy ice. He had come to the end of the passage. Stone would play with him— the cat and the mouse stuff—then would rub him out.

'If . . . if you're figuring on bumping me off——'

Stone closed the door. He moved across to the other side of the desk. His hard eyes looked down on the man who had ruined his life.

'A good suggestion,' he agreed evenly. 'I'll give you a minute or two for confession first. After you killed Harrison

74

Brock was it Gilbert's idea to hang it on me? Or did you think of that yourself?'

'I didn't kill him,' Ford said hoarsely.

'Why lie to me? We're alone, for the first time in ten years. If I decide to let you live, I couldn't prove what you had admitted.'

If I decide to let you live. From that clause Ford snatched a ray of hope. At the worst he had a few minutes reprieve.

'Sit down, Stone,' he said. 'Let's talk this thing over. Maybe we can fix it up.'

The ex-convict sat down, his chair not too close to the desk. He did not want to be hampered if there came a time for swift action.

'You do the talking,' he ordered curtly. 'I'll listen.'

An idea came to the trapped man. 'Have a snort with me. I'll get a glass.'

'You'll stay where you are.'

'I thought——'

'Don't think. Talk. I asked a question. Answer it. Did Gilbert put you up to framing me? Or did he come in afterward, in time to arrange the lies that convicted me?'

Ford moistened his dry lips. Maybe he could talk the other out of killing him. There were no witnesses. It did not matter what he said, if only he could placate for the time this long, lean avenger whose hard, reckless face looked across at him with stony menace.

'Lyn fixed it. He coached me up what to say on the stand. I was in a kinda jam, and I was sore at you. So I came through with the stuff he told me to say. O' course I hated to do it, and when you got out I was sure glad.'

'Don't lie, Ford,' Stone said quietly. 'It doesn't do any good . . . How deep was Cheyenne in it?'

The Bar B B foreman followed the lead, a little too eagerly. 'I wouldn't aim to throw down on Cheyenne or anything, but —if you've got to know—it was Cheyenne shot Brock. I came in later, to sorta protect him.'

'Another lie. You killed Brock. Cheyenne was seen on the Dunne trail at the time of the murder. What was he doing there—waiting to get Brock if he took the short cut?'

'Well, yes.' Ford attempted a defense. 'Brock wouldn't have been hurt if he hadn't reached for a gun. It was him or —the other fellow.'

'More lies. He was shot in the back of the head from ambush. You're not only a killer, but a dirty, cowardly assassin.'

Gordon's right hand moved swiftly, to disappear under his coat. The door of the room was opening. Glenna Ford stood at the entrance. Her plump, pretty face had a look of puzzled, ludicrous surprise. She had heard the last sentence spoken. Her big eyes fastened on the stranger.

She murmured, 'Gordon!'

He rose, suavely and ironically polite. Once he had been in love with her and she with him, but before he had been in prison three months she had married one of the men who had ruined him. The color flooded her cheeks. She had never been happy at her desertion, but the pressure of circumstances had been too strong for her weak will.

'The bad penny again, after so many years,' he said. 'Your husband doesn't seem glad to see me.'

'What did you say about—an assassin?' she asked tremulously.

'Never mind what he said,' Ford cut in roughly. 'You're not in this.'

With Glenna there had come into the room new hope for him. Ruthless though he might be, Stone could not kill him in the presence of his wife. That would be too raw.

'On the contrary, Mrs. Ford. I'm very glad you came,' their uninvited guest differed. 'I want to see Miss Gilbert. May I ask you to bring her here?'

'Stay where you're at, Glenna,' her husband told her harshly. 'Don't leave this room.'

The scornful gaze of Stone rested on the foreman. 'Don't be afraid,' he jeered. 'I'm not going to kill you—tonight.'

'What you want with the girl?'

'My business.' He added, with compelling gentleness that veiled a threat: 'I'm in rather a hurry, Mrs. Ford, if you don't mind.'

'All right. Do as he says, Glenna. And don't be long.' Ford growled it out of the corner of his mouth. He accepted the word of his enemy at face value. He was a liar himself when it suited him not to tell the truth, but he had always known that Gordon Stone's word was good as a bond.

'Better mention to Mrs. Ford that she is not to tell anybody but Miss Gilbert I am here—if she wants to find you healthy when she gets back,' Stone said, a silky warning in his smooth low voice.

'You heard him, Glenna,' the woman's husband snarled.

Glenna looked from one to the other, a troubled frown on her face. She had been given looks but not brains. There was something about this she did not understand, and it frightened her. For nine years these men had hated each other. It was conceivable that Gordon had come to kill her husband because Curt had testified against the boy and almost sent him to the gallows. But why come to the Bar B B, where there were a dozen of his enemies within call? Why not drygulch

76

Curt while he was riding the range? And what did he mean by calling Curt an assassin?

She turned and walked out of the room. Gordon watched her go, amazed at himself that he could ever have been desperately in love with this untidy, helpless woman who was developing a triple chin. His bitterness against her had long since passed. No doubt she had been under a coercion too strong to resist. He did not wish her any harm. It was a fair guess that any happiness she might find in life would not come from any consideration given her by her husband.

Ford looked at the clock. The time was half-past ten. There was no use expecting Webb for many hours yet. Nor were they likely to be interrupted by any of the Bar B B men. He wished he could think of a way to summon help without arousing the suspicions of his visitor. It hurt his vanity that he was sitting there submissively, hands on the desk, under compulsion of an enemy too contemptuous even to draw a gun on him.

A bitter rage welled up in him. One of these days he would wipe the slate clean.

16. Ford Sees His Guests on Their Way

KAREN was lying on the bed reading when Glenna entered with the news that Gordon Stone was in the house and wanted to see her. In one swift sinuous movement she was on her feet, excitement shining in her eyes.

'He's here—alone?' she demanded. 'What does he want? Is he mad?'

Tears filled the blue eyes of Glenna. 'I'm afraid there will be trouble. I don't know why he came, unless it was to pick a quarrel with Curt. I used to be his girl, before he went to prison. Maybe he thinks I should have waited for him to get out.'

'Let's go,' Karen said quickly.

Her heart was beating fast as they walked downstairs. Glancing at the plump matron beside her, she thought it very unlikely that the suggested explanation was the true one. Glenna was a good sort, still pretty in a comfortable, fleshy way, but not exactly the person to inspire a hopeless, perpetual passion.

At sight of Gordon, so sure of himself, rising at their entrance with such careless and indifferent ease, a tumult of emotion flooded her breast. He was, she thought, a man among ten thousand, for stark strength and force.

'You . . . wanted to see me?' she asked.

'Yes. Stand over there, please. You too, Mrs. Ford, unless you would rather sit.'

77

The women took the place to which he had directed them. Karen understood that Stone was dominating the situation. He did not want them behind Ford. No guns were drawn, but she felt that the roar of them might be not far distant. The hands of the foreman were not resting on the desk because he enjoyed keeping them there. He was acting under the compulsion of one who had the drop on him.

'Why did you come here?' Karen wanted to know. In her tremulous voice was expressed the stress of a dismayed anxiety. 'If the men found out——'

She left the sentence suspended in air. There was no need to finish it.

'I came to talk with you,' he answered. 'In Barranca I was told your uncle was holding you here against your will. Is that true?'

'Yes, it's true, in a way.' She stared at him in amazement. 'You don't mean you walked into this nest of enemies to find out what I'm staying at the Bar B B for?'

'To take you away, if you want to go,' he explained. He added, sharply, to Ford: 'Keep your hands on the desk.'

Karen felt drums of excitement beating in her throat. 'Take me where?' she inquired.

'It's a wide world,' he answered. 'Why burden Lyn Gilbert's hospitality?'

'I'll go,'' she replied with swift decision. 'Have you a car?'

'Yes. I left it in the brush down the road.' He turned his sardonic smile on the foreman. 'Mr. and Mrs. Ford will see us on our way, I expect.'

'I'd like to see you in hell,' the man at the desk retorted, an ugly rasp in his voice.

'But pending that happy day you'll walk down the road with us, won't you?' his visitor drawled.

'If I had a gun handy——'

'But since you haven't——'

Ford lowered at his enemy, torn between fury and the fear that Stone might yet kill him. 'You've got the drop on me,' he growled. 'You're free to go when you've a mind to. What are you scared of?'

'I'm loaded with suspicions you would rouse the ranch as soon as we left,' Stone told him cheerfully. 'So I'll ask you to stroll along with us a little way. You and Mrs. Ford will enjoy the walk back in the moonlight.'

Was this a trick to get him out of sight of the ranch house and kill him, the foreman wondered? Stone must hate him, bitterly, for what he had done to him. He would never get a better chance for revenge.

'I'll not go a step of the road, fellow,' the Bar B B man said. 'If you're aimin' to kill me you can do it right here.'

'When I kill you there will be a gun in your hand. Take your choice. Walk along with us to the car or stay here. But if you stay——'

Ford read significance in the thin grim smile accompanying the truncated sentence. 'All right,' he flung back defiantly. 'Say I stay.'

'Okay with me,' Stone replied suavely. 'I'll have to knock you cold to keep you from squawking for help from your thugs.'

Glenna thought it time to act as peacemaker. 'How can you talk that way, Gordon?' she said in her sweet, faintly simpering voice. 'Life is too short to hold grudges. Just because you didn't like each other when you were hotheaded boys is no reason for quarreling now. Live and let live, I say. Shake hands and make up.'

She had, Stone perceived, not the faintest idea of the depth of the gulf separating him from her husband. He spoke to Ford, ignoring her olive branch.

'Do you go or stay?' he asked curtly.

'I'll go, seeing you have the deadwood on me,' the foreman said sullenly.

'Good enough.' Stone spoke to the girl without lifting his gaze from the man at the desk. 'Pack your suitcase, Miss Gilbert. Be back here as quick as you can. We'll wait in this room for you.'

Karen moved to the door.

'I'll go help you,' Glenna said.

'You'll stay here,' Ford snapped.

'Why do you get so cross about nothing, Curt?' his wife complained amiably.

'Your husband isn't at his best tonight,' their guest suggested. 'He likes to be top dog and give orders. I'm sure he doesn't mean to be impatient.'

Glenna looked at Stone. 'You sure have changed, Gordon,' she said.

'Time stands still only for you,' he answered with mock gallantry.

'I've took on flesh,' she admitted complacently.

Karen returned with the suitcase.

'You took yore time,' Ford growled.

'Swing out from the right side of the chair and fold your arms,' the other man gave instructions. 'The ladies will walk together, in front of us. I'll be a step behind you, Ford, with my hand on the butt of a six-gun. If you make any play for help or get away I'll drop you in your tracks.'

They walked out of the house into the yard. As they started down the road a man came out of the men's bunkhouse and walked across to the corral.

'That you, Curt?' he called. 'The bay mare has done got her colt.'

Ford felt the pressure of something hard against his ribs. 'See she's looked after properly,' he ordered gruffly. 'I'll be around after while.'

'Sure,' the man answered, and moved on his way.

'You did fine,' Stone said ironically to his prisoner. 'He may be wondering who your friends are, but he figures it isn't his business to be inquisitive. Soon as we've started you can mobilize your army and hit the trail after us. I don't expect it will buy you anything, but you might as well keep the boys busy.'

'One of these days I'll get you where I want you,' Ford said, with a low savage curse.

Derision was in Stone's hard laughter. 'You're one of these by-and-by gents. Not today, but maybe tomorrow . . . We turn to the left here.'

The car was in the chaparral, back of some mesquite. Gordon helped Karen into the front seat and himself took the place behind the wheel.

'It has been nice to see you,' he said to the Fords. 'We've enjoyed our visit. Think I'll mention it to the society editor of the *Courier*. A pleasant time was had by all.'

He pressed the starter and engaged the clutch. The car swept in and out among the brush and angled back to the road. They drove for a few hundred yards in silence.

Karen was the first to speak. 'You're improving,' she said. 'You've learned to laugh. It isn't exactly a gay one yet, but anyhow you've made a start.'

'I've learned a lot of things,' he said quietly. 'I came back to Barranca with just one purpose, to be an efficient machine for revenge. I wanted to live for that and nothing else. Thanks to one good friend—and others who showed their kindness even though they were almost strangers—I discovered it wouldn't do. Life is never squeezed dry, as long as you face facts honestly and unafraid. The sun is still shining somewhere over the hill. While the blood runs warm in you it is an unforgivable sin to close your heart to good.' He stopped abruptly, then added with a wry grin: 'Sermon by Gordon Stone, convict. Text: Vengeance is mine; I will repay, saith the Lord.'

'I'm glad,' the girl said warmly.

'You ought to be, since you're partly responsible for the change.' He dropped the subject, embarrassed at his explanation. He had forced himself to this confession, because he felt he owed it to her as an apology. But he hated mawkishness and sentimentality. A man had to be hard to travel rough trails. 'I borrowed this flivver to make a quick getaway if you decided to leave the ranch.'

'Where are you taking me?' she asked.

'Up to you to say. You must have friends in Barranca who would protect you from your uncle.'

'If I go to any of them I'll bring trouble to their door.'

'Isn't that what a friend is for—to take on your griefs when it is necessary?'

She smiled. 'You are too generous. Most friends are just fair-weather ones. They don't want to go to war for you. But I'll decide where to go before we reach Barranca—if that is our destination.'

'I'll have to cut up into the hills and take a roundabout way. Ford will telephone to his boss, and Gilbert is likely to arrange a reception for us.'

'Yes,' she agreed. 'Don't take any more risk for me. I can get to town some way. You've done too much already. Going to the Bar B B was a foolhardy risk.'

'I got a kick out of it. To make Curt Ford sing small is a pleasure.'

'Well, don't indulge it too often. The man wanted to murder you. And don't forget that he is a venomous reptile.'

They turned up a rough road into the foothills. It was full of ruts and rocks, so that their conversation died down. But Karen was happy. Joy flooded her being. She was riding beside the man she loved, and he had just risked his life to rescue her from an unpleasant situation.

17. The Night Drive

THE little car rocketed along a narrow, poorly defined road. Brush leaned into the road and snatched at the wheels. In the background junipers rose out of the shadows vaguely and vanished in the rear.

Karen had not the slightest idea in what direction they were going, nor did she care. They were climbing higher into the hills, and the stars were thick in the sky but infinitely far. She and this man were alone, a thousand miles away from the encompassing troubles that beset them. In the clean night, here in the uplands, all difficulties fell away and became nothing.

He was not the kind of man she had expected to love. His orbit and hers scarcely touched. In spite of a certain wildness of the blood she had lived a tame and conventional life, whereas his reckless feet had carried him along devious and probably crooked trails. His path would be a steep and dangerous one, even if he survived the pitfalls ahead. But she cared nothing for that. She wanted to tread it with him. Obscurely she realized that there is a deadline between good and evil. Gordon Stone had come to it and had made his choice. He meant to fight, for no other course was open to a man of his character. But he had turned his back forever on the road that led to shame.

At the top of a wooded slope he drew up the car, for the engine was boiling. A wind swept the pines mournfully. It blew from the north, and it brought with it a sound that caused Gordon to shut off the engine and listen attentively.

'Do you hear anything?' he asked presently.

'Is it the bawling of cattle?' she inquired.

'Yes. Driven cattle. They have come some miles, and they are being pushed.'

'Who would be driving them at night?'

'Some gents who wouldn't want to be seen trailing them in the daytime,' he answered grimly.

'You mean—rustlers?'

'Yes. I'm going to find out who they are.'

A chill swept her, as if the night had suddenly turned colder. 'How? If they are rustlers and are discovered, they will shoot to kill.'

He did not answer her protest. His mind was busy with ways and means. 'They must be coming down Elk Creek Pass,' he said, more to himself than to her. 'Think I'll run across and have a look.'

He started the car.

'But there will be a lot of them. What can you do alone?' Karen asked.

'Don't know yet. I'll see how things work out.'

Gordon had spent all his youth in this part of the country and knew it like the face of a friend. Leaving the road, he swung the car down a slope that ran into a grove of cottonwoods. Here once more he stopped to listen. The bellowing of cattle could be heard plainly.

'You'll only get killed,' the girl pleaded. 'It's foolhardy to try to stop them. I wish you wouldn't.'

'Don't worry. It will be all right. I'm only going to slip down to the foot of the pass to investigate. I'll play my cards close.'

A pulse of fear beat fast in Karen's throat. 'If I went with you it would be safer,' she suggested timidly, knowing her offer would be rejected. 'They wouldn't dare kill you with a witness like me present.'

'Rustlers are outside the law. They would be forced to rub out all the witnesses. If you went with me it would only double the risk.' Gordon's smile was warm and friendly. 'But I'm much obliged for the offer, partner. You're a gentleman.'

'Why do you have to know who they are?' she demanded. 'It isn't your business. You haven't any cattle in the hills.'

'If my enemies are rustling I'd like to catch them at it. Don't be disturbed. I don't mean to throw down on myself. It really isn't very risky. But there's a chance I may have to follow them. In case I'm not back in an hour run back up to the road and head for town.'

'Without knowing whether——'

She stopped, afraid to put her fear into words lest she make the danger more real by expressing it. The man saw her face was white and stricken.

'Buck up,' he said cheerfully. 'I'll promise to come back sound as a dollar. If you hear shots don't worry. Nobody is going to hit me. But understand, I'm not looking for trouble of any kind.'

He waved a hand at her as he vanished into the night.

Gordon passed through the cottonwoods and climbed a rock-covered hill beyond. It brought him to a bluff which looked down on Elk Creek Pass. As he clambered down there came to him two or three times the resentful bawl of a cow. In his high-heeled boots he slithered along a steep descent of loose rubble until he reached a boulder bed below.

The drive was close to him now. At the bend in the pass, just above him, he could make out a blur of motion. Out of it details began to shape. A man on horseback—cattle—another rider—more stock. The distance was too great for him to tell faces, but among the blobs of moving figures he was almost sure he made out those of three men. There would be one more, bringing up the drag.

A plan of action came to him. There was risk in it, but also there was a chance of success. He moved out from the rocks, crouching low, gun in hand. Most of the drive had passed, but a few stragglers were bringing up the rear. The drag driver came around the bend. If he saw the crouching figure at all he took it for an outcropping boulder. When he made his discovery it was too late.

'That you, Pete?' he called uncertainly.

Gordon was beside him. One hand held the bridle, the other pressed a revolver against his stomach.

'Slide out of the saddle—this way,' Stone ordered. 'Don't make a sound. And keep your hands in the air.'

'W-who are you?' the rider faltered.

'Never mind about that. Do as you're told.'

The trapped man looked down the dark and dusty cañon. His companions were so far ahead that they could be of no assistance to him. If the man holding him up meant business he would be dead long before help arrived.

Stiffly the night rider swung to the ground beside Stone.

He was a slim young fellow not much over twenty. His eyes were a skim-milk blue, his mouth and chin weak. Peering into the face of his captor, he gave a little gasp of dismay.

'It's you!' he exclaimed. 'I thought——'

'You thought it was one of Fleming's men,' Gordon hazarded.

He had not seen the brand on the stock yet, but it was a fairly safe guess the bunch belonged to his uncle and had been ranging the Three Buttes district.

'I didn't say that. Fact is——'

The rustler stuck. He had not thought out a story yet that would explain this night shift of cattle into the high hills.

'Go ahead. I'm listening.'

'Fleming hired us to move this stock.'

It was a lame story. Stone laughed harshly and let it go. He ordered his prisoner to take the rope from the saddle and drop the loop over his head. Stone swung to the saddle, the other end of the lariat in his hand.

'About face,' he ordered. 'We're going on a little journey.'

'Where you taking me?' demanded the cowpuncher, trying to keep his voice hard and confident.

'I'll ask any questions necessary. Get a move on you.'

For about a quarter of a mile they traveled up the cañon, then swung up a steep narrow gulch that ran into the pass. It brought them to a plateau. To the right was a blurred shadow that meant trees. Toward this Stone directed his prisoner.

'This is a nice, quiet spot and it will do nicely,' he said, dismounting under a huge live-oak. 'I'm going to ask some questions and you are going to answer them. I advise you to talk—and to tell the truth.'

'What you want to know?' the boy inquired sullenly.

'I want to know first the names of the men riding with you tonight.'

'I've got no information on that subject,' the rustler replied.

Stone tossed the end of the rope over a limb of the tree and drew it taut.

'You're going to come clean, or else——'

The youngster looked into his hard, steely eyes and drew scant comfort from what he saw. He moistened his lips. From a dry throat came a croaking protest.

'You wouldn't murder me?'

'In the cow country it isn't murder to rub out a rustler,' Stone retorted callously. 'But I'm giving you a chance before I do it. If you talk—you don't hang.'

'I'm only a kid,' the other man said in a cracked voice.

'Not too young to steal other men's cattle. What's your name?'

'Parke Rogers.'

'I'm asking a question, Rogers. Remember that lies won't serve you. I want the names of the men who rode with you tonight.'

Rogers swallowed a lump in his throat. 'I've never done you any harm,' he said hoarsely.

'I've never done any harm to the Bar B B men who have been combing these hills to kill me,' Stone answered, his voice hard and metallic. 'If you expect me not to hit back, you've got another guess coming . . . Cough up the names of your partners.'

Huskily the rustler gave names. 'Tom Webb—a fellow called Slim—Lute Purdy.'

'Gilbert send you out to steal Fleming's stock?'

'No. Gilbert isn't in it.' Reluctantly the man let leak another name. 'Curt Ford was aimin' to dispose of the stock.'

'Where?'

'I dunno.'

Gordon thought this was probably true. Ford would not take his associates too much into his confidence.

'Any reason for picking on Fleming's stock?'

'Gilbert had a row with him today. He drove the boss off his property.'

'Thought you said Gilbert wasn't in this?'

'He isn't. Anyway, Tom Webb told me so. Maybe Curt figured it would be an open season on Fleming now.'

Gordon dragged the rope down from the limb of the tree and mounted again. He directed his prisoner to strike across the plateau. As they traveled, he asked questions. That he had been fortunate in capturing the right man he realized. If Tom Webb had been the drag driver instead of Parke Rogers he would have got nothing from the Hairy Ape but a stony look of defiance. A bluff with a rope around his neck would not have been enough to make him talk.

But the capture of a man like Rogers had not been sheer luck. On such a drive the youngest and least experienced man would naturally be chosen to bring up the drag while the top hands directed the herd. Gordon had nipped in after the others had passed just in time to get him.

18. The Prodigal Returns

KAREN waited tensely for the return of Gordon Stone. The minutes crept past, as always for one in a stress of anxiety. She listened, intently, for the shot that would tell her he had been discovered and attacked. Nothing broke the silence, except the occasional slight soughing of the wind in the tree-tops. She walked up and down under the cottonwoods, too restless to sit or stand quietly. Sometimes it seemed she could not stay there, waiting for news that might break her heart. If she had not let him go, or if she had insisted on going with him! But why think of that, since she had done only what he had made her do?

There was no use trying to follow him. She would get lost in the hill waves. All she could do was wait. It was of no use to remind herself that he was strong and of good courage. Neither of these could help him against a bullet winging through the night.

Yet he was gone less than the hour he had suggested. She heard the sound of a horse's hoofs striking rubble, and found no hope in that since Gordon had left on foot. But she knew his voice when he called, and her heart lifted at the sound of it.

She ran to meet him, and stopped when she found two men instead of one. The first was on foot, a rope around his throat. He was a young cowboy named Parke Rogers from her uncle's ranch. More than once he had been her guard when she rode.

Stone swung from the saddle. 'My luck stood up fine,' he said cheerfully. 'I brought back one of the rustlers as a souvenir for you.'

'What about the others?' she asked. 'Didn't they object to letting him go?' She tried to keep the joyful relief out of her voice.

'No. They didn't even miss him. His name is Rogers. So he says. We've had a cozy little chat. He confided to me the names of the waddies who were with him. Tom Webb—Lute Purdy—Slim. Do you know them?'

'Yes. They all work for my uncle.'

'Curt Ford is in it too. Our young friend here is going to make an affidavit to that effect. We'll have the records all cluttered up with sworn statements soon.'

'Are you going to take him with us to town?' Karen asked.

'Not just now. We're going to drop in to the J F Ranch and have a little talk with my uncle first.'

Rogers spoke up. 'I'm not going to the J F. You got no right to take me there.'

His captor did not answer in words. He tied the hands of the prisoner behind his back and ordered him into the rear seat of the car.

'Afraid you'll have to sit beside him and see he behaves himself,' Gordon told Karen. 'He might get notions if you don't.'

When they arrived at the J F an hour later all lights were out. It was past midnight, and in the cattle country the day begins and ends early.

Gordon hulloed the house. He called several times before there was an answer. At last a head was thrust out of an up-stairs window, a shaggy gray one with bristling eyebrows.

'Who is it? What you want?' John Fleming demanded.

'A bunch of your stock is being driven into the hills,' his nephew answered. 'I've brought one of the rustlers with me.'

'I'll be down,' the ranchman snapped, and withdrew the head.

With no warning the front door opened a few minutes later. Fleming stood there, a rifle in his hands. He had put on boots and trousers. The lower part of his nightgown was thrust into the jeans.

'Who is it close-herdin' my stock so careful?' he inquired suspiciously.

Stone moved into a better light. The old man let out a startled exclamation. For a moment neither of them spoke.

Abruptly, Fleming said, 'I'll light a lamp.' From inside he called, 'Well, ain't you comin' in?'

Gordon Stone walked into the house from which he had been driven many years before. With him he brought Karen and the prisoner.

By the light of the coal-oil lamp old John's leathery face betrayed emotion. His hands trembled.

'I'm listening,' he said harshly, eyes fastened on the face of his nephew.

Gordon Stone wasted no words. 'This is Miss Gilbert. She has been a prisoner at her uncle's ranch. I was taking her back to town in a borrowed car when we heard cattle bawling at Elk Creek Pass. So I investigated. This fellow here was bringing up the drag and I cut him out from the rest. The rustlers are Bar B B men and Curt Ford is running the steal. I came here because it is your stock they are taking.'

An oath jumped from the throat of the startled ranchman. He apologized in two words to the young woman. 'Wait here,' he added. 'I'll rout the boys out.'

He went to the bunkhouse and beat on the door, calling to his men to rise. They wakened from deep sleep and took his orders to catch and saddle.

Fleming strode back to the house. 'Where are they taking my stock?' he roared at Rogers.

The Bar B B man looked at him sullenly without answering.

The ranchman walked up to him and shook a fist in his face. 'I won't take a thing off'n you,' he announced. 'You'll talk, or get a rawhidin' you'll never forget.'

Rogers decided to talk. 'They're headin' for Pyramid Park,' he said.

'They'd better be,' Fleming flung back. 'If you're lying to me you'll catch hell.'

'I don't think he is lying,' Gordon said. 'They were pointed in that direction.'

Without reference to the past old John wiped it out in one gesture. 'If you're going to lead our boys tonight I'd better have a horse run up for you, Gord.'

'Yes,' assented the returned prodigal. 'We'll have to hurry. As soon as Webb misses Rogers he'll push the stock fast.'

'What about Miss Gilbert?' asked Gordon. 'She'll have to stay here till I get back.'

From under his grizzled eyebrows Fleming looked at the girl. He knew the story current about her difficulties with her uncle.

'Miss Gilbert can stay here long as she has a mind to,' he answered. 'We ain't fixed with luxuries, but I reckon we can make her comfortable. Susie will look after her.'

'You're very kind,' Karen said.

'I wish I could ride with you, son,' old John told his nephew, 'but with this rheumatism I reckon I would just hold back the party.'

'We'll make out to get the stock back if we're lucky,' Gordon replied. 'No use you waiting up. It will be day long before we're back. You want to keep this fellow locked up close till we get his sworn statement signed before a notary. Probably you'd better send for one to come out here. We don't want Gilbert getting at Rogers before he goes on record.'

After the J F riders had left the ranch Fleming roused his old housekeeper and asked her to prepare Gordon's old room for their guest. Susie made the bed, hung towels on the rack, and filled the pitcher in the bowl with fresh water.

The room was a small one with a sloping ceiling. On the walls still hung the pictures Gordon had put there when it was his. There was a snapshot of him on a bucking bronco and another in chaps and wide-rimmed Stetson taken in company with Jack Turnbull. Both of the youths looked very callow and self-conscious. A lot of water had run down the Cache since that far day.

Karen felt a strange emotion at occupying the room. She had been a little girl when he lived here. All she had known about him was that he had gone bad and been sent to prison for his crimes. She had not even been sure of his name, only that he was a nephew of John Fleming, also a man of evil. Neither of them meant anything to her. They did not even remotely touch her life.

Now this young criminal was the man she loved. In spite of his indifference, his active resentment of her interest in him, she could not look at him without an odd, breathless excitement. Emotion had flamed up in her like tow set afire when the jolting of the automobile had flung her body against his. He cared nothing about her, of course. She was a shameless woman no doubt, and gloried in it. For she meant to have him for her mate if it was possible to weave a charm that would enchant him.

Nothing in her life seemed more strange than this, that she had known many men, a lot of them in her own group with similar tastes and interests, and had felt for them only indifference or at most friendliness, yet at almost the first sight of this released convict had been aware of a heat running through her lithe, brown body, or a passionate attraction toward him that dwarfed all her other experiences.

To be here in his room, where she would touch the quirt he had used and pick up a book he had read, sent a thrill through her veins. She thought of Susan Marr Spalding's poem, 'Fate.'

Two shall be born the whole wide world apart,
And speak in different tongues, and have no thought
Each of the other's being, and no heed;
And these o'er unknown seas to unknown lands
Shall cross, escaping wreck, defying death,
And all unconsciously shape every act
And bend each wandering step to this one end—
That, one day, out of darkness, they shall meet
And read life's meaning in each other's eyes.

Surely it was going to be that way with them. It was not possible that he could hold her quivering heart in the hollow of his hand and toss it from him as something of no importance.

19. War in the Park

GORDON made no attempt to pick up the trail of the rustlers, but cut across toward Pyramid Park as directly as the contour of the country would permit. His men swung straight into the hills. Through a cleft in the rock rim they passed into a gulch that took them up a stiff trail toward the front range. The way was rough and rocky, but the sure-footed cow ponies clambered forward like cats, the ropy muscles standing out on the sweat-stained skin.

The path climbed one side of the cañon. It was so narrow that the precipice along which the men rode fell away with no margin of safety from the hoofs of the horses. The deep gorge at their right was a lake of blackness the bottom of which could not be seen. If an animal lost its footing on the rubble the rider would plunge down hundreds of feet to the rocky floor below.

The cañon brought them to a mesa dotted with junipers.

Across this they traveled, stopping to pick up Jack Turnbull and Lincoln Conway from their night camp.

Since Gordon had been away so many years, he was not sure of the way to Pyramid Park. With the exception of Turnbull none of the other riders had ever been there, but Jack led them correctly, twisting in and out of wood pockets until they stood on the lip of the park, from which the horses slithered down, carefully picking each step of the descent.

The rustlers had not yet arrived with the stolen bunch of stock. Though the night was cold, with a chill wind blowing, Gordon lit no fire. He divided his force. Three of them, Turnbull in command, were hidden in the brush near the foot of the slope down which the drive must come. The others were disposed of in the long hogan built long ago by rustlers for a shelter. He himself waited among the young pines that fringed the precipitous southern wall of the park. His idea was to be in a position where he could keep in touch with both parties.

The night was black, in spite of the glitter of the stars, but along the horizon line above the bluffs ran a faint hint of coming dawn. Gray was beginning to sift into the eastern sky.

Stone felt uneasy. Had Rogers fooled them after all? Or had the rustlers become frightened at his disappearance and abandoned the steal? Soon now they must be here, if they were coming at all.

On the wind drifted the bawling of a cow. They were coming. Already they were at the lip of the park, pushing the drive down the slope. Presently Jack would close in behind them silently and cut off the retreat.

Voices floated to Gordon. A casual laugh rang out. Evidently the Bar B B men saw no occasion for quiet. They had no suspicion of a trap. As they rode across the valley toward the hogan their minds were at ease.

'Here at last,' one of them called to another. 'Me, I'm ready to turn in and sleep around the clock.'

'Grub first,' the answer came. 'After that, sleep.'

A voice shook them out of their serenity, startled them like the explosion of a bomb.

'Welcome to Pyramid Park,' it drawled, and rang clear as a bell in the night silence.

'Goodlemighty!' one of the rustlers cried. 'Who's that?'

'The name is Gordon Stone. Don't go crazy with the heat, boys. My men have blocked the trail. A lot more are in the cabin. You're bucked out.'

Webb answered with hardy defiance: 'That's yore story, fellow. You ain't got any men, except maybe Jack Turnbull and that li'l squint Linc Conway. Skin outa here sudden, or we'll hang up yore hides to dry.'

'I have all of John Fleming's riders with me,' Stone called back. 'Hullo the hogan and name any one of them. See if he doesn't answer.'

Webb shouted the name, 'Billy Preston.'

From the cabin a voice yelled back, 'Here!'

'Tim Sanders.'

'He's with the crowd holding the trail outa the park,' Stone explained.

'So you say.' Webb flung back a snarling question. 'What's the big idea, jailbird? Whyfor do you claim you're here?'

'We're after a band of rustlers. I'll name them—Tom Webb, Lute Purdy, Slim. We've caught them with the goods. Don't get this wrong, Webb. You're trapped. Drop your guns and shove your hands into the air.'

'Like hell we will!' Webb cried. 'Fellow, if you want me come a-shootin'.'

'Wait a minute. Don't push on the reins, Webb. I'll talk to Slim and Purdy. Why let him fool you, boys? Dead or alive, you're going back with us.'

'If you've got all the men you claim——' Purdy began uncertainly.

'No if about it. I have.'

The roar of Webb's gun came back in echoes from the cliff. He whirled his horse. 'Come on, boys. Let's get outa here.'

The noise of the battle filled the night. Voices screamed, amid the drumming of rifle fire. There was a turmoil of milling cattle. A raucous oath ripped the night. Slashes of lightning tore the darkness.

Gordon ran forward toward the churning mass. He found what he was looking for, a horseman just emerging from the frightened herd. The man fired toward the cabin, at the men boiling out of the hogan. He did not see Gordon until he was being dragged from the saddle. The long barrel of a .45 wiped his head and he collapsed.

Out of the reach of pounding hoofs Stone dragged the limp body. The cattle broke, stampeded. As suddenly as it had started the gunfire died. The crash of bodies whipping through the brush grew faint. Silence flowed back into the night.

Jack Turnbull's voice cut into it sharply. 'Everything okay, Gordon? You all right?'

'Yes. Keep that slope covered, Jack. It's the only way they can get out.' Stone called to the cabin: 'One of you boys drift this way with a rope. I have a prisoner.'

Billy Preston appeared.

'Any of you boys hurt?' Stone asked.

'Nary a one. Who is this bird?'

Preston stooped over the unconscious man. 'It's Slim. You shoot him?'

'No. Pistol-whipped him, after I'd dragged him from his horse. I reckon Webb and Purdy got away. We'll comb the park for them soon as it's light.'

Two other riders joined them.

'I never did hear so many guns poppin' at once,' a tanned young Hercules drawled. 'I can see how this will make me a liar for the rest of my life, tellin' how I won the war . . . That guy is coming to. I'll help myself to his hardware, so he won't make any mistakes.'

Slim groaned, opened his eyes, and felt his head.

'Better get him to the house,' Gordon suggested. 'I'll have to wash and tie up the wound. Expect he'll have a headache for quite some time.'

'You busted me one with yore gun,' Slim complained sourly.

'So I did,' Gordon admitted. 'It seemed a good idea. You were wanging away at the boys with yours.'

They supported the prisoner to the cabin and looked after his hurt. Meanwhile two of the J F men busied themselves about getting breakfast. Day was breaking over the hills. Soon the park would be flooded with light.

After those in the cabin had eaten sandwiches and drunk some hot coffee a detachment relieved Turnbull and his men.

'We collect Webb and Purdy, then hit for the J F Ranch.'

Jack grinned 'Hmp! The hairy ape will sure be some bear to collect. He's one bad combination, a fighting fool without sense.'

'That's right,' Linc Conway agreed. 'He'll go through, I reckon.'

'Likely he's up in the rocks against the north wall,' Jack guessed. 'We'll have a nice time digging him out.'

Gordon said nothing. He was staring out of the window, eyes narrowed to shining slits. The stretch of park in front of him he did not see. What he visioned, in imagination, was that field of boulders below the cliffs at the far end of the valley. Two men were crouched there, back of cover, ready to make a fighting finish of it. No chance of getting them out with no casualties. Not by a frontal attack. But it might be done from above, by expert marksmen. Jack would do for one.

He turned to Tim Sanders. 'Who is the best shot with a rifle among you J F men?'

Sanders was a heavy-set man with a brick-red face. 'I hate to brag,' he grinned.

'Good enough. I want you and Jack to ride out of the park and swing around along the rim until you get back of Webb and Purdy. Take your time. Don't expose yourself, but crawl forward till you can see where they are holed up.

Then begin shooting. You're not to hit them, but you are to drop bullets so close that they will have to quit the rocks and take to the brush up against the opposite wall. Understand? I don't want them killed or even hurt. But we have to get them out of there. We can't wait to starve them out, because Curt Ford will send someone to find out what is wrong that they didn't come home.'

Turnbull looked at his friend, with a searching eye.

'Say we drive them into the brush. What then?'

'We'll be waiting for them.'

'Webb will still have his gun, won't he?'

'Yes, but not the cover of the rocks.'

'You aim to meet him in the chaparral?'

'Yes.'

'You—and who else?'

'I'll have the boys scattered around in the brush. My idea is to get near enough to talk with Webb and Purdy if I can.'

'Yeah!' scoffed Turnbull. 'If you're near enough to talk they'll be near enough to shoot, won't they? That's not so hot a plan.'

Gordon grinned at his friend. 'I didn't invent this situation, Jack. We have to take it as it lies. Maybe you can suggest a better plan. Webb is a bad man with a gun, and I don't want anybody killed if I can help it—not even a Bar B B man.'

What Turnbull really objected to was his assignment. 'Why send me up to the rim? Anybody can plug at these guys and drive them out of the rocks. The war is down here in the valley.'

'I'm hoping there won't be a war.' Stone led Turnbull aside. 'It's this way. I don't know my uncle's riders. Sanders looks to me like a cool, dependable customer. We've got to have somebody up there who won't get buck fever and shoot up these rustlers. That's why I'm asking you to go.'

Jack grumbled, but went. His parting word was a warning.

'Don't get funny with Webb. That fellow is poison. If he takes a crack at you it won't be outa loving kindness. Betcha a hat peace talk won't go as far with him as you could throw a three-year-old bull by the tail.'

Stone watched the two men ride out of the park and vanish back of the rim. He left Conway and two of the J F riders to guard the exit from Pyramid Park. The others he took with him.

He drew up at a clump of aspens. 'We'll tie our horses here and move through the brush on foot. I'm going to send you in over to the left there, Bart, and the country close to the wall will be yours, Sim. Keep under cover every minute. Under no circumstances expose yourselves. I want you to go forward about fifty yards and lie doggo there. When I was

93

a boy I hunted in this park. A brushy arroyo runs out from the rocks where these fellows are probably hidden. They will likely try to slip out by way of the arroyo. If they do I'll be waiting at the gate for them. I'm going to propose a surrender, provided they give me a chance. Purdy may accept. I don't know about Webb. When Purdy comes through the brush with his hands up, if he does, you take him back to the cabin. Throw a rope over him before you start. Stay there and guard the prisoners till I come.'

'*If* you come,' Bart amended with wry grin. 'I figure Webb will fight. Maybe Purdy will to.'

'I said *till* I come,' Stone insisted quietly.

The party moved into the chaparral and deployed.

20. 'Everything Fine as Silk'

GORDON worked his way up the arroyo carefully, examining every rock and every bit of shrubbery as he went. The men he was looking for might be hidden there already instead of in the rock field. The unwariness of a moment could cost him his life.

Above the eastern rock rim of the park the sun appeared and flung long rays of light across the foliage. In the brush some cattle were grazing. One of them, a two-year-old heifer, stared at Stone, uncertain whether to bolt or not. On the fore right shoulder the man read the J F brand. No doubt this was one of the herd driven in the night before.

From the rock rim in front of Gordon came the crack of a rifle. Jack and his companion getting into action. They had discovered the fugitives and were driving them from the boulder field.

He took a position behind a large outcropping of quartz with fifty yards of open sandy wash in front of him. If the rustlers tried to escape by way of the arroyo he would have them at a great disadvantage.

How long he waited he did not know. There were more shots from above, and answering fire out of the rock field. For a long time there was silence. Gordon began to fear that the hunted men were not coming his way.

A bush snapped. There was the sound of a pebble rolling beneath a weight. A hairy face peered round a clump of cactus. After it came a hulking body.

'Okay, Purdy,' Webb called back in a low voice.

Another figure came round the bend. The two moved forward cautiously. They were on foot. It was likely that they had cached their mounts because it gave them a better chance to escape being seen.

Stone waited until they were about thirty yards from him before he spoke.

'I'll ask you to stop there,' he said. 'You're covered from every side. Drop your weapons in the hand.'

Purdy's jaw dropped. Panic rode his voice as he answered. 'Don't shoot. I'll surrender.'

'Fling down your gun and drift this way,' Stone ordered.

The cowpuncher did as directed. While he was moving forward Webb clambered up the side of the arroyo, stirring up a cloud of dust from his slipping feet. Stone flung a shot in his direction as the man vanished in the brush.

'Keep coming,' he told Purdy curtly.

Swiftly he ran his hand over the man's body to make sure he had no concealed weapons, then called to Bart.

'I have a prisoner for you!' he shouted. To Purdy he said: 'Get a move on you, fellow. I'm in a hurry.'

They met the J F rider on the way to meet them. Stone turned over to him the captured man and wheeled at once to set out in pursuit of Webb. He knew the direction to take. The rustler could not go back or go forward. He must keep going, if he traveled at all, in the direction of the cabin at the other end of the park. But this would take him into more open terrain. In all likelihood he would slacken his pace, uncertain what to do. Perhaps he would try to cut back. The chaparral in which he was trapped had a very limited extent, for a large part of the park was open grazing ground.

Stone traveled swiftly but cautiously. His gaze swept the mesquite ahead of him, ready to pick up any suspicious movement. He knew that Webb was a dangerous man, dominated by a gusty passion and an untamed savage resolution. Though he had no power to think a situation out shrewdly, he could fling bullets fast and straight. Very likely he had that sixth sense of danger which comes to fighting men, the instinct born of experience that tells what to do in an emergency.

A sound of some heavy body crashing through brush came to Gordon. His guess was, a horse and rider. They were moving fast, with no attempt to conceal the slash of vegetation into which they tore.

Stone deflected his course, to intercept them if he could. He ran, dodging mesquite and cactus as he went. Webb had stumbled into the bunch of horses left by his hunters at the edge of the clump of aspens. The man racing on foot to meet him did not need any proof to know that.

Through brush less dense Gordon caught sight of the animal plunging recklessly toward the arroyo. Webb was close to the edge of it, and evidently meant to hurl the cowpony at the deep gully without slackening the pace.

Stone flung up an arm and fired. The horse stumbled, at the very brink of the ravine, and went down into it headlong. Gordon hurried forward. He heard a voice rip out a furious oath. A moment later he looked down, to see horse and man pinned fast in a V-shaped fissure at the arroyo edge. Webb's leg was under the saddle, and he could not extricate it on account of the weight of the gelding. In his hand was a revolver. At sight of his pursuer, thirty yards down the gulch behind him, he twisted his head, reached an arm over his shoulder, and flung a bullet toward him. Hampered as he was by his position, the rustler had no chance to take aim.

'You're wasting, lead,' Stone told him coldly, his eyes bleak, without malevolence, without pity. 'Why tempt me, Webb? I can kill you and run no risk. No sense in being a fool. Throw your hand in the discard. A busted flush won't beat a full house.'

'Shoot and be damned,' the pinioned man shouted, and again sent a shot crashing across his shoulder.

Gordon saw that rage was burning hot in him. The man was too excited, too furious to listen to reason. Better let his anger spend itself, or at least drive him into a position of complete helplessness. Stone took shelter behind a tree and fired a bullet just over the head of the other. From Webb's gun a third shot roared.

'Not within five feet of me,' Gordon taunted. 'I'm telling you that you're bucked out.'

Webb fired, wildly, the explosions of his gun echoing back from the cliff. His foe kept count, and after the sixth strode forward.

The hammer of Webb's gun fell on an empty chamber. Gordon put the barrel rim of his .45 against the back of his captive's head.

'Which is it to be, a sensible surrender or a slab in the morgue?' he asked harshly.

Webb strangled his wrath. 'Have it yore own way,' he said bitterly. 'Get this damned animal off'n me.'

Gordon unfastened the rope from the saddle and tied the hands of his prisoner behind him.

'You killed yore own horse,' Webb jeered, with momentary satisfaction.

'I don't think he's dead,' Stone answered. 'I shot to crease him. Let's have a look.'

The cowpony stirred, lifted its head, and tried to struggle to its feet. Gordon took the bridle.

'Try again, Baldy,' he urged. 'You'll make it this time.' He coaxed the animal to its feet.

With his eyes on the prisoner he petted the trembling Baldy, soothing the fright of the horse with gentle touch and soft words. Webb attempted to get up, but a leg collapsed under his weight.

'Broken?' asked Stone.

'Gone dead on me,' the hairy man said sullenly. 'I don't reckon it's busted.' Resentfully he added: 'You tricked me into emptying my gun.'

'Thank me for that. If I hadn't I might have had to rub you out.'

Someone could be heard breaking a way through the brush. The cowboy, Sim Randolph, burst into sight through screen of mesquite. He stopped, staring at the two men.

'Everything okay?' he asked of Stone.

'Fine as silk. I had a little talk with Webb and he agreed with me it was better to surrender.'

Webb gulped out a string of savage oaths.

'Don't mind his language, Sim,' continued Stone. 'He's a diamond in the rough, and his bark is worse than his bite.'

'I heard him barking and biting plenty while I was hot-footing it here,' Randolph said dryly. 'How come with all that lead spilt nobody got hurt?'

'The gent's horse fell on him,' Gordon explained. 'He had his arm wrapped around his shoulder when he was making the fireworks. Sort of trying for a happenstance hit with no luck. After he had emptied his gun he got friendly, the way he is now.'

Webb wasted some more violent expletives.

'We'll drift back to the hogan after I've called the boys down from the rock rim,' Stone said. 'Soon as we've rounded up the stock we'll get out of here.'

He stepped into the open wash where he had first caught sight of the two rustlers and fired three shots rapidly into the air. From the bluff above a rifle boomed in answer.

Within the hour all of the horses and cattle had been rounded up and the party was ready to go.

Jack Turnbull rode beside his friend, just back of the three prisoners. 'You're sure the luckiest guy I ever met,' he said, with a derision that covered admiration. 'You meet four rustlers and collect them all, single-handed, your own self, without getting a scratch. Don't you reckon maybe that's a world's record?'

'You chose the right word—luck,' Gordon answered.

'Like heck I did. They all had guns in their hands and were ready to plug you if they could. You've got the darndest knack of makin' yore own luck. You bust in, with sixshooters poppin' at you but never hittin' you, and in a coupla minutes it's all over but collecting the prisoners. How the Sam Hill you keep from going to join the angels I wouldn't know.'

'I've always noticed that the safest way to meet a danger

is to walk right at it,' Gordon said. 'When you get close it usually isn't there.'

'Fine, until the 'steenth time. After that yore friends listen to the preacher tell what a fine guy you used to be.'

It was afternoon when the party drew into the J F ranch.

21. Cheyenne Contemplates Matrimony

BARRANCA buzzed like a busy beehive with the news that Gordon Stone had rescued Karen from her uncle's ranch and that four Bar B B punchers had been caught red-handed while rustling John Fleming's stock. No sporting event could have held as great an interest for the town as this warfare between the returned convict and the man who had sent him to prison. Financially and politically Gilbert was far stronger than his enemy. He had a preponderance of ten men to one. Yet in every encounter between them so far Stone had been the victor. Posses scouring the hills for him had come on his smouldering campfires, but the man they wanted was gone. His great mobility and his unexpected shifts had been too much for his foes. The enthusiasm of those who hoped he would win began to approach confidence.

Gilbert himself was no longer certain of the issue. There was something uncanny in the luck and adroitness of this man. He came out on top every time.

The owner of the Bar B B was sitting slumped before his desk when Ford and Cheyenne walked in on him. The little eyes in his leathery face fastened on the latter.

'So you're back,' he piped.

'You guessed right,' Cheyenne said. 'I drapped in to report progress.'

'Meaning that you did the job?'

'Meaning that the gent had lit out before I got to Carbondale—with your friends Stone and Turnbull.'

'The boys say the little skunk Conway was with Stone's crowd when the Pyramid Park business was pulled off,' Ford said harshly.

Gilbert shifted his gaze to the ranch foreman. 'Do you and your bunch of rustlers steal beef from me as well as my neighbors?' he asked, with insult in his high voice.

Ford lowered at his boss. 'Don't get heavy with me, Lyn. I was aimin' to cripple Fleming by runnin' off his stock. You know that.'

'I don't hire you to send my men out on private night riding of your own. Though I hadn't a thing to do with it, the Angel Gabriel couldn't persuade this town I wasn't back of that crazy business. I wash my hands of it. The whole passel of you can go to the penitentiary for all I care. Folks as dumb as you are deserve it. A rustler has to be a smart man to get away with his steal these days.'

'You ought to know, by all accounts,' the foreman retorted angrily. 'And don't talk that washing-yore-hands-of-us stuff. You'll work yore pull to get us out of this for all its worth. I know too damn much about you.'

'The other four boys are in the calaboose waitin' for you, Curt,' Cheyenne grinned. 'They claim it ain't so bad in the pen these days, what with baseball games and movies and all.'

Gilbert continued his indictment, ignoring the interruptions. He slammed a huge fist on the desk, shrilling his complaint with splenetic bitterness.

'I have a fine bunch of lunkheads working for me, or rather for themselves. This convict shows you up proper. First he lams the tar outa you, Curt, when your foot slipped, as you was so particular to explain to me, with all the cackling gossips of the town having grandstand seats. Then when you send out a posse to arrest him, Cheyenne bungles it so *he* gets captured instead and one of my riders goes to the hospital and runs up a bill on me.'

'I didn't hear anything about arresting him,' Cheyenne said hardily. 'My instructions were to bump him off.'

'Not so loud,' Gilbert urged. 'Firkins or my stenographer is liable to hear . . . Then you comb the hills for two-three weeks, and all the satisfaction I get is a lot of excuses about how you just missed getting this scoundrel. Meanwhile he digs up an affidavit from Linc Conway that is liable to blow both of you sky-high.'

Cheyenne leaned back in his chair, chewing a tobacco cud comfortably. 'Not me,' he differed. 'I'm sitting pretty.'

'On top of all that he traps a bunch of my hired boobs while they are rustling his uncle's stock. I never saw the beat of his luck. That puts me in bad and fixes him up with old John Fleming and all the other cattlemen who spend their time hating me and figuring out ways to cripple my interests. Read the stories in the *Courier*. Every fool in Barranca is laughing his head off at the way this fellow makes a sucker out of me.'

'They've been waitin' a long time for that belly laugh, Lyn, and you hadn't ought to grudge them a deep one,' Cheyenne said, with mock sympathy. 'But it sure looks like you and Curt were unlucky when you picked this guy Stone for an enemy. Too bad the hanging didn't go through as scheduled when you framed him for the Brock killing. You ask for a hundred per cent success from yore hired hands, but you weren't very thorough that time your own self, I notice.'

'Too much sentimental pity for him on account of his youth. The governor weakened and commuted his sentence.

Not my fault.' The top of the desk cut into Gilbert's fat paunch as he leaned forward, lowering his voice still more. 'Boys, you've got to get him, before he gets you.'

'That's right,' assented Ford sourly.

'You mean before he gets you two,' corrected Cheyenne. 'I told you once before, Lyn, that I'm one of these-here innocent bystanders looking on.' He added maliciously: 'Enjoying the fun, as the fellow said when his mother-in-law was bit by a rattler. Looks like Stone has the Indian sign hung on you. Well, you've had a long run of luck for yore money, Lyn. It can't last always. You've heard of this-here law of averages.'

'Don't fool yourself, Cheyenne,' his employer rasped in a whisper, shaking a fat forefinger at the rider. 'I'll mop up this two-spot like I always have done those who tried to fight me.'

'Will you do this mopping up personal?' asked the saturnine puncher, a hint of irony in his murmured question. 'Or by deputy?'

Gilbert did not answer. He turned to his foreman. 'That beef-buyer is staying down at the Kenworthy Hotel. Go talk with him about that bunch we have in the north pasture. Don't let him rim you. I'll want to okay it before you close with him.'

Ford rose. 'Might as well be drifting, Cheyenne. Keep me informed how things go, Lyn.'

'He means about whether you've pulled enough to fix the district attorney so he won't have to go to jail,' Cheyenne explained.

'I can tell him what I mean without any help from you,' the foreman flung out belligerently. 'Let's go.'

'Cheyenne is staying,' Gilbert said. 'I want a little talk with him.'

'Hmp! Private business,' Ford commented offensively. He was suspicious of everybody these days.

'Exactly,' his employer answered.

'Thought I was foreman of the Bar B B,' growled Ford.

Cheyenne was looking out of the window. He laughed shortly.

'Talk of the devil,' he drawled.

The gazes of the other two men slanted through the window to the street below. Three men and a woman were getting out of a car. The men were John Fleming, Dave Landers of the Scissors Ranch, and Gordon Stone. The woman was Karen Gilbert.

The cowpuncher made derisive comment, pointed at his two companions.

'Coupla days ago he was on the dodge—holed up in the hills and dassent show his nose in town. Now he's straddlin' down the street, easy to find as a bell-mare. I'd say his stock is lookin' up. See what respectable company he keeps. Old John musta killed the fatted dogie after his nephew rounded up a passel of Bar B B rustlers. And there's Dave Landers stickin' closer than a cockleburr. Seems like I've seen the young lady somewheres.' His sardonic grin slid over his employer and back to the street. 'Why, I'll be dad-blamed if it isn't Miss Gilbert. We'll all be one nice happy family soon.'

Gilbert did not answer. His pachydermous exterior gave no hint of what he was thinking, that his enemies were getting together and coming out into the open. He must move fast—and against Gordon Stone, who was the spearhead of the opposition.

'We could get him, right now while he's in town,' Ford whispered.

'Sure you could,' jeered Cheyenne. 'Hop to it, Curt. There ain't nobody sittin' on yore shirt-tail.'

'If a man watched his chance.'

'Dig up the tomahawk and paint yoreself for war, Curt. We all know you'd fight a rattler and give him first bite.'

The foreman looked at him angrily. 'I ain't scared of him, and I've heard plenty from you, Cheyenne.'

'That'll do, boys,' the man at the desk interrupted. 'Thought you were on the way to the Kenworthy, Curt.'

'You're the doctor,' snapped his major-domo.

After Ford had stamped out of the room Gilbert hitched his chair a little nearer the desk. 'Come closer, Cheyenne,' he said.

The cowpuncher's reply was derisively frank. 'I see you've picked me as the deputy to do that mopping. Much obliged for the compliment, but I wouldn't choose to accept. Don't forget I'm on another job right now.'

'We'll forget that little scoundrel Conway for the present. I have other business for you, Cheyenne.'

The bowlegged rider reached for his hat. 'Sure. I know all about that. Good of you to remember me, Lyn, but I'm plumb busy and haven't time. I'll be saying "Adios." ' He started toward the door.

'Sit down, you condemned fool!' Gilbert snapped. I'm paying your wages.'

Cheyenne teetered back on his high-heeled boots and sat down close to the desk. 'I'm listening,' he mentioned.

Gilbert waited a long time before he spoke, his gimlet eyes fastened on the blank wall face of the other.

'This is big money for you, Cheyenne,' he said at last. 'I'm going to show you a way to make a stake in the country, so you'll be fixed for life.'

On Cheyenne's dark face there was a smile. 'Fixed in the penitentiary?' he asked. 'How can you be sure of that, Lyn? They might hang me.'

Gilbert waved that aside as persiflage. He appeared to study the cowboy, as if he were appraising his quality. 'You're not such a bad-looking fellow, Cheyenne. You have that reckless devil-may-care look women are supposed to like. And you're old enough to have some sense. How would you like to get married?'

If the Bar B B cowboy was surprised his wooden expression did not show it. 'I've been married,' he said. 'And you've just done told me I'm old enough to have some sense.'

'You're not married now, are you?'

'No, sir. My wife had sense too. She divorced me.'

'I'm not talking about romance. You and I are men of the world. How would you like to marry my niece?'

Before Cheyenne's mind flashed a picture of Karen's dark young beauty, keen as a blade.

'Did she ask you to propose to me?' he inquired, with drawling sarcasm.

'She doesn't know what's good for her. I reckon she'll kick around a while, but she'll come to time in the end.'

'I'm good for her, you figure?'

'She's like a colt that needs to be ridden with a firm hand. You're the man can do it.'

'I see.' Cheyenne did not attempt to conceal the insolence in his voice. 'You're thinking of what's best for her. And that's me—rustler, bad man, killer. Can't you do better than that for her, Lyn?'

'You can reform, can't you?'

'After I've rubbed out Gordon Stone, you mean.' The eyes of the man were points of slitted light.

'The L B is a good ranch. Of course that would go with her, since she owns it.'

'I know the L B well as you do. No need to sell it to me.' He added, after a moment: 'You're a hell of a guardian. Miss Gilbert sure got a bad break in the uncle she drew. What's the idea in offering her to a man like me?'

'You'd make as good a husband as Gordon Stone, wouldn't you?'

'Stone.' The interest in the narrowed eyes quickened. 'What's he got to do with it?'

'Only that the little fool thinks she's in love with him. I can't have her marry a convict. You may be a hard case, but you are not a disgraced man.'

Cheyenne thought, swiftly, in flashes. If it was a choice between him and Stone, that was different. It was true he had been liked by many women in his time. His insolence and his recklessness had fascinated several, usually to their sorrow in the end. But there could be no happiness for Karen Gilbert in a marriage with Stone any more than one with him. Given a chance, it was possible the girl might take a fancy to him. She looked capable of wild and impulsive decisions.

'Aren't you trying to swap nothing for something, Lyn?' the puncher asked, dragging the words lazily. 'Miss Gilbert won't take your say-so about a husband. She's free, grown-up, and sassy.'

'She'll do as I say, after thrashing around a while. Don't worry about that.'

I notice she didn't stay at the Bar B B when you told her.'

'She would have stayed if that fellow Stone hadn't got her to leave. Fellows like you and him fascinate her. That's one reason I'm picking you. She might fall for your type. I'm not claiming to be any dear friend of yours, but you suit me a lot better than he does. You can put your money on it that if he lives he'll marry her.'

'He ain't sick, is he?' Cheyenne asked.

'Not right now.' The little eyes of Gilbert held fast to those of the other man. 'But I'm wondering.'

'If I take a crack at this, how do I know you'll stick to your agreement?' Cheyenne asked.

'Why, you know I'd do what was right,' the Bar B B owner murmured in a grieved voice.

'Sure.' The puncher's words dripped with sarcasm. 'You're honorable as all get out. Ask anybody about that. But I don't want any misunderstanding. If Miss Gilbert can't see me for dust—even after you have explained what a swell catch I am—where do I get off, Lyn?'

'Oh, I'll handle the girl.'

'Maybeso. And maybe not. But let's suppose Stone oozes out of the picture and after that I don't get to first base with the girl.'

'No use figuring it that way. I'm telling you——'

'Yes, I heard you before. Since you're so certain, I'll let you back yore opinion with hard cash. When Stone . . . quits annoyin' you . . . if you can't deliver the L B ranch and its mistress, you'll crash through with five thousand cash and I'll light out of here for keeps.'

After much whispered argument Gilbert assented. In his mind he held a reservation. It might be possible to avoid payment by charging Cheyenne with the murder of Stone and so getting off scot-free.

The killer read his mind. 'I know what you're thinkin', Lyn,' he said in a low voice, his shallow, flinty eyes fixed on the other. 'But it won't be thataway. You'll settle, if it's the last thing you ever do in this world. I'll never let you welch. Be sure of that.'

'I wouldn't think of doing such a thing,' Gilbert protested indignantly. 'I don't rue back on my bargains.'

'Not when you can't help it.' Cheyenne rose and sauntered toward the outer office. 'See you later.'

'Wait a minute.' The squeaky voice came oddly from Gilbert's mountain of flesh. 'Don't go off half-cocked, Cheyenne. You want to get at this thing right, so there won't be any comeback.'

'If I blast him off the map he can't come back, can he?' the killer asked. 'Or are you afraid of his ghost?'

'Nobody need ever know who did it—if it's done right.' The beady little eyes of Gilbert fastened on a letter file without seeing it. They were narrowed in deep thought. 'No use hunting him down in the brush. He'd be as liable to get you as you would him. The thing is to lay a trap. Couldn't we use my niece as bait? Have him walk into a spot where you're waiting for him? I'll figure out something before night.'

'That'll be okay with me. I'll take all the breaks I can get against that bird.' The cowpuncher moved toward the door again.

'You want to be careful,' his employer whispered across the room at him.

'Don't I know that?' the bad man answered. 'When I'm hunting a wolf like the one I'm after. He'll never know what hit him.'

Cheyenne bowlegged out of the office, his wide hat tilted at a rakish angle.

22. Gordon Meets the District Attorney

As KAREN walked down Dolores Street with Gordon Stone, his uncle and Dave Landers bringing up the rear, a quick excitement stirred in her. She could not match his long stride, but she moved with the light, free step of one who loved the air and the sun.

She knew the little procession was being watched, and that the story of it would run like a prairie fire all over town. This was the first time in many years that Barranca had seen John Fleming and his nephew together. It was evidence that they had buried the hatchet and were again friends. The presence of Landers was important too, for he had much influence with the smaller cattlemen and was accepted as a leader by them. More interesting still from a dramatic angle was this public confirmation of the report that Lyn Gilbert's niece had formed an alliance with his enemies.

Karen was no exhibitionist, but it was a pleasure for her to appear in the sight of her little world beside this strong, brown man who was just now so much in the popular eye. It identified her with him, made a bond between them. This was one more thread that tied them together and perhaps made possible her heart's desire. Maybe what she hoped for was a mirage, but she would travel toward it as long as she could.

The trip to town was an excursion into what had been enemy territory. Here Lyn Gilbert owned the machinery of the law, but Gordon Stone was playing the hunch that his foe was too wise to outrage community sentiment by moving legally against him or by enforcing his guardian's rights over the girl. It would be more like him to pose as an injured and maligned man and to strike at them from under cover.

Karen was coming to town to stay with her friend Rhoda Pinckney, a granddaughter of old Jasper. After the party had dropped into the office of the *Courier* for a conference with the publisher Hatfield, Gordon drove the girl to the home of her friend.

A vivid young thing ran down to the gate to meet them. She was a slim girl about eighteen, with eyes like wood violets and hair painted by the sun's rays to a ruddy gold.

'Darling, I haven't seen you for a thousand years!' she cried. 'Everybody's so *excited*. You've had such *thrilling* adventures. I can't wait to hear about them. I'm just *dying* of envy.'

She was a young woman who dealt in superlatives. Her speech italicized important words with enthusiasm.

Karen introduced her companion to Miss Pinckney.

The wood-violet eyes looked Gordon over swiftly. 'My goodness, are *you* the man who has turned this town upside down? *Everybody* wants to meet you. Are you really so devastating?'

'Not at all,' he assured her. 'I'm a gentle soul greatly maligned.'

'Then my grandpap is an awful liar. You nearly gave him heart failure that day at Pratt's feed store. But come in. I want to brag to the girls that you've actually been in the house.'

"You mustn't mind Rhoda's impudence,' Karen told Gordon. 'She's just that way and can't help it.'

'I'm not impudent at all,' her friend protested. 'I admit I have enthusiasms.'

'You look very shy and innocent to me,' Gordon said gravely, walking beside her to the house with a suitcase in his hand.

'Oh, that's just those deceptive violet eyes,' Karen explained. 'They are deadly weapons when our Rhoda uses them.'

'Don't believe her, Mr. Stone. She is trying to prejudice you against me, because she wants to monopolize the most exciting man in town. The rest of us girls are going to *gang up* on her.'

'Interesting but not authentic,' he commented.

'Just because she knew you first is no reason for her to *close-herd* you.'

'An unsophisticated child from the cow-country,' Karen said. 'Her talk is just full of ranch expressions.'

'Mr. Stone and I ought to celebrate this historic occasion. Will it be a cocktail? Or do you take yours straight?' Rhoda asked him.

'I'm a non-drinker. Got into the habit during my years of retirement.'

'You don't have to *stay* that way, do you?'

'It seems wise, for the present. I'll be moving along to keep an appointment. Nice to have met you, Miss Pinckney. Your grandparents and I used to be great friends. I wouldn't like to say how near I came to eating them out of house and home by dropping in just at mealtimes.'

'Mother has a good cook too,' the girl said demurely.

'Don't forget I warned you, Mr. Stone,' Karen reminded him.

Gordon smiled. It was pleasant to listen to the badinage of these young ladies, none the less because it marked how far he had come on the road to rehabilitation. Only a pronounced change in sentiment, one so complete that it viewed him no longer as a criminal but as an innocent man who had been much wronged, could explain Rhoda Pinckney's attitude toward him. Karen had declared herself, in action if not in words, before public opinion had crystallized, but Rhoda was swimming with and not against the tide. She approved him because the crowd she went with had voted him its moral support.

Stone drove downtown from the residence district to the Longhorn Club. He had made an appointment to meet his uncle and Landers there. Neither of them had arrived, but he found Jasper Pinckney and three other substantial citizens playing whist. At sight of him Pinckney gave a whoop and turned his hand face down on the table.

'Look who's here,' he announced. 'Nobody but Jack the Giant Killer. Boy, we been talkin' about voting you a medal as Barranca's most useful citizen.'

He shook hands eagerly, then introduced the young man to his friends. One of them Gordon had known in the old days, a ranchman named Venner. Another was a hardware

106

merchant, the third a realtor. All of them met Stone in a friendly spirit, though he noticed they did not endorse his old friend's vituperation of Lyn Gilbert. Perhaps they privately agreed with him, but as yet they did not care to go on record. None the less Gordon sensed a critical resentment of the political clique that had been running the affairs of the county. If they felt there was a chance to defeat the present administration, they would probably come out into the open against it.

Gordon realized that he had been fortunate. His activities had blown into flame a long-smouldering hatred of the methods of Gilbert. He knew that as yet he had done nothing to justify the public faith in his ultimate success. All he had accomplished was to undermine the position of his enemies. The sworn statements of Lincoln Conway and Parke Rogers had shaken the security of Gilbert by changing whispered suspicion into open challenge. Gordon's arrest of the rustlers had been a lucky break. But outside of these advantages he had managed only to stay alive while he was being hunted.

'Glad you came to town and showed yoreself, son,' Jasper said. 'It knocks into a cocked hat all Lyn's talk about you being an outlaw holed up in the hills. And when you caught that bunch of plug-uglies runnin' off yore uncle's stock it didn't help Gilbert's rep any with honest folks.'

Venner nodded agreement. He was a full-blooded man, with the color high in his veined cheeks. 'That's right, Stone. You're showing sense. You might have killed two-three of these Bar B B warriors and got away with it. But you didn't. People understand now that you've got plenty of gravel in your gizzard but are not on the prod looking for trouble. Lyn is about as popular as a wet dog at a church social, but until you showed up it has been many a year since anybody stood up to him. I'm not criticizing him, you understand, but mentioning points that occur to me.'

'I'll criticize him from hell to breakfast!' Jasper exploded. 'For a long time we've run our boot-heels over sidesteppin' any difficulty with Czar Gilbert. I'll cut the deck deep for you, boys. Till this lad showed up we all had a streak of yellow down our backs a foot wide.'

The hardware merchant picked up his cards. 'Who dealt?' he asked.

Gordon understood this to be a hint that the conversation was becoming too publicly partisan. 'Don't let me interrupt the game, gentlemen,' he said, 'I'll read a paper while I wait for my uncle and Mr. Landers, if I may.'

Half an hour later old John Fleming and the owner of the Scissors outfit came into the room. Gordon rose, and his uncle stamped across to meet him. Anger flamed in the bright eyes of the cowman.

'We met Curt Ford on the street,' he burst out, half the room still between him and his nephew. 'He served notice on you to get outa town, or to come a-shootin' when you meet.'

'Curt had been drinking,' Landers explained.

'I told him where to head in at, that he wasn't cock-a-doodle-doo in this town, and that I expected to see him behind bars for running off my critters. We mighty nigh had trouble right there.'

'Glad you didn't,' Gordon said. He added, in his slow clear drawl: 'Seems to me Mr. Ford is hard to please. He's been combing the hills for me, claiming I was hard to find. Now I'm here, and he wants me somewhere else.'

With mind divided, Jasper trumped his partner's king and lost the rubber. 'If that brand-blotter has served notice, he'll have to go through, Gordon,' the old man warned over his shoulder, chair tilted back on its rear legs. "You want to go heeled. Have someone trail behind you to see he doesn't git you in the back.'

'How about getting out of town before trouble starts?' the hardware man suggested.

'That will be fine,' Gordon said dryly, 'if Mr. Ford wants to leave.'

'We came in to talk with the district attorney, Fleming mentioned. We haven't seen him yet. Our appointment is at five. After we have done our business in town I expect we'll go. Curt never saw the day he could make Gordon go hunt a tree.'

'Maybe he won't meet you,' Venner said.

'I hope he won't,' Gordon answered quietly. 'I'm not looking for trouble. If we have a difficulty, it will be because Ford forces it on me.'

The district attorney, Driscoll, met the three Kettle Hills men with cool reserve. He was youngish, well dressed, with more than a hint of the supercilious in his manner. Seated in the office when the ranchmen arrived was Sheriff Scott, middle-aged and heavy-set, a politician who scattered smiles promiscuously.

Driscoll indicated chairs.

'I understand you have come in to surrender,' he said to Stone curtly.

'Exactly what is the charge against me?'

'While resisting arrest at the hands of a lawfully appointed posse you shot down, with intent to kill, a deputy named Oscar Carlson, familiarly known as Yorky.'

'A Bar B B cow hand, isn't he?'

'That has nothing to do with it. He was a special deputy appointed by Sheriff Scott.'

108

'Driscoll is right, boys,' the sheriff corroborated genially. 'Yorky was a deputy.'

'There were about eight men in that posse,' Gordon said, his cold gaze challenging Scott. 'Can you name one who was not a Bar B B rider, in the pay of my enemy, Lyn Gilbert?'

The sheriff lifted one plump leg over the other and smiled disarmingly at the young man seeking information.

'If you had been a law officer long as I have, Gordon, you would understand a fellow has to get his posses where he can find them.'

'It must be nice to have someone like Gilbert to get them for you.'

'He listened to his master's voice,' Fleming cut in harshly.

'Now—now, John, that's no way to talk,' the sheriff reproved.

'All this is outside the record,' Driscoll said impatiently. 'Have you or have you not come to give yourself up, Stone?'

'You are in a hurry, Driscoll. We came here to talk things over. You know as well as I do that two first-class unprejudiced witnesses—Hal Ferguson and Miss Karen Gilbert— are prepared to testify this posse of Bar B B warriors attacked us and in their opinion intended to wipe out me and Jack Turnbull. One of the posse, Parke Rogers, has since declared under oath that the orders given them by the cowboy Cheyenne were not to bring us back alive.'

'That statement has since been repudiated by Rogers,' the district attorney snapped. 'He tells me it was obtained under pressure, with a rope around his neck.'

'I expected that,' Gordon countered. 'Does he deny that he was caught in the act of rustling my uncle's cows, along with three other members of this fine posse of Sheriff Scott?'

'They all deny it. What witnesses have you against them outside of yourself and Turnbull and a bunch of your uncle's men?'

'When we took them back to the J F Ranch they did not deny it. Miss Gilbert was one of those who heard them practically admit it. No doubt they tell a different story now.'

'They are nothing but a bunch of damned rustlers,' Fleming cried indignantly. 'Why wouldn't they try to lie out of the jam they're in?'

'Do you mean that you're not going to prosecute them, Mr. Driscoll?' asked Landers.

'When I'm shown the evidence against these men I'll examine it and see how strong it is,' the district attorney responded. 'Until then, you can't hurrah me into telling you what I'm going to do.'

'Maybe you'll tell me what you mean to do about me,'

Gordon said. 'I'm here. The sheriff is here. Is he going to arrest me and throw me in the calaboose?'

Driscoll did not answer at once. He was in a tight spot. A great hullabaloo had been made over the hunt for Stone and Turnbull while they had been on the dodge. It had been given out that they were desperate criminals wanted by the law. Editorials had been written about them and sermons preached. But since then the tide of public opinion had turned, at least temporarily. Gilbert did not want Stone arrested. There would be an outcry against it, in view of recent developments.

'If I release you in care of your uncle, to be delivered to me whenever I ask it——'

'Better put the cuffs on me now you have me,' Gordon interrupted with a satiric smile. He appreciated perfectly the position of the district attorney. The offer of the hunted man to surrender was embarrassing. Out in the hills he could be played up as a lawless criminal, but under lock and key he would be a liability.

'No, I won't do that. I'll ask Mr. Fleming to go bond for your appearance.'

'I'll guarantee it, but I won't put up any security,' Fleming said. He too realized that Driscoll was in a hole.

'You promise that when I want him Stone will give himself up?'

'Yes, if we figure there's no shenanigan about it,' the old man amended bluntly. 'He won't come in to be massacred.'

'I resent that,' the district attorney said stiffly. 'As any honorable man would.'

'My uncle is a little forthright, Mr. Driscoll,' mentioned Gordon, a suggestion of an apology in his smile. 'You may gather that he neither likes nor trusts Lyn Gilbert.'

'That has nothing to do with me.' Driscoll rose from his seat, to indicate the interview was over. He was annoyed. What he had expected was to release Stone after he and his friends had sufficiently placated him and had filed bond for his appearance at a required time. Instead of which they had challenged him to do his worst.

He turned to the sheriff, after the others had left the office, and flung out a vindictive comment.

'I'd like to have my hooks in that fellow on a murder charge that would stand up. I'd certainly put him over the hurdles.'

'He's a tough nut to crack,' Scott admitted. 'Some changed since he was a kid sent up for killing Brock. I'd hate to have him on my tail.'

Driscoll thought the same.

23. 'Don't Let Your Fingers Get So Twitchy, Webb'

OUTSIDE the courthouse Gordon said to his companions, 'Got to see a man, but I'll meet you at the car in half an hour.'

'What man?' asked his uncle sharply. 'Don't you know you can't go jumping all over the lot like a chicken with its head cut off?'

Gordon corrected his error at once. 'Did I say a man?' he asked, and grinned sheepishly.

'You sure said a man, but if it's that girl you have to see I reckon there won't be any tying you till you've had yore powwow.' Fleming eyed him with a frowning gaze. 'Boy, you quit foolin' with girls till you're outa the woods. They'll only buy you trouble.'

'Did I mention any girl?' Gordon said innocently.

'You don't have to name her. I've been watching you an' her for two-three days. Well, mosey along. Curt won't be lookin' for you out in the residence section. An' you be back in half an hour, like you promised.'

The young man turned away from the business part of the town, but as soon as the oldtimers were out of sight he swiftly retraced his steps. He had said he was not looking for trouble, and that was true; but he did not intend to run away from it. It was his opinion that the safest way to avoid danger was to walk straight at it and to challenge its reality. He meant to do that now.

The favorite hangout of Curt Ford and the other Bar B B men was the bar of the Kenworthy Hotel. Very likely the foreman was there now, fortifying himself with Dutch courage. Gordon moved along the street rapidly, with a long, light stride that seemed effortless. He went to the side entrance of the hotel and passed into the bar by the rear door.

His swift glance swept the room. Except the bartender and himself there were only four men in it. One was his friend Pete Milan, the little cobbler. The second was Curt Ford. With him were two of his riders, Lute Purdy and Webb. Milan sat at a little table by himself. The others were ranged along the bar.

Milan caught sight of Gordon, started to speak, and strangled the words in his throat. He gathered instantly that his friend had not come to talk with him. With fascinated eyes he watched Stone move noiselessly to the bar, watched him stop close to the foreman, who had his back half turned to him.

The gaze of Purdy, facing his boss, grew glassy. Webb's glance followed. 'I'll be damned!' he exclaimed.

'You seen a ghost,' Ford sneered, and turned to find out what was disturbing them.

As he did so a .45 was gently withdrawn from the holster at his side and pressed against his stomach.

'Take it easy, gentlemen,' Gordon jeered. 'Don't get abrupt. I'm scared to death and my hand's shakin' like an aspen leaf. Too bad if this gun went off.'

'W-what do you want?' Ford blustered.

'You told my uncle you were looking for me, so I drapped in to find out what for . . . Don't let your fingers get so twitchy, Webb. If a bullet drilled Curt it would pass right into your bread-basket. Better shove up your hands . . . I said, *put 'em up,* all of you.' The mockery had passed out of Stone's voice, and into it had jumped an ice-cold savage threat.

Webb delayed a moment, after the other four hands had gone up. 'You're great, when you've got a gun in yore hand and the other fellow hasn't,' he sneered.

'Get 'em up, you fool,' ordered Ford. 'Do yore beefing some other time.'

The Hairy Ape raised his arms.

'Have to ask you, Mr. Milan, to collect the superfluous hardware. Make sure you don't leave any with them.'

Milan did as Stone requested.

'Now we'll all relax,' Gordon said. 'I didn't expect to find you and Purdy here, Webb. Gilbert must have just sprung you out of the calaboose. That's fine. I reckon you'll be going on another night ride soon. I really came to see Curt, because I heard he wanted me to get out of town *muy pronto.*' Again Stone's voice had taken on the note of drawling derision. 'Naturally I was scared stiff, and I figured if I could talk it over with you, Curt, maybe you would let me off this time.'

The shock had banished the fumes of whiskey from the brains of the foreman. 'I'm not lookin' for you,' he said hoarsely.

'That certainly takes a load off my mind. Uncle John told me you were.'

'I guess I was some excited,' Ford mumbled. 'Been drinking.'

'But you're not excited now? You're going to let me stay long as I like?' Gordon mocked.

'It's a free country,' the Bar B B major-domo was heard to growl.

'For those who aren't locked up in the penitentiary. I've done my whack at it. Now that the three of you are due to have your turn I've an idea you won't feel any too free in stir. But it won't last more than eight or ten years before you'll be out again.'

'We're not going to the pen,' Webb snarled.

'You're sure an optimist. Don't you know that Gilbert will drop you like hot potatoes when he feels the heat? Did he ever go through for anybody in his life when it didn't pay him any longer? Right now he's figuring on feeding you-all to the wolves and explaining how disappointed he is to find you such bad waddies. Good old Lyn, he always fixes it for somebody else to take the jolt for him.'

'What'll I do with these guns?' Milan asked.

'I'll take them with me,' Stone said. 'Friendly though the boys are, they might get frisky and start some fireworks. Well, see you at church some time.'

Gordon gathered the weapons, backed to the door, and vanished through it. Once outside, he lost no time in putting distance between him and the Kenworthy. Five minutes later he joined his uncle and Landers at the car.

'Did you see yore girl?' Fleming asked.

Gordon drew the guns from under his coat and dropped them in the rear seat of the car. 'You mentioned a girl, not I,' he said. 'It was a man I went to see.'

'Where did you get all that artillery?' Landers inquired staring at the weapons.

'I got it from the man I went to see and from his friends.'

John Fleming's bristly eyebrows drew together in a frown. 'What man are you talkin' about?'

'The name is Curtis Ford.'

'You been seeing Curt Ford?'

'Why, yes.' Gordon looked at his uncle with bland innocence. 'He told you he was looking for me. I thought he might be at the Kenworthy bar and dropped in there.'

'You dashed idiot!'

'He wasn't expecting me. Fact is, he was doing a little celebrating with some friends. Gents by the name of Webb and Purdy.'

'They might have blasted you full of holes,' Fleming said excitedly.

'That idea didn't seem to occur to them,' Gordon drawled.

'Did you have trouble with them?' Landers wanted to know.

'No trouble. I asked Curt if he was looking for me and he said he had changed his mind. So we had a few pleasant words and I came away.'

'But—the guns. How did you get them?'

'Oh, I had Curt's forty-five jammed against his belly and he didn't feel comfortable. I think he sided with my notion

113

that it was good medicine to collect his friends' hardware before ideas occurred to them.'

'You took Curt's gun from him?'

'Before he knew I was among those present. I eased it out of his holster as he turned toward me.'

'How in Mexico did you get away with that? You're the luckiest coot I ever knew,' his uncle said.

'Don't you think a little good luck is due me?' Gordon asked dryly, 'after I spent over eight years in the penitentiary for a killing I didn't do?'

Old John dropped a hand on his shoulder. 'Boy, you deserve all the luck in the world. But you know by this time we don't all get what's coming to us. Don't ride yore luck on the spur against these gunmen. Howcome you to pull off so crazy a stunt?'

'He served notice on me it was to be a showdown. If I had left town without seeing him he would have spread it all over the hills that I ducked out to miss meeting him. I couldn't afford that, not just now. Somehow I've picked up a rep I don't deserve, that I come out on top every time I brush against the Bar B B men. That's a good impression to have in circulation.'

'Yeah, so long as *you* stay in circulation and don't get pumped full of lead,' Landers said. 'Webb and Ford are both handy with a gun. What made you think you could get away without a battle?'

'I've noticed that if a man comes into a barroom quietly where others are drinking he can be right at the elbow of his enemy before the fellow sees him. It kinda shatters his nerve to be taken so suddenly, especially when there is a gun in his ribs. I counted on that much of a break—and got it.'

'Well, don't count on it again,' his uncle snapped. 'If you don't look out some day you'll go one step too far, and that will be the last you ever take. Quit yore grandstanding. You do not need any longer to show this town you've got sand in your craw. Barranca knows that. From now on play it safe . . . Let's go.'

They climbed into the car and Gordon took the wheel.

24. Gilbert in Conference

FIRKINS stood in front of Gilbert's desk and received instructions regarding an overdue mortgage held by his employer.

'I'll dictate a letter immediately,' he promised.

' 'S all,' squeaked Gilbert, his eyes already running over a proposed contract for the purchase of water rights.

114

The clerk shifted on his feet. He gave his hands a dry wash.

'About—er—Miss Gilbert,' he began.

The owner of the Bar B B put a fat forefinger on the paragraph he was reading and looked up to fix his beady little eyes on Firkins.

'What about her?' he demanded.

'I—er—think it my duty to mention that she is accepting a good deal of attention from young Ferguson.'

'Why pick Ferguson? A dozen men play around with her.'

Firkins stroked his little black mustache. 'She is, one might think, more—er—friendly with him—is seen with him more often. Tonight, for instance——'

'Yes?'

'Some of the Country Club set are going, if I have been correctly informed, to a picnic at the Red Rocks this evening.'

'Ferguson is taking Karen?'

'So I learned from Wally Henderson at my boarding-house this morning. Wally is one of the party.'

'Probably they will all pile into two or three cars and go together.'

'Not all of them. Ferguson is taking your niece in his new roadster.'

Gilbert asked more questions and came to a decision.

'Don't tell anyone you've mentioned this to me,' he ordered. 'I'll take steps to put an end to this nonsense.'

'Yes, sir. If your plans in regard to—er—Miss Gilbert and me are to come to fruition it will be necessary for me to get into closer contact with her socially.'

'You don't seem to be an impassioned lover,' the big man jeered. 'Why don't you sweep her off her feet?'

'I never get a chance to see her,' the clerk complained.

'Maybe we can remedy that. The little fool has had rope enough. It is time I taught her who is master . . . Better get that letter about the mortgage off at once.'

Firkins departed, aware that the subject of his relation to Karen Gilbert was for the present closed. He was far from satisfied, for he did not know whether his boss had changed his mind. In fact he was not positively sure that Gilbert had not been playing with him for amusement.

Slumping deeper into his chair, Gilbert reached for the telephone and called up the ranch. He got Ford on the wire and told him to report in town at once.

'Something doing?' asked the foreman.

'I said I'd see you at my office,' Gilbert snapped, hanging up the receiver.

Driscoll dropped in on him, plainly worried and annoyed. He carried with him a copy of the *Courier*.

115

'Seen this editorial?' he asked. 'Hatfield keeps pounding away at me. Wants to know whether rustlers control this administration. Twenty people have asked me within two days what I am going to do about it. I'll have to take some steps.'

'Why not?' Gilbert queried. 'Make a gesture. Indict the boys. Pull a nice line of talk about all lawbreakers looking the same to you. We'll have the case adjourned from one term of court to another and finally dropped.'

'I could make a bluff of pushing the case hard until after the election,' Driscoll proposed. 'After a while people will forget how red-hot they were for a conviction.'

'By that time we will have given them something else to think about,' Gilbert said significantly. 'I've put up with all I'm going to from that convict Stone.'

'The sooner you put him out of business, legally, the better I'll be pleased,' Driscoll answered. 'I don't like the fellow. He's as insolent as the devil.'

Gilbert's leathery grin was an ugly thing to see. 'You know I wouldn't do anything that wasn't legal, don't you, Driscoll?' he whispered across the table.

The lawyer rose. He did not want to know anything about any plans that might be in the other man's mind.

'Of course not. Well, I'll fix up indictments against your four men. Unless I'm pushed to it I'll leave Ford out of it. It's a pity they pulled off that night raid. Gives a handle for your enemies.'

'Cow hands have no brains,' Gilbert explained. 'If they had, they wouldn't be riding for thirty dollars a month. But you'd think after all these years Curt would have more savvy than to get caught.'

To Ford, an hour later, his employer was as brusquely plain.

'Try not to bungle this business,' Lyn said waspishly. 'You never had a head worth a hill of beans, but you used to be able to bull things through until this fellow Stone got your goat.'

'He hasn't got my goat,' the foreman protested, his full-blooded face purple with anger. 'Just because he came into a saloon and got the drop on me is no sign I'm scared of him.'

'I might believe that if he hadn't made you eat dirt twice before that. See you don't slip up on this little job. If you do, there will be another foreman at the Bar B B. And understand, Ferguson isn't to be hurt under any circumstances, even if he shows fight. I don't want this whole damn town down on me.'

'He won't be hurt,' Ford made sulky answer. He added resentfully: 'Easy for you to sit here and say, "Do this and

116

do that," like you were Napoleon Bonaparte and the Kaiser rolled into one, but if you had to put over the job yoreself it would be different. Why blame me if things go wrong? You're slipping, Lyn. You ain't the big mogul you were. Talk about Stone showin' me up! Why, he makes you look like a two-spot.'

'You think so, Mr. Ford?' Gilbert sneered, expressionless as the pachyderm he resembled. 'But *I'm* not the one he is going to send to prison for life if he cuts the mustard. You're the guy elected, unless I can work it to keep you out. Don't make a mistake, Curt. If you don't tie to me you're sunk.'

'Quit ridin' me all the time. I'm doing the best I can. And don't you make a mistake either. I'll do a hell of a lot of squawking before I go to jail.'

Ford leaned across the table, his brindle head thrust forward. The shallow, flinty eyes in the harsh face challenged his boss.

Gilbert watched him steadily. 'Nobody ever squawked on me—and lived to brag about it. Go slow, Curt.'

It was the gaze of the foreman that faltered at last. 'What's the sense in us quarreling?' he growled. 'Like you say, we're in the same boat and got to stick together.'

The owner of the Bar B B nodded. 'That's better . . . Call me up tonight after you've done this job. Don't mention any names. If everything is okay say so.'

For a long time after Ford had left the office Gilbert sat slouched in his chair staring at nothing.

25. 'Time for Her Friends to Take a Hand'

IT CAME abruptly out of the night, the summons to surrender. At the same moment Hal Ferguson caught sight of a log tossed across the road in front of the car. He flung on the brakes and killed the engine.

A man stepped out of the brush to the side of the automobile.

'Tumble out,' he ordered.

'Is this a holdup?' Hal asked.

'I said, get out,' the voice repeated harshly.

Karen leaned forward to see the man. It was light enough for her to recognize him.

'We're going to a picnic at the Red Rocks,' Hal explained. 'I have fifteen dollars with me. You can have that.'

The door was opened. An arm reached in and seized the young man by the coat collar. He was dragged out of the car like a sack of meal.

'Do like you're told, you fool,' the owner of the strong arm said.

Several others had by this time joined their leader, who now turned his attention to the girl.

'I'm askin' you to step out, Miss,' he repeated.

Before he had finished speaking Karen was beside him.

'What do you want with me, Curt Ford?' she demanded.

'I represent your guardian, Miss,' the foreman told her, civilly enough. 'He wants you back at the ranch.'

Hal interrupted: 'Look here, you can't pull anything like that. Miss Gilbert is a young lady grown. She doesn't want to go to the ranch, and she doesn't have to do it.'

'So *you* say,' Ford replied, his lip lifted in an ugly sneer. 'I say different.'

His hard, shallow gaze fastened on the young man contemptuously. He was a gunman and Ferguson was a playboy from the city. That was what his jeering regard said. If he had any sense he must know he was overmatched. Hal did know it. His opposition would get him nowhere. It would probably be very unfortunate for himself. But he was not a coward and he had to go through for the girl he was escorting.

'Nothing doing,' he said hardily. 'This bandit stuff doesn't go nowadays. I'll not stand for it.'

One of the men spoke up defensively. 'We're not bandits, mister. Lyn Gilbert is this young lady's uncle and her guardian. He wants to have a talk with her at the ranch. Nothing wrong with that, is there?'

'Quit beefing,' Ford snapped. To Ferguson he gave instructions. 'Turn that car and beat it back to town, young fellow.'

'And leave Miss Gilbert with you? I won't do it.'

'No use, Hal,' said Karen quietly. 'It's going to be the way they say.'

'I'm going with you,' he said stubbornly.

Ford gave a signal and two of his men seized Ferguson. He struggled, uselessly, and was flung to the ground.

'Wait a minute,' Karen intervened. 'There's no need being rough. You see how it is, Hal. I'm in their hands, and you can't do anything about it. You may as well agree to drive back to town.'

Hal tried to throw off the men who held him. 'No, I'll not do it!' he cried.

'All right with me,' the foreman agreed. 'Tie him up, boys. Not too tight.'

They left him there a few minutes later, tied hand and foot, on the seat of the car.

As soon as they had gone Hal set about freeing himself. The knots were tied loosely, and after working at them for some time he was able to slip his left hand out of the loop which bound it. Shortly he stepped out of the rope encircling his ankles.

He was unarmed. There was no use following the party to the Bar B B. It would be better to hurry back to town and get help.

But from whom could he get help at Barranca? If he went to Sheriff Scott that suave politician would explain to him, with his tongue in his cheek, that Gilbert was entirely within his rights as the guardian of Karen. An appeal to Driscoll would be as useless. The district attorney would probably suggest he have a talk with the owner of the Bar B B. In imagination he could hear Lyn Gilbert tell him to mind his own business. Among the younger set Karen had plenty of friends, lads of spirit who would ask nothing better than to attempt a rescue. Reluctantly Hal gave up the idea of calling on them for aid. This was not their kind of a job. They were young fellows recently out of college, most of them. In a free-for-all fist fight they would give a good account of themselves. But this would not be that kind of an affray. Guns might flash, and very likely some of the boys would be killed or wounded. It would not do to bring them into it.

His mind went back to the one man he knew who might be able to cope with this situation. Gordon Stone had rescued Karen once from her uncle. Maybe he could do it again.

Hal did not go back to Barranca. Instead, he drove to the J F Ranch. Old John and Gordon were at supper when he arrived. They listened to his story, the old man with sulphurous comment and his nephew in a tight-lipped, grim silence.

'Lyn wants his hands on her so he can keep control of her property,' Fletcher hazarded angrily.

'That's only part of it,' Hal explained. 'Karen told me that he's been putting pressure on her to make her marry Edgar Firkins.'

'Who is Firkins?' asked Gordon.

'His clerk. Of course Mr. Fletcher is right. Gilbert is promoting the marriage because he can control Firkins.'

'What kind of man is this clerk?'

'A sly, underhanded little man—not bad-looking—a fellow of no character, I would guess. But I hardly know him. He doesn't belong to the crowd I go with, nor to Karen's crowd either. She has never been alone with him for a moment and has never been in the least friendly with him.'

Fletcher slammed the table with his fist. 'Lyn can't get away with it! We're in the U.S.A., not in Roossia. By jolly folks won't stand for it.'

Out of bleak eyes Gordon looked at him. 'Who is that won't stand for it? He has got away with plenty in his time,

119

hasn't he? You don't think he'd stop at forcing a girl into a marriage she hated, when he has never batted an eye at robbery, murder, and the framing of innocent men to prison? Folks, as you call them, have taken anything from Gilbert he wanted to hand them. They will keep on taking it. Public opinion will go so far and no farther.'

'Miss Karen has sand in her gizzard. She's a li'l thoroughbred. Lyn can't bully-puss her.' The old man offered this dubiously. He did not believe himself that it was a sound argument.

'She'll fight him long as she can,' Gordon said. 'And how long will that be? You've seen plenty oppose him. How did they come out? Name one that beat him.'

'I'm looking at one now, boy,' Fleming said. 'You've skinned the old devil at every play.'

'Don't forget he put me away in prison for eight years, and that I haven't been back more than a few weeks yet. He isn't through with me.'

'All right. What's the idea?' old John asked irritably. 'Do we sit on our hunkers and let him do as he damn pleases with this girl?'

'No.' The eyes of his nephew were cold and steely. 'We get busy, without waiting for "folks" to do anything about it. Time for her friends to take a hand.'

'That's the way to talk,' Hal applauded. 'Count me in from start to finish.'

'How you aim to play that you are drawing, son?' the rancher wanted to know. 'And what kind of a hand is it? A busted flush won't stand up when it's called.'

'If it's called,' Gordon corrected. 'I can't answer your questions, Uncle John, since I haven't picked up my cards yet. Have to think this out before we shove in our chips.'

Jack Turnbull stood in the doorway. He looked from one to another, aware that something was in the air. 'If it's not too stiff a game I might take a hand,' he drawled.

Ferguson explained: 'Lyn Gilbert's men held up Karen and me while we were going to a picnic. They tied me up and took her with them to the ranch.'

The reckless face of Turnbull lit up. 'Do we bust in to the Bar B B and pull a young Lochinvar?' he asked Gordon.

'Not exactly,' his friend answered dryly. 'We wouldn't get as far as I could throw a load of hay uphill. Not with all Lyn's gunmen waiting for a crack at us. I don't mean to play the old fox's game for him.'

'You didn't have such bad luck when you dropped in on Curt Ford last time,' Jack suggested.

'Once is enough. Have to try something else next time.'

'Try what?' Fleming said testily. 'If you're aimin' to play poker with that wise old owl Lyn Gilbert——'

Gordon interrupted, a gleam of purpose in his harsh face. 'You're sure shouting, Uncle. If I play poker with him I've got to put my legs under the same table as the old villain and size up his stone-wall face before and after the draw. Think I'll go to town and pull up a chair. Gilbert certainly will give me the glad hand.'

The old man grunted. 'Hmp! He'll give you a busted flush and himself an ace full. I know that old devil, and so ought you by this time.' Excitement brought a glow of color into the wrinkled, leathery face. 'If you're figuring on any kind of deal with him you'd just as well forget it. He'd double-cross his own grandmother. Don't go making any fool mistakes like that. Lyn hasn't racked along all these years without having wrinkles on his horns. He's smart as all get-out. Look how he muddied the water so I threw down on you at the time of yore trial, boy.'

'I'm not forgetting a single one of all his kindnesses to you and Jack and me,' his nephew said quietly. 'He couldn't sell me a bushel of freshly minted dollars for fifty cents. But I'd like to find out if I can what's in his mind.'

'You know damn well what's in his mind!' Fleming exploded. 'He means to rub you off the map and put me out of business. You're not so dumb you don't savvy that. Keep away from him, I say. He sits in his office like a great, fat spider spinning a web to catch flies like you an' me an' his niece an' swallow us up. No, sir. Do yore talkin' with that buzzard when you're in the open with no brush around inside of half a mile. You never can tell when some of his dirty gunmen may be drawin' a bead on you.'

'Maybe you are right,' Gordon admitted. 'I expect you are.'

But under the surface of his spoken words he was considering ways and means. There might be profit in establishing contact with the old fox.

26. Hell-Bent for Trouble

GORDON STONE had always bulked larger in the community than his financial position justified. As a lad, fearless and reckless and undisciplined, he had stood up to Lyn Gilbert until the great man of the district had wiped him from the map. After many years, during which the owner of the Bar B B had grown fatter and richer, he had come back from prison still fighting. Barranca and the Kettle Hill cow-country accepted him as a symbol. He stood for the opposition to Gilbert and his coterie, for that individualism which in the West can always be relied upon eventually to challenge despotic power. One of these days, if he could keep alive till then, public support would come rolling in like a great wave and sweep aside Gilbert's predatory greed.

Until then he had to outguess as well as outfight his enemy. No doubt Hal Ferguson was right in thinking that Karen's uncle had seized her to prevent any chance of losing control of her property. The marriage of his ward to Firkins might suit him exactly, since his clerk was only a white chip in the big man's game. But Gordon's suspicious mind probed deeper. The old scoundrel had a way of killing two birds with one stone. There might be another motive, one not yet apparent. The young man was of opinion that he was a factor in the situation. Some bait would be spread before him, to draw him into a trap.

What he had suggested to his uncle recurred to him. He had not seen Lyn Gilbert since the last day of his trial. It might be a good idea to surprise him by a personal visit. He might get a line on what the old fox had in mind. Such a meeting would have to be properly staged, so that it would seem not to be of his seeking. For trouble might flame up out of it.

Gilbert always dropped into the Longhorn Club about five o'clock for a whiskey and soda. He usually stayed half an hour to chat with the oldtimers present. It was his one concession to the need of any social contact. Often he picked up gossip that helped him in a business way.

The club would be a good place to meet Gilbert. There would be present substantial citizens who might be useful later as witnesses.

Gordon contrived to meet Jasper Pinckney as the old man was on his way to the Longhorn. He wangled out of him an invitation to come in and have a drink. Other oldtimers were at the club ready to begin their late afternoon whist game. Asked to join them, Gordon declined on the plea that he would have to be leaving shortly. He sat back of Jasper and watched the play, a glass of lemonade on the small table at his side.

Into the room walked Gilbert, accompanied by his rider Webb.

From back of his hand Pinckney volunteered information. 'The old buzzard mostly packs one of his hired warriors with him these days. A compliment to you, Gord, I reckon. You got him goosey.'

Gilbert shuffled to the large easy chair he usually occupied and lowered himself carefully into it. His little beady eyes picked Gordon up and fastened on him. To the man beside him he murmured a warning:

'Stone present.'

Instantly Webb began to bristle. This was his fourth meeting with this lean, hard stranger. In each of the three first he had been bested. Because of him he was under an indictment on a criminal charge of rustling beef. The pent-up rage in the Bar B B rider was dangerously near the point of explosion. Silently he glared at Stone, his hairy wrist hovering close to the butt of the revolver scabbarded beneath his left arm.

'Keep your shirt on, Tom,' his employer snapped. 'I'm playing this hand.'

One of the card-players, shuffling the deck, glanced up and recognized Gilbert. He called across a greeting.

'Is this a gentleman's club, Venner?' Gilbert squeaked, 'or is it open to riff-raff from the jails?'

Pinckney took up the challenge swiftly, pretending to misunderstand the point of the question.

'Maybe you oughtn't to have brought Webb while he is under indictment for driving off another man's beef, but we're kinda liberal-minded and know he hasn't been convicted yet. Don't worry about it.'

'I'm not worrying about that,' Gilbert retorted. 'You know damn well who I mean, Jas. That convict sitting there at your elbow.'

Gordon rose. He said to Pinckney in his soft, even drawl, 'I wouldn't want to make trouble in your club, so I'll just drift.'

'You don't have to go,' old Jasper piped up belligerently. 'Lyn don't own this club.'

The pachydermous face of the big man was immobile, but when he answered Pinckney his voice shrilled. "Keep outa this, Jas, unless you're hunting trouble. I'm telling you that this scoundrel's presence is an insult to me. I won't stand for it.'

'Maybe, since we've met accidentally, Mr. Gilbert, we might clear the ground by talking things over,' Gordon suggested coldly. 'Understand, I don't like you any better than you do me. I think you're an underhanded, double-crossing, murderous reptile. If you had what was coming to you it would be a ten-foot drop from a gallows. But God has not appointed me a representative to blot you out. I'll not do it, except in self defense. Ever since I came home your hired assassins have kept crowding me. I could have put an end to three-four of them, including the gunman standing there beside you. I'm giving you notice. Lay off me and my uncle. I've had a-plenty of you and your warriors.'

'That's a threat!' Gilbert screamed.

'Not a threat,' the young man corrected. 'A warning. I won't be drygulched by you if I can help it.'

Edgar Firkins came into the room and walked up to Gilbert. 'I've brought your car, sir,' he said. 'It's outside.'

With a wave of his fat hand Gilbert brushed the clerk aside.

'If Governor Hillcrest had had any guts you would have been hanged eight years ago,' he said to Stone venomously. 'If it were legal I'd offer a reward to anybody who would rid the world of you.'

'When did you get so legal?' Gordon asked, his voice dripping icy contempt. 'You've had a reward hung up for me ever since I came back. If I'm shot—as I am likely to be —your orders will be responsible for it, you yellow-backed coyote.'

Venner said a word from the whist table. 'Gentlemen, this has gone far enough. You must not bring yore quarrels here to settle.'

'You're right,' Gordon replied instantly. 'Please remember I didn't start it. I'm on my way out now.'

'Wait a minute.' With the rolling walk of the cow puncher Webb moved swiftly to the door. 'What was that you called me, fellow?' he demanded thickly.

'Don't be a fool, Tom,' the man's employer yelped shrilly. 'Let him go . . . now.'

'I've let him go too long,' the hairy man answered harshly. 'It's gonna be him or me this time.'

Firkins dived for safety beneath a lounge. Without lifting his eyes for a fraction of a second from the gunman Gordon knew that those at the card table were making a break for cover. An attendant went through the barroom swing door as if he had been fired from a catapult.

Webb's hairy hand was on the butt of his .45, but he had not yet drawn. His crouched body swayed forward, as if he were rooted to the ground. The eyes in his swart face were dull as boiled gooseberries, and they held fast to those of the man he hated. Driven by the seething passion in him, he had elected to go through to a fighting finish. Already he realized it was a mistake. Stone could have been waylaid and shot down from ambush if a brittle and too urgent temper had not betrayed the Bar B B man. It was too late to go back now. He had to kill or be killed.

The cold, hard face of Gordon did not leave the hairy, brutal face of the gunman. Thought flashes raced through his brain. Was it to be two against one? Would Gilbert back with a gun the play his hired man was making? Or would he hang back, as he usually did, and be full of hypocritical regrets later?

From Webb's thin-slitted mouth poured a stream of pent-up venom. That he was working himself up for the kill Gordon knew. When he was primed for it his arm would sweep out and the gun would roar.

Gordon waited, nerves alert and muscles keyed. It would be soon now. The man was near the explosive point. Still Stone did not draw. He had studied Webb, during the long ride back to the J F Ranch from Pyramid Park, and he had noted that the man was logy and muscle-bound. The puncher might be a good shot and probably was, but would be slow in action. Gordon himself was fast as a flash of light. Not for nothing had he practiced in the hills with a revolver hours every day . . . In a moment the killer would telegraph his intent by a change of expression or by a shift of position.

Webb's arm whipped up. Two guns crashed, almost as one. A bullet splintered the wood paneling back of Gordon. There were no more shots. On the face of Webb appeared a strange, bewildered look. It lopped forward, as the knees buckled and the heavy body swung half round and sagged. Heavily the awkward figure fell to the floor with arms outflung.

Without a second look at the lax and motionless gunman Gordon whirled on Gilbert. The ranchman had not moved. His immense, gross body was still huddled in the chair. Only the gimlet eyes, fastened on his enemy, were quick with life.

'What is it to be, Gilbert?' asked Gordon, his voice low and deadly in its gentleness.

'You fool!' shrilled the big man. 'Have I lifted a hand?'

'Not in person. Only through your hired killer.' The words of the young man were etched in acid. 'Chalk his death up to your account. One more on the list. You destroyed him, not I.'

Gilbert began to set in order his story for the public. His philosophy was that the best defense is a vigorous attack.

'You lay in wait for me here, you murdering devil—knew I always dropped in every afternoon,' he screamed in his high, fluty voice. 'If Webb hadn't happened to be with me I would have been lying there where he is. Your finger is itching to kill me now, but you haven't the guts, not with these witnesses to testify against you. Go ahead, you wolf. I'm unarmed. Finish the job.'

Pinckney and Venner had come out from behind the furniture where they had sought cover. The club attendant was peering through a slitted opening of a partially closed door. One of Firkins's feet could be seen projecting from under the lounge where he had dived.

'You can't get away with that, Lyn,' Pinckney snapped. 'Gord told you he wasn't hunting trouble. All he asked was for you to lay off him. He started to leave, so as to avoid a difficulty. But yore man wouldn't have it that way. He called for a showdown. Not this boy's fault he had to rub him out.'

'You heard me tell that lunkhead Webb to sit tight,' Gilbert roared. 'You heard me give him orders to let this convict go. Everybody in the room can swear to that.'

'If you fed a tiger raw meat and led him around on a leash you wouldn't expect him to stay put when you took him into a herd of sheep, Lyn,' suggested Venner. 'This man Webb was dangerous. We all knew that. 'Course I don't need to be told that you regret this business as much as anybody. Neither you nor Stone were to blame, the way I look at it. Bringing Webb here was a mistake. No doubt about that. But you didn't foresee Stone would be present, so it can't be helped now. I would say this is a good time for you two to patch up yore differences. Shake hands and forget this feud. It's bad medicine.'

'Why call it a feud, Mr. Venner?' Gordon asked evenly. 'All I have done has been in self-defense. I've stayed inside the law ever since I came home. But I'm not going to shake hands with a man who robbed me of my ranch and rigged up false testimony to send me to the penitentiary.'

Gilbert heaved himself out of the chair in which he sat. 'Nor am I going to call a man friend who came here today to murder me,' he snorted, and waddled out of the room.

Gordon looked down at the prone figure on the floor. 'I wish to heaven this had not happened here, gentlemen. We'd better send for the police and the coroner.'

Firkins crept out from under the lounge. He took one look at the body on the carpet and started to hurry out of the room. All the color had been driven from his face.

'Like to speak to you a minute, Mr. Firkins,' Gordon said quietly.

The clerk gave him a startled look. Fear stared out of his eyes.

'I—I gotta be going,' he answered, from a dry throat.

'After we have finished our little talk.' Gordon led him into the pool room adjoining the lounge. Nobody else was there.

'I . . . hadn't a thing to do with this,' Firkins said, his legs trembling.

'I understand that.' Gordon fastened a hard, steely gaze on the man. When he spoke it was without raising his usually low voice. 'A story has reached me that you have talked with Lyn Gilbert about marrying his niece.'

The little man swallowed. He tried to speak twice before he could form words. 'I—I—Mr. Gilbert thought——'

'You are out of your depths, and you'll find the waters

126

rough,' Gordon said, still holding him steadily with unrelenting eyes. 'You saw what took place just now in the other room. Gilbert uses men as pawns to serve his ends and lets them be sacrificed for him. What happened to Webb might come to another man, if he got tangled in the plots of Gilbert. Is it worth it, Mr. Firkins?'

'Good God, no!' Firkins shuddered. 'I—I—I'm not in this —er—arrangement you mentioned. Not any longer. I thought —if Miss Gilbert—er—wanted it that way—— But I withdraw. I won't be trapped. I'm a man of peace, Mr. Stone.'

Gordon pressed for an explicit promise. 'You mean that you will not be an ally of Gilbert in forcing his niece to marry you, no matter what he promises. No doubt he had made a covenant with Webb—and you see what it brought his dupe. I'm not threatening you, Mr. Firkins, I'm asking you to sidestep the snares laid for your feet. For God's sake, take my advice.'

Firkins said fervently he would, and hurried from the room, still ashen-faced.

27. In the Matter of Bond

So SWIFTLY had the peril leaped up that Gordon had found no time for fear. A cold, wary instinct for self-preservation had swept aside all emotion. But with the danger past a weakness amounting almost to sickness ran through him. He had never killed a man before, and the shock of what he had been forced to do unnerved him.

He leaned against the billiard table and fought down the weakness. It would not do to let people guess how much he was shaken. His reputation as a superman, cold and inhuman and invariably successful, was just now an asset he could not spare. The morale of those supporting Gilbert was already below par. Gordon knew he would be watched warily by eyes searching for panic in him. His bearing must be so impassive as to discourage hope in them.

When he walked back into the lounge he was again sure of himself. Chief of Police Morrissey flung open the outer door and entered. He was a member of the club and had been not more than a block away at the time of the shooting. Word had reached him, almost on the wings of the wind, that there had been a killing at the Longhorn.

He looked down at the body on the floor; then his keen gaze swept the room. 'Who did this?'

Gordon said quietly, 'I did it.' He attempted no justification. Better let his friends do that for him.

Pinckney did not disappoint him. 'He tried to duck it, Chief, but Webb was hell-bent for trouble. He wouldn't have

127

it any other way. When Gordon tried to walk out he beat him to the door and said it would be a showdown right now. He poured out a mess of private cuss-words that b'iled. This boy didn't lift a hand till Webb drew. Ask Venner. Ask Carson. It was plain self-defense.'

'How did it start?' Morrissey asked.

The chief was a well-built, soldierly man in middle life. Gordon liked his looks.

Old Jasper explained the circumstances.

After verifying them by the testimony of the others present the chief said he thought Stone had better go with him to the district attorney. 'As a formality,' he added, 'I can't see you were to blame in any way.'

Driscoll did not quite take the same point of view. Already he had been in telephone conversation with Gilbert.

'What was Stone doing at the Longhorn Club?' he asked waspishly. 'He's not a member. Everybody knows Lyn Gilbert drops in there afternoons. How do we know he wasn't waiting there to get Lyn?'

'Gilbert didn't lose any time getting to you, did he?' Gordon drawled. 'A telephone is sure handy when you're in a rush.'

'That's my business,' the district attorney countered. 'I'm telling you that I'm not satisfied with your story. Looks to me as if you egged Webb on to draw.'

'Unimportant to me what you think,' Stone said indifferently. 'I expect Gilbert's hired men to think what he puts in their mouths.'

'You're all swelled up like a poisoned pup, aren't you?' rapped Driscoll. 'Want everybody to be afraid of you. Well I'm not. I'll treat you the same as I would any other criminal who comes before me.'

'Alleged criminal,' corrected Gordon gently.

'All right—alleged. You're going to jail until I can look into this story.'

'I've been there before.' The satiric smile on Gordon's face did not reach his cold eyes. 'Kindness of Gilbert the last time too. He won't be as lucky now. He can't monkey with the testimony on this occasion. The witnesses are a little too high-class.'

'You're making a mistake, Driscoll,' the chief told the other official. 'I have looked into this business. Talked with Pinckney, Venner, Carson, and the club attendant. They all tell the same story. Gilbert started to ride Stone soon as he saw him. There was some talk back and forth, but Stone said in so many words he had no intention of hurting Gilbert. He tried to leave the club, but Webb wouldn't let him. This Bar B B puncher said they would settle the trouble right there. He was the first to draw. It's an open and shut case of self-defense.'

'I'll expect you to hold this man a prisoner,' Driscoll said arrogantly. 'When I'm ready to have you free him I'll let you know.'

'I'll hold him until his bond is fixed, anyhow. If you want him held longer you will have to file the proper papers and get the court to refuse bond.'

Gordon sat in the office of the chief while he telephoned his uncle what had taken place. The old man grew excited at once.

'Didn't I tell you to stay away from that old fox?' he sputtered. 'You're so doggoned bull-headed you've got to go ram-stamming off to play a lone hand . . . I'll be right in soon as I can get there.'

The chief offered his prisoner a cigar. 'I don't reckon I'll bother locking you up. You look to me like a cool customer. If I left you here alone I expect you'd still be here when I came back.'

'Couldn't be pried loose from this chair except legally,' Gordon told him with a smile.

John Fleming brought with him to town three other stockmen from the Kettle Hills district. Landers was one of them. The remaining two owned the Triangle V and the Box Open A brands. All of them were men of first-class reputation, though their combined holdings in land and beef were less than half as much as those of Gilbert. They were out in the open at last. The fight of Gordon Stone was their fight. They had come to go bond for the prisoner, and they knew that the owner of the Bar B B would regard it as a personal affront. If he won out in this struggle, as he had often done before, he would see it cost them plenty.

The Kettle Hill men found Gilbert in the chambers of the judge when they went to apply for bond. The district attorney was also there.

Fleming glared at his old foe and fired the first broadside. Better let that boy of mine alone, Lyn,' he snarled. 'He won't leave you any killers unless you drygulch him.'

'We'll cut out talk of that sort, Mr. Fleming,' said Judge McMurdo severely. 'I presume you're here on business. If not——'

'I'm here to get my boy outa the calaboose, Judge,' old John said defiantly. 'Any objections?'

'I haven't heard of any, if you are prepared to put up bond,' the judge said with dignity.

'How much?'

'A mere nominal sum. Two thousand dollars.'

Fleming was surprised. This was too easy. He grew suspicious. 'What's the catch, Gilbert?' he demanded.

'Always looking for a nigger in the woodpile, aren't you, John?' the Bar B B man jeered. 'A young fool when first I knew you, and an old one now. There's no catch. That boy of yours, as you call him—a murderous ruffian if I ever saw one—was waiting at the Longhorn Club to kill me. Luckily for me Tom Webb was there. He defended me, and your fine nephew killed him instead. But Tom was born and died a lunkhead. He lost his head and put himself in the wrong. Your lucky convict slips out again. Keep him out of my way, John. I'm fed up with the scoundrel.'

'Lyn, you're crooked as the hind leg of a coyote,' the Kettle Hill rancher hurled back at him. 'You wouldn't know a straight man if you met him. I'll tell you now that you're a liar. Gordon never went to the club to kill you.'

'If I hear any more of this kind of talk I'll refuse bond,' McMurdo said sharply.

Fleming glared bleakly at him. 'I'm through, Judge. Nothing to say to Lyn I haven't told him before.'

The papers were made out.

An hour later Gordon left town in the Landers flivver.

'We've got the old scalawag on the run!' Fleming exulted jubilantly. 'Lyn wanted to hold you but he didn't have the guts. He was scared the town would get up on its hind legs about it.'

Gordon was not so sure of that. He wondered whether he had not been turned loose because Gilbert wanted him free. If so, why?

28. Karen Writes a Note

KAREN sat on the porch of the Bar B B ranch house reading the *Courier*. Her eyes were racing through a front-page story, one with a seven-column head. It was an account of the killing of Webb at the Longhorn Club. The news shocked her and set the blood in her veins strumming with excitement.

Obviously Webb had been the aggressor and had forced Gordon Stone to shoot in self-defense. Karen was deeply glad her friend had come through unhurt, yet was greatly disturbed at what had occurred. It showed how determined his enemies were to destroy him. Moreover, she was afraid of the effect of this encounter on Gordon. Of late he had been growing less hard and bitter. An appreciation of the value of life had been renewed in him. He had learned to laugh again. But one who kills has the mark of Cain stamped on him. In the thoughts of those about him he is set apart from others. It is brought home to him that there is a barrier which makes him a stranger. Karen did not want him driven back inside himself. She wished she could get word to him that she was on his side now more than ever.

A rider of the Bar B B was sitting in front of the bunk house mending a stirrup leather. Probably he was there to keep an eye on her and see she did not wander too far. The man was Parke Rogers, the youngster who had signed and later repudiated a confession of rustling J F stock.

He came to the house to get some rivets. Searching through the tool chest on the porch, he seemed to have a difficulty in finding what he wanted. Karen became aware that his skim-milk eyes drifted her way more than once. She guessed he wanted to speak to her and did not know how to begin. Since she was used to attracting a good deal of attention from men, she wondered if he was getting sentimental. In that case she would have to nip his approaches in the bud before they became annoying.

Not until he was passing her on the way back to the bunkhouse did he find courage to speak. 'Kinda mosey down my way, careless-like, and stop to talk,' he muttered out of the corner of his weak mouth.

Karen was interested, not in the man but in his suggestion. This did not sound like an entering wedge for anything of a flirtatious nature. It was taking too much for granted. Yet he had something to say to her he did not want anybody else to hear.

Presently she rose, stepped down from the porch, and played with a collie dog which had been sitting in the sun with adoring eyes fixed on her. Accompanied by the dog, she wandered slowly in the direction of the bunkhouse.

To Rogers she said, 'You have something you want to tell me?"

He nodded, after making certain they were out of hearing of others. 'Yes, ma'am. A message from yore friend Hal Ferguson. He's been fixing up a plan to help you escape from here. I was to tell you that he'll have a car waiting for you tonight on the road outside the southwest corner of the big pasture. You're to send him word through me that you'll try to be there.'

'How can I be there when I'm watched all the time?'

'Mrs. Ford likes you and feels kinda sorry for you. We figured you could talk her into letting you slip away. He says for you to write him a little note. Don't put his name on it, in case it should be discovered. Just tell him you'll be there at a set time. If you can't make it the first night maybe you can the second.'

'When did you see Hal Ferguson?' she asked.

'Yesterday, when I was in town. On the street.'

'Are you a friend of his?'

'You couldn't exactly call me a friend,' admitted Rogers. 'We say "Hello!" '

'You are one of Lyn Gilbert's men. Why would you be bringing messages from Mr. Ferguson about helping me to escape?'

'Lyn ain't bought me body and soul,' the young man said with weak violence.

'You're in trouble about rustling and you are expecting him to get you out of it, but you want me to believe you are working for me and against him. Is that reasonable?' Her keen eyes searched his putty face.

His face flushed. 'A fellow has to look after himself. Lyn is playing his own hand, all right. I'm just a chip in his game. If he feels like it he'll feed me to the wolves. Don't you know it?'

'Yes, I know it. But how are you looking after yourself by helping me? You'll have to be plainer.'

Rogers was embarrassed. He looked down and drew a mark in the sand with one side of a worn boot. 'If you got to know, Ferguson crashed through with fifty dollars for me to get this message to you. You'll have to keep yore mouth shut or I'm sunk, Miss Gilbert.'

This sounded probable. Karen pointed one more question at him. She knew he would not have any money from his wages until the end of the month. 'Can you show me the fifty dollars?'

He looked at her resentfully. From the hip pocket of his Levis he drew slowly a roll of bills. After a swift glance around, to make sure they were not observed, he flipped back the edges of the notes to show they were tens.

'Seeing is believing,' she said with a little nod. 'Excuse me for doubting, but you know I'm in the enemy country.'

'I'm driving in to Barranca this aft to get supplies. If you figure you can slip away tonight—and it looks to me like you could—write a note for me to give Ferguson.'

Karen wrote a note and handed it to the puncher an hour later. She did not entirely trust him, but she could see no reason why he would find it to his advantage to deceive her. If she slipped out to the rendezvous and did not find Hal there, there would be no profit in it for the cowboy.

After the midday dinner Karen saw Rogers start for town in an old car. The foreman gave him instructions, and after the man had gone walked back to the house. At the porch he stopped to turn his ugly grin on Karen.

'Having a nice visit here?' he asked.

There was something disturbing in his manner, as if for some reason he was gloating over her. She wondered if Rog-

132

ers had betrayed her to Curt Ford. If so, she could find no logical reason for it. Neither her uncle nor his major domo had anything against Hal Ferguson. It would do them no good to spring a trap on him, if that was what was in their minds.

Karen gave him a lead. 'It's almost over,' she said. 'I'll be leaving soon.'

'That so?' he jeered. 'Decided just when to go?'

His wife was seated in a rocking chair on the porch, her plump hands folded over an ample lap. Glenna could do nothing for a long time with no visible discontent.

'I expect Miss Karen is getting bored by us,' she volunteered. 'It's nice to have her here, but she must miss all the good times she has in town.'

'I do. But you've been very nice to me, Mrs. Ford.'

The foreman sat down. 'We've certainly tried to make Miss Gilbert feel we wanted her to stay. The welcome sign is hanging right out for her.'

'I've noticed that,' Karen mentioned. 'But after all a guest ought not to impose on her hosts. Time I was going.'

From the corner of his cold, shallow eyes the ranch manager slid a look at her.

'Maybe you might get one of yore friends to pick you up and run you to town.'

'Why, we could get her to town, Curt,' Glenna told him reproachfully.

'So we could, when it's time for her to go,' Ford agreed.

Karen thought, furiously. So it had been a trap after all. Surely Ford had not arranged it only to humiliate her. That would not be reason enough. There must be an advantage in it somewhere for him or for her uncle. But where? The thing did not make sense. They were tempting her to try to escape, yet Ford was practically admitting this by openly exulting in the frustration of her hopes. Apparently their plan—if there was one at all—did not depend upon her unwitting cooperation, since the foreman was making it clear she could not get away. Was it possible that something had taken place which made it necessary for them to get Hal Ferguson into their hands? It did not seem likely. How could he be a menace to Lyn Gilbert?

Ford was off on another subject. 'Yore friend the convict has broke loose again. I expect you read the story in the *Courier*. Hatfield didn't tell it the way it happened. He'll turn black into white any day to do us dirt. Stone lay in wait at the Longhorn Club for Lyn. He would have got him too if yore uncle hadn't of took Tom Webb with him. So poor Tom gets rubbed out instead. The killer couldn't get them both.'

'If it's the way you say, why did Judge McMurdo release Mr. Stone on two thousand dollars' bond?' Karen asked.

The eyes of Curt Ford gleamed with evil triumph. 'I reckon the damn convict is asking himself that question too. He'll find out . . . right soon. Before morning, we'll collect the wolf's scalp.'

'How will he find out? What do you mean, you'll collect his scalp?'

Ford pulled up abruptly. He realized he had been talking too much. The steady gaze of the girl was fixed on him. 'Never mind. None of your business.'

'Why, Curt, that ain't any way to talk to Miss Karen,' his wife protested plaintively.

Her husband rose to walk into the house, but turned at the door for an explanatory word. He spoke to their guest, in a voice meant to be suavely disarming. 'Reckon you're right, Glenna. I don't mean a thing, Miss Gilbert, except that he can't kill an innocent man these days and get away with it. He'll learn there's law in the land.'

For Karen the sunshine lost its warmth. A chill breath of winter swept through her. The face of the man betrayed him. There was etched in it such a look of sly and furtive cruelty that she knew some deviltry was under way against Gordon.

29. 'I'll Thank You All My Life'

BEHIND a closed door Karen sat down in her room and tried to think out the meaning of the enigma with which she was faced. Carefully she checked all her impressions and remembrances of the hours between the time when Parke Rogers had spoken to her and the moment when Curt Ford had made a belated attempt to obliterate from her mind his threat of immediate vengeance against Gordon Stone. She essayed a reconstruction of what had been said. Everything done and spoken she weighed critically. That there was a connection between the letter she had written Hal Ferguson and the foreman's triumphant certainty of getting rid of his enemy during the night she was convinced.

A word of the cowboy Rogers came to her mind and brought sudden light. He had told her not to address her note to Hal by name for fear it might be discovered. His warning had struck her as unnecessary, but she had obeyed it. Now she knew why it had been given. The note was to reach Gordon Stone and not young Ferguson. It was to draw him into an ambush where his enemies would be waiting for him. She had been used as a lure for his destruction.

Karen tried to recall how she had worded the note. Was there anything in it to make Gordon suspicious of the rendezvous? Had she mentioned the message sent by Ferguson? She was afraid not. All she had written was that she would be on the road outside the southwest corner of the big pasture about ten o'clock that evening (Tuesday) if she could slip away unnoticed.

He would walk into the trap and meet a blast of gunfire. It was four o'clock now. In six hours, unless she could save him, his splendid, supple body would be lying lax and lifeless in the dust. She could see his enemies standing above him making ribald jokes to be greeted with cruel laughter. Drygulched at last, the man who had challenged her uncle's brutal power and almost shaken it down would be obliterated forever. Lyn Gilbert would be more than ever lord of the Kettle Hill country.

Just now Karen cared nothing about the Bar B B man's struggle to maintain his power. The terror rising in her throat was for the man his enemies meant to murder. She had to prevent it. All her life was wrapped up in his. With the hard and reckless force that was Gordon Stone wiped out, existence would have no meaning. The world would be a desert waste too empty for travel.

She fought down her panic, to consider ways and means. In the evenings Glenna was her companion, a chaperon given the task of making sure she was locked in her room after they separated for the night. There were others in the house, a maid and the Chinese cook Sing Toy. Of late a guard patrolled the place from sunset to sunrise. Curt Ford was never in evidence after supper.

The most important obstacle to escape was Glenna. With her help Sing Toy and the maid could be decoyed to another part of the house. Karen would have to take her chance with the sentry. But first Glenna had to be won. This would not be easy. She was a good sort, indolent, kindly, of a pliable disposition. Her impulses were all to friendliness. But she had a deep-rooted fear of her husband. He was a man of violent temper, harsh and dominating, and when he was angry he lashed out at her as he did at his horse. She had been a complaisant wife, had never crossed his will in any matter of importance. If she ever did, he would make her pay with savage and enduring cruelty.

After supper Karen enticed Glenna to her room for a chat. There was no difficulty in that, for she was a never-failing source of interest to her hostess. The older woman was interested in clothes, in the point of view of the younger generation. The personality of this vital and independent girl fascinated her. Glenna was soft as putty. Under pressure she had given up what she most wanted in life. But she could and did admire a woman who fought valiantly for her own.

Karen put Glenna in the most comfortable chair and attacked.

'Do you hate Gordon Stone very much?' she asked.

Mrs. Ford looked at her, surprised. 'Why, no! Of course I don't. We used to be engaged. If it hadn't been for his troubles——'

The girl cut in. Her hostess was inclined to talk at length, and there was no time now for reminiscence. 'Because if you do you can satisfy it tonight. He is going to be murdered.'

Glenna dropped her double chin and stared at Karen. She was too amazed to speak.

'In about three hours,' Karen continued. 'At the southwest corner of the big pasture. They're using me to lead him into a trap.'

'How do you know?' Glenna asked, big-eyed.

Karen told her. After she had finished, the other woman shook her blonde head.

'No, dearie. Curt is hard, but he wouldn't do that. You're just imagining things. He talks a lot, Curt does. I've learned that a lot of it doesn't mean anything.'

'This means the death of Gordon Stone,' Karen protested. 'Can't you see how it all fits into place? The man Rogers was chosen to get me to write the note. He told me not to use Hal Ferguson's name and just to say I would be at the meeting-place at ten o'clock tonight. Like a fool, I fell into the trap. The note wasn't to go to Hal. That's why I wasn't to write his name. After I had written it your husband didn't trouble to keep secret from me that it was a plot. You heard him jeering me about getting one of my friends to run me to town. He knew all about it. Since I am a prisoner he didn't care if I found out I had been duped. But in his triumph he said a little too much. He told me just when Gordon is to be killed. So he tried to wipe that from my mind by talk about the law getting Gordon. Oh, Glenna, don't let them do this awful thing! Help me to save Gordon.'

'How can I help save him?' the older woman asked helplessly. 'Curt wouldn't change his plans because of me. I have no influence with him.'

'You can let me escape in time to warn Gordon.'

'I couldn't do that, dearie,' Glenna said at once. 'Curt would never forgive me if I interfered. I don't know what all he would do to me. He's . . . not gentle, you know.'

'We could make it look as if I had escaped without your help.'

'That wouldn't matter to Curt. He would blame me just the same.'

136

'You loved Gordon once. He never did you any harm. I don't want to tear open healed up wounds, but I think your conscience has always troubled you because you deserted him and married the enemy who helped send him to prison. This is your great chance to make up for the wrong you did him, Glenna. Help me save his life tonight and you'll never need to be ashamed about him again.'

Glenna began to cry. 'It's all very well for you to say help save him, but like as not you're just frightened about nothing. Mr. Gilbert says for you to stay here. If I let you go Curt will go on something awful. I'll be the one he's mad at, and I'll be here and have to take it. I just can't do it, and I don't think you ought to ask me.'

'It's to keep a man from being killed, Glenna.'

'That's what *you* say, but I don't think so. You're worked up about nothing because you are in love with Gordon. Curt isn't mean enough to do such a thing.'

'If Gordon is killed I'll testify in court about the plot and that your husband told me it would be done tonight.'

Through her tears Glenna looked into the young face of tragic woe. 'That's the way men are, dearie—stubborn and bull-headed. We women have to put up with it. If you marry Gordon you'll find he's that way too.'

Karen brushed that aside. 'I'm not talking about marrying him, but saving his life. I won't let you stop me. Can't you see how horrible this is for me? If he dies, it will be because they used my letter to draw him into the trap.'

For nearly an hour Karen urged, cajoled, threatened. At last Glenna gave way, bullied into surrender.

'We'll have to wait a while,' she said, plainly worried. 'You can't start while so many of the men are moving about.'

To this Karen agreed. She changed to riding breeches and boots, in order to appear less conspicuous. This done, she waited in a fever of impatience. The minutes dragged. Glenna weakened, and had to be convinced all over again.

The activity outside died down. Karen looked at her watch. The hands showed eight-thirty.

'Time to start,' she decided.

'You're still set on going, are you?' Mrs. Ford asked.

'Yes. I must, Glenna. Be sure you get Nelly and Sing Toy in the back of the house and keep them there as long as you can.'

Glenna sighed heavily. 'I'll do my best.'

'I'll thank you all my life, dear,' Karen said fervently.

Nelly was in her room, but Sing Toy was not to be found.

'Mr. Ford came for him and took him away right after supper,' the maid explained. 'He didn't say what he wanted with him.'

This fluttered Glenna. She did not know whether to go back to Karen and report or remain with Nelly as originally planned. After some hesitation she stayed with the maid. When ten minutes later she returned to her guest's room that young woman had vanished.

30. A Cry in the Night

LINC CONWAY limped to the house and stuck his head in the doorway. 'Fellow to see you, Gordon!' he yelled.

Stone came out to the porch and looked around. The darkness of night was sinking down over the land. A few stars showed in the sky. There would be many more later.

'Over here by the smokehouse,' Conway called.

Gordon walked in that direction. He found with the former sheepherder another man, a Chinese.

'Claims he's got something important to tell you,' the little lame man said. 'Wants to see you alone.'

Since there were few Chinese in the cattle country, except in the laundries and restaurants of the towns, Gordon was surprised at the presence of this one. He might have come to get a job as ranch cook, but that did not call for any secrecy.

The Oriental turned oblique eyes on the young man. 'Me Sing Toy,' he said. 'Me cook at the Bar B B Lanch. Lady give me letter for Missa Stone.'

They had walked a few yards to one side. 'What lady?' Gordon asked.

'Missie Gilbert. She say give it only him.'

'I'm Gordon Stone. The letter is for me.'

'Maybe you give me ten dolla.'

'Maybe,' Gordon agreed. 'Let me see the letter.'

'All light. Yo no fool Sing Toy.'

Gordon struck a match and read the note. It was signed 'Karen,' but did not mention his name.

'I shall try to be on the road at the southwest corner of the big pasture at ten o'clock tonight (Tuesday).'

That was all. Two lines, and no more.

'Did Miss Gilbert give you this herself?' Gordon asked.

The cook nodded assent.

'How did you get here?'

Sing Toy moved his thumb in the direction of a shadowy horse hitched to the corral fence. 'Me lide blonco pony to go see Hop Lee. Me come here instead.'

The yellow face was as expressionless as the sphinx. From it Gordon could read nothing. He asked more questions, aware that he would learn no more than Sing Toy wanted to tell him. The Chinese might be bringing him a message in perfectly good faith, or he might be inviting Gordon to ride to his death. The answers of the cook were blandly innocent. Miss Gilbert was treated well at the ranch but not allowed to wander out of sight. She and Mrs. Ford seemed to be good friends. He did not know how the prisoner expected to slip away from the house and reach the road. No, he did not like the foreman. Nobody did. He was a bully. For nearly a year Sing Toy had worked at the Bar B B, but he was tired of it and meant to quit to start a laundry at Barranca.

Gordon gave the man the ten dollars he wanted and let him go. But Sing Toy had not vanished into the darkness before Gordon had given orders for two horses to be saddled. He called Jack Turnbull from the house. In two sentences he told his friends what had taken place.

'We'll ride after Sing Toy and see where he goes,' he added. 'Maybe somebody is waiting up the road to get a report from him.'

The two armed themselves and mounted. They followed the cook down the road.

'Looks kinda fishy to me,' Jack said. 'Why would Miss Karen pick this Chink to bring her message? One of the Bar B B riders could have brought it easier. I don't reckon this slant-eyed biscuit-slinger can much more than stick to a saddle. When he gets on a bronc folks would notice it.'

'That's true,' Gordon agreed. 'But he may be the only man on the place Miss Karen could trust. She couldn't be choosy in her messenger. I'm not comfortable about this, but I've got to stay with it till I find out whether it's a sure enough note from her or a trap to bed me down nice under the daisies.'

'Sure,' Jack assented. 'Got to play out the hand . . . Say, ain't that the Chink ahead?'

They slowed down, not to get too close. If Sing Toy knew he was being followed they would learn nothing. He was too wily to give himself away. The care they used not to be seen was responsible for losing him. The cook left the road in the darkness, and whether he had turned to left or right they did not know.

The trailers drew into the brush and consulted in low tones, for it was possible the enemy might be huddled not far distant.

'No use looking for him in the mesquite,' Jack said. 'If we jumped up anyone they would hear us coming and smoke up.'

'Yes. He must have turned off to meet someone waiting for him. I don't like it.'

'Well, anyhow, we've had our warning,' Turnbull mentioned, with a thin grin. 'Any ambush we walk into will be

139

one we're expecting. If we go slow they're as liable to lean against bullets as we are.'

'Maybe.' Gordon was doubtful about that. 'How many of Gilbert's hands will be out for this turkey kill? Will there be quite a mess of them? Or will the job be given to a couple of them, say, with Cheyenne bossing it? The latter, I'd think. No need letting a lot of fellows in the know, one of whom might blab later under pressure, when all that is required is one blue whistler sent to the right address.'

'Cheyenne's chore,' Jack guessed. 'Either alone, or with another guy to help him. Too bad the invited guest won't be present at the party.'

'We'll drift out of this vicinity,' his friend said, 'and decide what to do later.'

They were a mile nearer the Bar B B before either of them spoke again.

'What we got to decide?' Jack asked casually. 'And why are we heading this way?'

'I've got to make sure Miss Karen isn't depending on me,' Gordon explained. 'There's an off chance she sent me that note by Sing Toy. If she did I can't let her down.'

'That's right. Are we making for the road back of the pasture?'

'We'll come up on it through the brush from the south on foot. Then if there's a surprise party we'll be giving it.'

They left the road, to turn into a stretch of desert thinly covered by cactus and greasewood. More stars were coming out, and the night was growing lighter. The horsemen moved at a road gait, not hurrying, but steadily drawing in the miles between them and their destination. The country looked peaceful as old age under the silvery moonlight. Its harsh and bristling aspect, the dry, desiccated appearance of its vegetation, were magically softened by the gentler touch of the myriad candles burning in the sky.

'Likely this is a one-man job, Jack,' his friend said after a long silence. 'I ought to send you home.'

'Try it, and see what luck you'd have,' Turnbull said cheerfully. 'No objection to you going back to the ranch, though.'

They came into a region of denser thicket. They were no longer in a greasewood district. Prickly pear, cholla, and mesquite predominated. Their mounts turned in and out among the thorny growth with the skill of long practice in following cows.

Gordon drew up in a dry wash. 'Road is two-three hundred yards ahead of us,' he said. 'We'd better cover that on foot.'

'Yep, and make haste mighty slowly,' Turnbull said,

140

swinging from the saddle. 'We're ahead of time, but the gents from the Bar B B may be early birds too. I'd hate to be mistaken for a worm.'

They tied their ponies and moved up the wash in the sand. Presently Gordon led the way out of the dry creek bed into the thicker chaparral to the right. He advanced with infinite patience, studying the shadowy bulk of each clump of bush that advanced to meet them from the hidden depth of the night. No step was taken without the knowledge that a dry stick would not snap beneath the foot. If he made a mistake now he might not live to make another. The men he was approaching, provided this was a trap, were as trail-wise as he and Turnbull. They were not amateurs at ambush. To survive, a killer has to have the sixth sense that warns of approaching danger. Cheyenne could not literally sniff their presence on the breeze as a deer might do, but he might feel a prickling of the spine from no logical cause that stirred unease in him. The slightest sound would startle him to wary and alert suspicion.

Jack breathed in his ear, 'We must be close to the road.'

'They may be lying in the fence corner on the other side of it,' Gordon whispered. 'Let's stick right here and wait.'

A cry reached them, the shrill, high scream of a woman.

Gordon snapped to his companion, 'Stay here,' and dashed into the open. He ran across the road as a bullet whistled past his head, and dived behind a clump of prickly pear.

He lay there, not stirring, nerves tense and senses alert. Somewhere back of the fence, in the obscure shadows of heavy mesquite or cactus growth, crouched one of the men who had come to destroy him. For the present he dared not move. It was impossible for him to know whether other assassins were concealed back of the penumbra of darkness fringing the moonlit road. The woman's cry still rang in his heart, but it would be folly to answer it now. The next move must come from the enemy. He had to wait motionless until they had in some way declared themselves. It might be by a hail of lead or by a concerted rush upon his position. Not knowing their strength or their whereabouts, he could not try to slip away without running the risk of jumping up a nest of them.

To him came the clop-clop of galloping hoofs. Somebody was leaving the scene of action. He did not know why. Possibly to get reinforcements. Through his mind trooped thought flashes, beneath the wary watchfulness with which he held himself keyed to attention . . . Was it Karen who had flung out that cry of distress? . . . If this was a trap, what was she doing here? . . . What was Jack Turnbull doing? Not waiting

141

where he had been told to stay. That was one certainty among many doubts.

The minutes dragged in heavy silence. Gordon became convinced that the number of his enemies was small. If there had been many he would have heard rustling and stirrings.

From his trouser pocket Gordon took a knife. He opened it, and with the point of the blade between finger and thumb flipped it at a shadowy clump of bushes twenty yards away. The knife tore through the foliage to the ground. A shot rang out. One of the enemy at least had been deceived and thought he was hiding behind that bit of shrubbery.

There was only one shot. Did that mean only one man was lying in wait for him? Maybe not. There might be one or two more, skillful enough in bush warfare not to betray their presence until the right moment.

A hubbub of sound filled the night, of men threshing to and fro in physical struggle. Jack Turnbull's rebel yell lifted into the air. There was a heavy, startled oath. Men's feet gripping the earth for a foothold shifted as their bodies moved.

Gordon went over the barbed-wire fence swiftly. He raced toward the battle field. A gun exploded, from a squirming mass almost within touch of his hand. Legs and arms tossed wildly with furious energy. Waiting only to make sure the man on top was Turnbull, Gordon reached across and brought the barrel of his revolver down on the head of the other. With a groan, the man he had pistolwhipped subsided.

'I'll take care of him,' Turnbull panted. 'Keep yore eyes peeled for his *tillicums.*'

No other sound disturbed the night. If the man had companions they gave no sign of interest.

Jack turned the face of his prisoner toward the light. An ugly scar disfigured the right cheek. 'Our old friend Buck Hayes,' the cowpuncher said. 'Coming back for more after we've both plugged him once. Must think he has as many lives as a cat.'

The Bar B B man groaned. His eyes flickered open. Into them came in succession a variety of expressions—bewilderment, wonder, fear.

'How many of you here?' demanded Stone harshly.

The ranch hand tried to stall. 'Why—I come down to fix a busted fence and——'

'Don't lie to me. I said, how many men with you?'

Hayes looked into the steel-barred eyes, cold and remorseless as the gleaming blade of a sword, and gave up without further evasion.

'Only Cheyenne,' he said, from a throat become dry and hoarse.

'Where is Cheyenne?'

'I dunno.' The man looked around, furtive gaze searching the brush. 'Looks like he fourflushed on me and beat it.'

'Not Cheyenne,' Turnbull differed. 'If he left he wasn't scared. He had some other reason.'

What other reason? That question stirred troubled thoughts in Gordon's mind.

'I heard a woman scream,' he said. 'Who was she?'

Their prisoner looked at him sulkily. 'I dunno anything about any woman.'

'You'd better know,' Gordon advised, a threat in his low icy voice. 'You heard and saw her.'

'I didn't either see her,' Hayes growled. 'I heard her, same as you did. She wasn't supposed to be here. I don't get it.'

'You know who she is?'

The gunman hesitated. 'I wouldn't say I know,' he said, after a moment of weighed silence. 'Sounded like the Gilbert girl, but she hadn't any business here.' He looked at Gordon with dull anger. 'Looks like I been double-crossed. Two horses galloped away, one of 'em mine. At least I'll bet one was. Too dark to make sure. Who was on those broncs? I don't know, but I can guess.'

'Guess,' ordered Gordon.

'Cheyenne on one and the girl on the other. The damned skunk left me cold.'

'To bushwhack me alone.'

'I didn't say anything about bushwhacking,' the man said sullenly.

'No, I mentioned that,' Gordon replied.

31. 'Safe as in God's Pocket'

KAREN stole softly downstairs from her room to the back door. Here she stopped to scan the horizon for enemies. A stir over by the blacksmith shop held her gaze. Presently a man detached himself from the gloom and came into the less opaque darkness of the open. She guessed he was the sentry and watched him, the door open an inch or two, stroll past the house toward the corral.

Clinging close to the wall, she reached the corner of the house. There seemed to be nobody in sight. Not too swiftly, she walked across to the root house. A voice hailed her, sending a wild flutter through her breast and into her throat.

'That you, Jim?'

Karen flung up a hand in answer, without speaking. She did not stop, but she felt her legs trembling beneath her weight. Only by sheer will could she conquer an almost irresistible impulse to run.

143

The man who had called was either satisfied or too indifferent to investigate further. He did not speak again, nor did he follow her.

She waited back of the root house for a few moments she could have sworn were hours. A garden fence barred her way. She crept over it and hurried through rows of beans to the other side of the vegetable patch. Another fence negotiated, she found herself close to the big pasture. When she came to the barbed-wire she lay down and wriggled beneath the lowest strand.

At this distance from the house her fear of getting caught was less acute. She began to run, driven by dread that she might be too late. The time was only twenty past nine, but Gordon and his enemies might keep the appointment early. Catclaw snatched at her trousers. Mesquite branches whipped her thighs. A sudden scurry of something in flight filled her with momentary terror. It was only a three-year-old steer getting out of the way.

She had to stop running. Her bursting lungs were clamoring for air. But she hurried on, at a gait half walk and half trot. The urge was imperative to make haste—make haste. She recollected that the pasture was a mile across. Angling as she was toward the southwest corner, it would be perhaps a mile and a quarter. Her course was as direct as possible, since she felt she had no time to detour to escape being seen.

Once she stopped to listen, but the night was filled with silence. Stars were filling the sky. A big moon was rising over the horizon. It was all so quiet that she doubted the need of this adventure. Had she been just silly in imagining Curt Ford was in a plot to destroy the man she loved? Perhaps she had been too anxious and had not thought straight. Soon she would find out.

She must have been going too far to the left, for the barbed-wire fence stopped her with no road in sight. Following the posts, she traveled toward the corner of the pasture designated.

A voice, curt and sharp, froze her in her tracks.

'Stop there. Stick 'em up. Who is it?'

Someone moved toward her cautiously. A squat figure came out of the darkness

'Make one crazy move and I'll riddle you,' the voice warned.

'It's Karen Gilbert,' the girl answered.

'Damn my skin if it isn't!' The cowpuncher Cheyenne stared at the girl resentfully, a frown on his brown-tanned face. 'Who the hell slipped up and let you out?' he demanded.

'Never mind about that!' she cried. 'I came to stop this . . . this terrible thing you plan to do.'

144

The eyes of the man narrowed. Somebody had been talking too much. It must have been either Gilbert or Ford, since nobody else was supposed to know about this except Buck Hayes and him. Pretty soon a dozen people would know about it, and they would make him the goat.

'What terrible thing you talkin' about?' Cheyenne asked craftily, searching for information.

'You're here to kill Gordon Stone,' she charged.

'Nothing of the kind,' he retorted. 'Where did you get that fool idea?'

'Curt Ford used my note to decoy him. He as good as told me so.'

'You must of misunderstood him. I come down to fix up a fence.'

His mind was quartering over the ground as he talked. He would show the Bar B B bosses whether they could play him for a sucker. The thing to do was to get out while there was still time. He wondered if Buck Hayes had been in the plan to unload the blame on him. Buck was a great side-kick of Ford and always played up to him. Maybe the foreman meant to swear to an alibi for his pal if any trouble rose after the killing. He had seen the two whispering together just after supper, off back of the corral where they thought they would not be seen.

'Are you alone here?' Karen asked.

'Sure I am.'

Her question had been unexpected. It had given him no time to consider an answer. He had spoken instinctively, to cover up the facts. But he decided swiftly to stand by what he had said. The doubt of Gilbert and Ford grew in his susicious mind to a certainty that he was marked for betrayal. He would decamp, with an unimpeachable witness by his side. Let Buck Hayes stay and do the job if he liked.

He knew this meant a break with Gilbert. There would be no place for him at the ranch after this. His thoughts had played a great deal with what Gilbert had proposed, that he tie up with him and marry his niece. That was out now, as far as Lyn was concerned. Very likely the old fox had just been stringing him along. Why not play a lone hand? This girl liked hard fighting men. Well, he was tough and reckless enough for her. If he had a chance to be with her for a time he could make her fall for him the way other women had. Into his mind slipped a mad urge. If she wanted a masterful man he would be one for her.

'Alone, except for you,' he added, dragging the words significantly.

With one swift glance her eyes swept him. She knew what that tone and manner meant when used by a man to an attractive woman. She wondered if he was going to be difficult. In any case she could cross that bridge when she came to it. The important thing was to get him away from here before Gordon arrived.

'If you are through fixing the fence we might as well go,' she suggested.

'That's right,' he agreed. 'No use sticking around here.'

He led the way through the brush to some mesquites where two horses were tied.

Like a flash the girl swung on him. 'You told me you were alone!' she cried.

The man stood there, taken aback, with no pat answer ready. He had forgotten the second horse would prove that he had lied. But he had made up his mind what he meant to do. Nothing she could say would change that.

'There's another man here,' she continued sharply. 'You're leaving him to murder Gordon Stone.'

'What do we care about him or Stone?' he said thickly. 'It's you and me, girl. I'm going to save you from that gray wolf Gilbert, and from that damned weasel Ford.'

'Forget that!' she ordered. 'I came to save Gordon Stone. We'll get the other man and take him with us.'

'Not on yore life. They'll play their own hands. You're going with me.'

He pulled the slip knots that fastened the ponies and brought them to her.

Karen faced him, eyes steady. 'I'm not leaving here unless the other man goes too.'

A heat burned up into his eyes as he looked at the slim, lovely young woman. Gilbert had told him to marry her. Well, by God, he would do it. All he asked was twenty-four hours alone with her. Given that long, he could make her see this his way. This was the first chance he had ever found to be alone with her. If he didn't make the most of it there would never be another.

He did not argue with her any further. His strong hand seized her wrist as he swung to the saddle of his horse, the bridle of the other animal looped over his arm. Stooping, he dragged her up in front of him. She screamed, trying to struggle free. A palm clamped over her mouth and he set the cow ponies in motion. Almost she succeeded in breaking free and wriggling to the ground.

'Be still, you little devil,' he told her, with no anger.

'Let me go,' she cried furiously, still attempting to loosen his hold.

The sound of a shot came to Karen. She stopped fighting, to listen. Beneath her ribs the heart of the girl died. There was no second explosion. The only sounds she heard were

146

the beat of the horses' hoofs and the swishing of the brush through which they charged.

A barbed-wire fence barred the way. Cheyenne lowered her to the ground, his fingers clamped round her arm, and slid from the saddle himself.

The faint pop of a distant gun explosion reached them.

'Let us go back,' she begged piteously. 'We may still be in time.'

With a wire-cutter he snipped the strands.

'We're not going back,' he said curtly. 'I'm taking you from that old scalawag Gilbert.'

'Taking me where?'

'Never mind where. You been trying to get away from him. I'm giving you the chance.'

'Let's go back first and stop the shooting.'

'No. Too late, anyhow. It's all over. Looks like Buck muffed the job. If he hadn't, there would not have been any need of a second shot ten minutes after the first. It would not surprise me if Stone had got Buck. Serve him right if he did.'

Karen turned and ran. The man grounded the bridle reins and followed. In his high-heeled boots he made an awkward figure as he covered the ground with long strides, but he overhauled her rapidly. She looked round, saw he was gaining, and dodged back of a cholla. Her thought was to cut back to the horses, yet she knew that to try it was useless. Before she had retraced one third of the distance his reaching arm had caught her shoulder.

'Nothing doing, lady,' he panted. 'Now you've cut yore rusty we'll take our little *pasear* together like I said.'

Her small bosom rose and fell fast in deep breaths. 'What do you want?' she cried. 'Have you gone crazy? You can't do this to me.'

'We'll have lots of time to talk about that, missy. I'm not a-going to hurt you any. Use yore head. Have I got to tote you like a sack of meal, or will you ride beside me nice and friendly?'

'If you'd only go back with me first and make sure——'

'I won't. That's done settled. We'll start from the chunk. Forget that fellow for a while. He's a criminal. I aim to save you from him and from yore old skunk of an uncle too. You're traveling with me. Question is, how?'

'You know what would happen to a man in this country who tried to kidnap a decent girl?' she asked, trying to speak quietly without hysteria.

'I'm not kidnapping you,' he grinned. 'I'm rescuing you. I done told you that se-ve-re-al times. Make up yore mind *muy pronto*.'

It would be better to seem to yield, she thought. On a separate horse she would find a chance to bolt and perhaps escape.

'All right,' she said. 'I'll go with you. But it's a silly business. What is it you want with me?'

'I want you to get acquainted with a man. With me, Cheyenne. If you take a shine to me we might get married. You need someone who can stick up for yore rights with that old scoundrel Gilbert. I'm the hairpin that can do it.'

'Much obliged, but I'm not looking for a husband,' she told him scornfully.

Undisturbed, he chewed his quid of tobacco. 'I reckon you don't know what you're lookin' for,' he replied. 'Give me time. You might find out I was the running mate you needed. Sure, I've been a tough citizen and helled around considerable, but you're the kind that needs a man of experience. Me, I've had it. In my day I have sure spread the mustard.'

'I'm not interested,' she said, disdain in her cold voice. 'You rode out tonight to kill a man for pay. That's all I need to know.'

'I've heard of one killer you're not so hard on,' Cheyenne retorted. 'And I'll say this for him, though I don't like a hair of his ugly head. I'd trust him a lot farther than I would that mealymouthed uncle of yours. There has to be some rock-bottom decency in a man that makes him draw the line somewhere. Lyn Gilbert hasn't got it.'

'And you have?'

He did not resent her contempt. It was entirely natural. He meant, if possible, to change her point of view. But that would take time.

'If a fellow hasn't gone rotten, if he lives by some law inside him, he can make a new start and run straight. It's like giving up drink. All he needs is to set his teeth in it.'

'Am I to understand that you are beginning a new life of righteousness by kidnapping me?' Karen asked.

There was a gleam of mirth in his saturnine face. 'Rescuing you,' he corrected.

When they had reached the horses she flung a question at him abruptly. 'Where are you taking me?'

Cheyenne knew that the slender, spirited girl who faced him with head up was smothering fear, and he admired her for it.

'I don't know just where right away,' he answered. 'Back to yore friends in town when I get round to it. But I expect Buck Hayes will report to Curt if yore friend the convict hasn't got him, and Curt will get busy on the telephone. It would annoy me to run into an ambush and get filled with

148

lead on the way in to Barranca. We'll have to hide out a while.'

'Why do you do this mad thing?' she pleaded. 'Don't you see that you are destroying yourself? Why play with words and talk about rescuing? The men who hunt you down won't do that. Kidnapping is what they will call it. You will just be a wild beast to them, to be hunted down like a wolf.'

'I'm taking a chance that in twenty-four hours you'll be on my side,' he admitted with frank hardihood. 'All my life I've taken long chances. I like to gamble for big stakes.'

'But I won't be on your side. What you are doing will make me detest and hate you. You are throwing away your life for nothing. It's not a gamble, but just madness.'

'I'm not of that opinion.' He swung a horse round and held the stirrup for her. 'Get on, Miss. We got to hit the trail.'

'Don't make me go,' she urged. 'If you have that rock-bottom decency you spoke of, you will ride back with me and see what—what has happened back on the pasture road.'

'No,' he told Karen harshly. 'I don't give a damn what has happened to either one of the two. Get on, or I'll throw you up.'

Karen pulled herself to the saddle and he adjusted the stirrups, letting the bridle trail as he did so. When he had finished he lifted his flinty eyes to hers.

'I'm letting you guide this horse, because we can travel faster that way. If you've got any sense you won't try any shenanigan. You wouldn't get fifty yards.'

Karen did not say anything. She was sick at heart and full of fear. The man she loved might be lying dead in a cactus jungle. For herself, she was in the power of a villain who was taking her alone with him to some hidden pocket in the hills.

They rode for miles in silence. He was the first to speak, apparently moved by her obvious objection.

'Buck up, Miss. It might be worse.'

'Will you tell me how it could be worse?' she asked, meeting his gaze.

She was thinking that they would be alone, all through the long night, far from any other human being, and she remembered the look she had seen on his face when he had mentioned their isolation.

Cheyenne read her thoughts. His cold, hard eyes held hers fast. 'You might be with a coyote like Curt Ford who would lose his head and go panicky if he had his back to the wall. Or with a skunk like yore uncle, who would sacrifice you in a minute to save himself. I'm a tough specimen. Anyone will tell you that. I burn powder quick. I have blotted brands a-plenty. Frequently I have been on the dodge, as we'll likely be for a while till I get you back to yore friends. But, by Godfrey, I fill man-size boots. I'll protect you from any harm.'

Her troubled gaze challenged him. What was in her mind flashed out with characteristic directness.

'Protect me from whom?'

'I told you that a man has to live by some law inside himself,' he said, dragging his words. 'While you are with me you will be as safe as if you were in God's pocket. All I'm asking is you try to meet me in a friendly spirit, not as if I was some kind of sidewinder.'

She drew what comfort she could from his promise, without being sure how much of a guarantee he was giving her. What sort of a 'friendly spirit' did he expect from her? Probably they thought in different languages. He was a villain by any ordinary code of living. Without knowing what crimes he had committed, she did not doubt they had been plenty. Even before tonight she had heard it rumored that he killed for pay. By taking her with him he was putting himself so far outside the pale that nothing more he could do would add to the penalty. But strangely, there was something about the virile scoundrel that she trusted. It was his strength. He was not weak, a victim of momentary impulse. If and when he sinned it would be by deliberate choice. He had mentioned rock-bottom decency. She clung to that word as a swimmer might have done to a life-buoy in a rough sea.

32. A Committee of Investigation

STONE and Turnbull tied up their prisoner and stuffed a bandanna into his mouth for a gag. He was trussed carefully hand and foot. His captors had urgent and dangerous business on hand, and they did not want him interfering with it.

'Maybe we'll be in too much of a hurry to come back and turn you loose,' Jack told Hayes cheerfully. 'But if you starve to death you'll be getting off easier than you deserve. A hired killer had ought to be boiled in oil.'

The friends retrieved their mounts, clipped the wire of the pasture fence, and rode through it toward the ranch house.

'I have a hunch we're barking up the wrong tree,' Gordon said. 'I'd say the horses we heard weren't heading this way.'

'Where would they be going, then?'

'That's what worries me. Cheyenne is a hardy scoundrel. If he was sent to bushwhack me why didn't he tie up the girl and stay to finish the job?'

'Search me.' Jack offered a suggestion. 'It might not have been Miss Karen we heard.'

'It was. I'm almost sure of that. She was frightened, and when she screamed somebody cut off the sound suddenly . . . We'll have to go slow on this job, Jack. I mean to find out if she is at the ranch all right, but I don't want either of us shot up.'

'You don't think anybody at the Bar B B would shoot one of us, do you?' the cowpuncher asked. 'When we're just two friendly inquiring lads.'

At some distance from the house they dismounted and tied their horses to the branches of a live-oak. Ten minutes later they were crouched back of the root house.

They saw the sentry saunter across the open and vanish behind the bunkhouse. Nobody else appeared to be in sight.

'We'll cut across to the house,' Gordon whispered to his companion. 'Now!'

They made a run for it to the kitchen. The room was dark, and they groped a way from it into a hall lighted by a coal-oil lamp. The stairway to the second floor invited their feet. Softly they took the creaking treads.

Neither of them knew which room was the one that had been assigned to Karen. Four closed doors confronted them, two on each side of the corridor. Since none had transoms and no light sifted through to the hall, one guess was as good as another.

Gordon did not tap on the door nearest him. He very gently turned the knob and opened the door far enough to look inside. Except for a faint glow of moonlight near the window the room was dark. Gordon's hand brushed along the coverlet of the bed. Nobody was sleeping in it. After Turnbull had shut the door behind him Stone struck a match.

The dress of a woman hung across the back of a chair. He recognized it as one he had seen Karen wear.

'Her room,' he whispered to his companion.

'They might not have brought her to her own room,' Jack murmured.

Footsteps shuffled along the hall. They waited, bodies rigid. Each of them had a gun in his right hand.

Whoever it was in the hall paused outside the room. The door opened, and Glenna walked in carrying a lamp in her hand.

Jack caught the lamp in time to keep it from falling out of the lax hand of the woman. Her startled eyes stared at Gordon. She opened her mouth to scream, but closed it when Stone put a finger to his lips.

'You!' she exclaimed. 'I thought—I thought——'

'Where is Karen?' Gordon asked.

'Don't you know?' Glenna asked. 'She went to warn you that . . . that . . .'

'Yes, I guessed that. Is she back?'

'No. Didn't you see her?'

Gordon shook his head. 'We heard her scream, then the sound of galloping horses. You're sure they didn't come back here?'

'I'm sure. I've been listening.'

'How many were on this job to ambush me?'

Glenna's hands lifted in a feeble gesture of helplessness. 'I don't know. I don't know anything about this. Karen found out and made me let her go.'

'How did she find out?'

'Put this and that together. Curt had been drinking and talked too much. I don't think they meant to hurt you, but only to make you prisoner.'

Neither of the men offered any opinion as to that.

'Did she write the note sent to me by your Chinese cook?' Gordon asked.

'She meant the note to go to Hal Ferguson. Did Sing Toy take it to you?'

'Yes.' Gordon's mind was wholly busy with the problem of Karen's disappearance. Were Gilbert and Ford back of it? Or was Cheyenne playing a lone hand? If the latter, what was in the mind of the cowpuncher? Did he mean to take her to her friends in town? Or did he intend to hold her for ransom from her uncle? There was another possibility. His next question pointed at it:

'Did this man Cheyenne show any special interest in Karen?'

Glenna was surprised, and showed it. 'Why, Karen wouldn't look at him.'

'I'm asking if he looked at her,' Gordon corrected.

'How would I know? I don't suppose so. He's just a hired hand.'

'Never noticed him hanging around her?'

'No. If he had, she would have sent him about his business.'

'Where is Curt?'

'I don't know. He hasn't been around since supper.' Tears of sef-pity welled into Glenna's eyes. 'He'll half kill me for letting Karen go.'

The clop-clop of horses' hoofs drummed into the yard. The same thought was in the mind of all of them. Cheyenne had brought Karen back to the ranch house. Gordon walked to the window and looked out. He turned, his face grim and harsh.

'We'll go downstairs,' he said.

'Is it Karen?' Glenna asked.

'No. Let's go. We'll leave the lamp here.'

The woman was frightened. 'Why do you look that way? Who is it?'

'You'll know in a minute.'

As they reached the foot of the stairs the front door opened, to let in Sing Toy and Curt Ford.

The foreman stood in his tracks and peered past his wife at the two figures in the dim light back of her. It took him an instant to recognize them. That eye-flash of time advantage was enough for Gordon. He moved forward with swift, light tread, gun in hand.

'Take it easy, Ford,' he advised softly. 'Reach for the ceiling . . . Close the door behind you, Sing Toy. We'd like a word with you, too.'

The foreman glared at his enemy. Written on his face were various emotions struggling for dominance—astonishment, doubt, hate, rage. His arms lifted, swept forward swiftly. They dashed from the pendant where it hung the lamp that lit the hall. He plunged at Gordon, pinning his arms close to the body.

Instantly the night was alive with tumult. Glenna screamed. Sing Toy bolted through the door and filled the night with the clamor of his pidgin-English shouts for help. In the hall were sounds of shifting feet, of grunts, of whistling breaths, of crashing furniture. A gun roared. A raucous voice ripped out a curse.

The threshing bodies tore the stair rail down as if it had been cardboard. Ford's sinewy hands found Gordon's throat and tightened. He had his foe pressed back against the treads. In the struggle the revolver had been knocked from the fingers of Stone.

Turnbull, looking for his chance, found it at last. His gun lashed down on the brindle head of the foreman. Ford swayed. He staggered back against the wall. The hinges of his knees gave way and he collapsed.

It was time to be gone. Jack could hear the slap of running feet, the shouts of the Bar B B men on their way from the bunkhouse.

'Gotta light a shuck, Gord,' he cried.

Gordon groped for his revolver, but gave up the search as the first runner flung open the door.

'Upstairs—quick!' Gordon ordered, and turned to follow his friend.

The Bar B B men hesitated. In the darkness they did not know foe from friend. This gave the intruders a chance to reach the back door.

From the floor Ford snarled an order: 'Get him, boys! It's Stone.'

153

The feet of the ranch hands clumped through the hall and out of the kitchen in hot pursuit. To Glenna, flung into a clothes closet by the rush of men, came the crash of revolvers.

Her husband struggled to his feet, clutching at his soggy hair.

'Where are you, Glenna?'

'I'm here,' she answered. 'You hurt, Curt?'

'He tried to kill me, the wall-eyed son-of-a-gun. Get water and fix me up. I'll be in the living-room.'

He staggered into the room and sank down in a chair. His wife brought water and bandages. She lit a lamp and attended to his hurt. The wound was a superficial one, though he groaned a good deal.

'Karen got away,' Glenna said, in fear and trembling, after she had finished.

'They must of come to get her,' Ford said.

His wife did not correct him. If he thought so, that would be a good out for her.

'That's just what they did,' the foreman continued angrily. 'Came here to collect her while I was away. She must have fixed it up with that wolf Stone somehow. I got no use for li'l vixen. If the boys spilt some lead in her as well as in her two friends I wouldn't go into mourning. Nobody would be to blame but herself.'

'I hope she doesn't get hurt,' Glenna said timidly. 'She's really a nice girl, Curt, when you get to know her.'

'How can she be nice when she goes racing around with outlaws and bad men all the time?' he demanded. 'Girls today ain't what they used to be . . . I wish the boys would get back with at least two scalps. They did enough shooting to wipe out a regiment. Listen. By gum, they're still at it.'

'I wish they would come back,' his wife said nervously. 'Someone will get hurt.' This was not her idea of a pleasant time.

Ford came to another angle of the affair, one quite flattering to his vanity. He began to boast of his part in the encounter.

'Told me to hold up my arms, the wolf. Well, you saw me hold them up. He had me covered, but I went for him all spraddled out. They been telling it that I was scared of Stone. Did it look thataway when I took those birds on, both of them armed, and me with my bare fists? If I'd had another ten seconds I would of squeezed the life out of Stone. That side-kick of his saved him by cracking me on the head. Any day in the week I'll handle that convict.'

The Bar B B men drifted back to the ranch singly or in pairs. Some of them were quite sure they had wounded the

154

interlopers, but did not know how badly. The hunted men had reached their horses, mounted, and ridden into the darkness. On foot the pursuers had not been able to follow.

33. Cheyenne Outfits for Two

THEY rode hours before Cheyenne stopped at a line camp in a pocket of the hills on the edge of the desert.

'We'll outfit here,' he told Karen, and helped her to alight.

'If that's a courtesy it isn't necessary,' the girl told him. 'I've been riding horses ever since I learned to walk.'

'You ride 'em too well,' he said, the drip of sarcasm in his voice. 'If I didn't look after you right careful you might not want to go with me.'

'Are we going farther? Or is this where we stop?'

'We haven't started yet,' he told her. 'This is going to be a real camping trip you'll remember all yore life. We'll step into this shack. Ladies first.'

Karen passed through the dark doorway, not without trepidation. They were alone. Probably no other human being was within miles of them. This man had chosen to step across the line which separates the average citizen and the hunted man. The thing he was doing, in a frontier country such as this, called for death swift and sure. In such a case a desperado might well reason that he could pay the penalty only once anyhow.

But Karen gave no sign of the fear rising to her throat. She knew that if she went panicky it would tell against her. It was imperative that she keep her chin up. Cheyenne held her by the wrist while he lit a lamp.

To her surprise the round cabin was neat as a pin. Whoever lived in it had swept the floor, made the bed, and washed the breakfast dishes before leaving for the day.

Cheyenne swung round a home-built chair for Karen and told her to sit down. From the bed he took blankets and packed them into a tight roll, which he roped. Into a sack he put coffee, flour, salt, bacon, beans, and other supplies.

'Here's a jar of raspberry jam,' he said, looking up. 'You like it?'

'Don't take it for me,' she replied indifferently. 'I don't expect to be with you long enough to do much eating.'

He grinned. 'That's what you say. Different here. I'll put in the jam. I want this to be a nice camping party for you. My friends claim I'm some cook, and I mean to demonstrate they are right.'

'You have friends,' she commented with polite insolence.

'You'd be surprised. You're going to be one.'

Karen rose and strolled to the kitchen table. He was between her and the door, but he watched her closely. 'What's the idea? I invited you to sit down.'

The idea had been to blow out the lamp and try to throw herself through the window. But Karen reluctantly gave it up. It was high, and he would seize her before she could escape. She would be in the dark, and in his arms. That would not be so good.

'I've been sitting for hours,' she answered.

She opened idly the drawer in front of her and took out a carving knife. The sharp point she pricked against the ball of her thumb. 'I don't suppose I could do it,' she said, as if to herself; and to him: 'You have to be a professional, don't you, to slip a knife into a man under the fifth rib?'

Her insolence made him chuckle. 'I've never used a knife, so I wouldn't know about that. The way to find out would be to try . . . By the way, toss me that pig-sticker. We'll take it with us. And get me the fry-pan and the coffee-pot.'

Karen started to do as told, but stopped with the frying-pan in her hand. There came to them the voice of somebody singing. She guessed he was riding toward the cabin. In her a wild hope stirred.

'Bud Cowell,' Cheyenne said, after listening.

Words of the song reached them, in a voice devoid of melody.

'Foot in the stirrup and hand on the horn,
Best damned cowboy ever was born.'

Cheyenne flung open the door to meet him. 'Come right in to the party, Bud, and bring yore song along with you,' he invited.

'Hello, Cheyenne, you old son-of-a-rooster, how-come you here?' Cowell shouted.

He stood in the doorway blinking in surprise. At sight of Karen his lank jaw dropped. He was a thin slat of a man with a putty face and a snub nose, burnt to a shiny red by liquor and an untempered sun. In point of fact he had just returned from a ten-mile ride to get a pint of whiskey. His gaze wandered from the girl to the roll of blankets and to the sack of provisions. What this meant he did not understand.

Swiftly Karen explained. 'This man is kidnapping me, Bud. He's packing your things to take with him. You'll help me, won't you?'

Even while she was making the appeal Karen realized there was no force in this man. He would not put up a fight for her against the tough, hard man who was taking her with him.

'Why, Cheyenne wouldn't do that, Miss,' he explained, sliding a look at the other man. 'It's one of his li'l joshes.

156

Cow hands are thataway. They're always loadin' someone.'

'We're borrowing a few things from you, Bud,' the gun-man told him. 'No objections, I reckon.'

'If you aim to take that bed roll I don't see how I can spare the blankets, Cheyenne. Or that grub either. Curt will raise Cain about it.'

'Tell him to charge it against what the ranch owes me.'

'You ain't figuring on leaving.'

'He is taking me away with him somewhere, Bud, against my wishes and by force, without any instructions from my uncle.' Karen walked across the floor to the line rider. 'Are you going to let him do it without lifting a hand for me?'

Bud was embarrassed and distressed. 'Why, you must of misunderstood Cheyenne, Miss. It wouldn't make sense to do a thing like that. O' course I'm a man of peace, anyhow. I don't even tote a gun. But there's no need of talkin' that-away. Cheyenne won't hurt you none.'

'How well you know me, Bud,' the other man said, with a cynical smile. 'Just what I've been telling the young lady.'

Karen told her story urgently, with emotion. She begged Cowell at least to get word to Gordon Stone that she was in the hands of Cheyenne.

'That'll be all right with me,' Cheyenne assented. 'Tell him I'll be waiting at the gate for him if he comes. And give that word to old Gilbert too, the mealymouthed hypocrite. He claimed he wanted me to marry his niece. Well, I aim to fix that up with her *muy pronto*.'

'That's fine, Cheyenne. I'm sure you wouldn't do anything that wasn't right by her,' the line rider said. He wanted to get in a word of warning to the Bar B B bad man without offending him. 'I don't reckon folks would like that, would they?'

'Time for us to burn the wind,' Cheyenne told the girl. 'We got to get up into the hills.' He added a jeering word for Cowell: 'Don't forget to tell Lyn I'll take care of his niece proper.'

Cowell hated himself for his lack of spirit, but the best he could do was to make a suggestion that maybe the young lady would be more comfortable if they stayed at the cabin for the night.

Promptly Cheyenne vetoed this. 'Miss Gilbert is a ranch girl. Camping out won't hurt her a mite. No, we'll be getting along.'

'I'm not going,' Karen said. 'I'll stay here.'

Cheyenne chewed tobacco, his shallow, flinty eyes on Karen. In them was a hint of sardonic amusement. 'I have to be on my way, Miss, and I wouldn't dare leave you with a hell-a-miler like Bud. His rep with ladies is something fierce.

I expect you'll just have to drift along with me. I ain't exciting like Bud, but I'm safe as Old Dog Tray.'

She faced him, her eyes stormy and her slight figure erect. 'I said I wasn't going.'

He shook his head, upon which he had just placed at a rakish angle a wide-rimmed Stetson. 'I heard you the other time. While I like to oblige a lady, it can't be that way. We'll hit the trail.'

The anger in her eyes died away. It had been only a surface emotion, summoned to conceal the anxious fear in her.

"There's still time for you turn back,' she begged in a low voice. 'You can walk out of that door and escape the vengeance that is sure to fall on you. Besides, I'll thank you all my life.'

'When I go out of that door it will be with you,' he answered. 'My chips are in the pot and I aim to draw cards. I started to rescue you from Lyn. I couldn't quit on the job.'

He had not raised his voice. He had been too sure of himself for that. Looking at the man's bowlegged, broad-shouldered frame, at his stony, weatherbeaten face, Karen knew she could not hold out against him. Fear did not move him any more than pity. He went his way outside the laws that regulated the lives of other men. To say more would be weakness, since no plea could avail. She guessed he admired courage. It was important to keep up a bold front before him.

She walked out of the cabin in front of him.

34. Cheyenne Weakens

THEY rode deep into the hills. As they climbed higher the way grew more rugged, the slopes steeper. Cheyenne rode knee to knee with Karen, or, if the path was narrow, close to the heels of the bay upon which she was mounted. There was no chance of escape here, since he was never twenty feet away from her.

It was a land of wild ravines, rocky cliffs, great peaks, and narrow valleys, at times so far below that the bottoms were not visible through the gulf of black emptiness into which she peered. The stars were out in countless numbers, far away and cold. If the sun had been shining on them it would have been comforting. But in the night anything was possible. She understood, as never before, what was meant by the Biblical phrase that men love darkness rather than light because their deeds are evil.

They turned into a black defile that led precipitously up a steep and rocky trough.

'You go first,' Cheyenne said. 'Give the horse his head.'

It was the first time she had heard his voice for an hour.

He seemed, she thought, to be immersed in a sullen resentment. Was he regretting what he had done and looking for a way out? Or was he nerving himself to go through?

The horses clambered to the top of the slide, though more than once Karen thought the bay was down. At the summit was a bare, sloping scarp terminating in some scrubby pines. Near the edge of these Cheyenne drew up.

'We'll camp here,' he announced.

Karen swung stiffly from the saddle. The long ride and her intense anxiety had tired her greatly. She felt a hundred years old. And she was afraid, as she had never been in her life before.

The cowpuncher gathered dead branches and lit a fire. The night was cold in this altitude. He saw she was shivering.

'Like some coffee?' he asked, almost curtly.

She told him she would, partly to keep his mind busy with the routine of camping. They drank out of tin cups and her despair lightened a little. He was in a talkative mood for a change, and to her relief his conversation was of the past. Through what he said she reconstructed the conditions of his youth—poverty, a jealous stepmother, an unhappy family life. It was easy to understand why he had 'gone bad,' as the telling phrase of the West has it.

She found herself asking questions and even sympathizing with him, though that was the last thing in the world he wanted from her. He told her of his first essay into crime. While riding for an outfit in West Texas he had gone on a spree at the nearest cow-town. An older man had proposed they rob a train, and almost before he knew it the lad had become involved in a holdup during which the express messenger had been killed. From that day the stamp of the outlaw was on him.

'You're tired,' he said at last, and rose yawning from in front of the fire where he had been sitting tailor fashion.

He warmed the blankets and arranged them for her. Karen thanked him, her heart pounding.

The eyes in his stone-wall face told no stories. What he was thinking she did not know.

'Your first job is to sleep,' he told her. 'Don't worry about anything till morning.'

Was that a promise? She was not sure. The intention in her mind was not to sleep a wink. He suggested that she would be more comfortable with her boots off, then strolled away into the darkness. The plateau was on a great promontory from which there was no descent except by the way they had come. She knew he would not leave that unguarded.

From the provision sack she slipped the carving knife. When she went into her blankets it lay close to her hand. To take it seemed a futile precaution. She could not imagine herself driving the blade into the body of a man, not even to save herself.

For years she had forgotten her prayers, but she went back to them now. The cry her heart flung out was to the personal God of her childhood, and she made her petition much as she had done when a very small girl. If He would save her now and if He had kept Gordon alive she would be good. The faults in her way of living trooped to her mind. She would amend them all. She would say her prayers every night and go to church on Sunday.

Cheyenne came back to the campfire. He sat on the other side of it from her and smoked a pipe. His dark, immobile face told her nothing of what he was thinking. From the bowl of the pipe he knocked the ashes deliberately. Furtively the girl watched him. He did not once look at her. When he rolled up in the blanket his face was turned away.

The lump of fear in her throat began to ease. In the pleasant warmth of the blankets she grew drowsy. More than once, with a start, she made herself open her drooping eyelids. She must stay awake all night.

Very quickly after that she must have fallen asleep. Once in the night she awakened, to rest her cramped limbs by turning over on her other side. He was sitting by the fire, his face flung into sharp relief by the leaping flames. It was a dark, sardonic face, harsh but not savage, for the moment not entirely drained of expression. The mask off, she saw he was a man at war with himself. Whatever he had done, however far he had strayed into roads of evil, there was some saving grace of good in his lost soul.

Yet he had tried to kill the man she loved. Perhaps his companion in crime had done it. All through the fear for herself that had been so acute ran the deeper dread for Gordon. She tried to build up defenses against despair. It could not be that he was dead. The second shot she had heard proved that he had not fallen a victim to the first one. The assassin had missed. Gordon would have been warned by it. Probably the second shot had come from the gun of her friend. Even Cheyenne had thought that likely. For a long time she lay awake troubled and disturbed. The sleep into which she fell at last was filled with dreadful dreams.

When Karen woke again Cheyenne was busy with the frying-pan and the coffee-pot. She pulled on her boots and walked through the trees to a trickle of a stream fresh from the snows above. After she had washed her face and hands as best she could, using her wisp of a handkerchief as a towel, she patted her hair into some order.

The sun was just breaking through the heavy morning

mist. Great lakes of fog lay massed in the deeps below, and out of them broke spires and islands gaunt and rocky. Farther to the right, where the jagged outline of the range rose higher, the pools of fog in the gorges were thinning beneath the streaming light. Soon the whole panorama would begin to clear. The opaque clouds banked in the cañon at her feet would vanish into mist.

Karen drew comfort from the analogy to her own situation. Last night a fog of fear had filled her world. There had not been even any twilight shadows in the gloom. But now the sun was out again. In the pines a noisy jay chattered gaily. Smoke rose from the friendly campfire where the bacon was simmering. Busy with her breakfast was a man. In the distorted lights of night his shadow at times had taken on the shape of a monster. Now she knew he was not that. He was a villain by all social standards. He had tried the short cuts of robbery and murder to gain wealth. But deep-hidden in all his viciousness lay a stratum of decency that made him draw a line he would not cross.

He called to her, 'Come and get it.' His voice was harsh, unfriendly.

'I'm so hungry I could eat a mail sack,' she told him cheerfully as she moved forward. 'Coffee—flapjacks—bacon. Food for a king.'

The man's dark face did not respond to her warmth. He poured coffee into her tin cup and filled her plate. The raspberry jam she had scorned he passed to her. But he had nothing to say. A heavy sullen silence had replaced the campfire talk of last night. Karen carried the burden of such conversation as there was. His contribution was limited to 'No' and 'Yes.' This adventure had gone sour to him. She thought she understood why. He had staked everything on one cut of the cards and lost. He had not been thorough villian enough to seize the stakes after he had failed to win.

During breakfast he volunteered only one remark. 'If you're not intending to use that carving knife you better put it back in the sack.'

Karen was disconcerted. That was exactly what she had meant to do as soon as she found the opportunity to get it back unobserved. The knife was still hidden in the folds of her blankets.

'If we're not going to stay here I suppose I had better do the dishes and pack,' she said, rising from where she sat. 'If you ever want a recommendation as a cook please refer to me. A swell breakfast.'

'No need to pack,' he said. 'We'll leave the plunder here.'

Karen waited, in her eyes an eager unspoken question.

'I'm taking you to town—or part way anyhow,' he con-

161

tinued harshly. 'I'll leave you with someone who will get you in with a car.'

'You don't know how glad I am,' she said in a low, warm voice. 'Of course I'll tell everybody you rescued me when I was a prisoner at the ranch.'

'Yeah!' he jeered. 'And who'll believe it? What d'you think Bud Cowell has been doing but saving face by spreading the news? After we left he was out of that hogan quicker than hell could scorch a feather.'

'But if I deny his story—if I say you did what I asked you to do——'

'Won't make any difference. Too late. It will hurt you and won't help me. They'll ask where we were all night. There's no answer to that. I'll have to light out of this country if I'm going to save my bacon. About this time the posses are starting out to collect me. Soon as you're off my hands I'll be pulling for the Rio Grande . . . I'll go rope and saddle.'

She watched him straddle away, rope in hand, a hardy and resolute scoundrel. The wish was strong in her that he might come through alive.

35. 'The Best Bet is the Heidemann Line Camp'

As GORDON STONE and Jack Turnbull raced across the back yard at the Bar B B they knew the ranch hands were pouring out of the kitchen like seeds squirted from a squeezed lemon. The fugitives had a start of fifteen or twenty yards, but before the darkness had swallowed them revolvers were barking furiously in the rear. Jack did not stop to return the fire, since hasty escape was imperative. At that distance, in the dim light of night, the shooting of the pursuers was random. If either of them should be hit, it would be by a chance bullet.

'Have to hit the gate farther down,' Jack told his friend. 'Can't risk getting hung up on the barbs.'

'Right,' Gordon agreed.

They were making for the big pasture where they had left their mounts. Jack reached the gate first and vaulted over it. A moment later Gordon was scudding after him into the mesquite. The drumfire of guns followed them.

Jack looked back. Vaguely he could see a mass of something swarming over the fence. The sound of voices drifted to him.

'They're still hell-bent to get us,' he panted. 'Hope we don't miss our broncs in all this brush.'

'More to the right,' Stone answered. 'Oughtn't to be far from here.'

'Over this way,' Jack called, not loudly. 'I see 'em.'

They pulled the slip knots and swung to the saddles. A man broke out of the darkness as they got into motion.

'Scare him,' Gordon said, and Jack turned in his seat to fire.

They plunged into the chaparral, paying no attention to the cactus spines that clutched at them or the branches that whipped their faces. Occasionally a revolver sounded, but they knew none of their pursuers were firing with any definite aim.

Through the brush they rode to the fence corner where they had left Buck Hayes. The Bar B B gunman had rolled around a good deal. They found him trying to cut the rope which bound his wrists on one of the barbs of the wire. So far he had managed to tear his hands a good deal more than the rope.

'Let me do that chore for you,' Jack said, and with his knife slashed the strands. From the man's mouth he removed the gag.

Hayes looked at his freed hands, then sullenly at Stone. 'What's it to be?' he asked. 'You fixin' to bump me off?'

Gordon found the revolver of the prisoner, which he had tossed into the brush after binding him. 'I'll borrow this permanently, if you don't mind. Left mine up at the ranch house . . . No, we're not exterminating you now. I suppose we ought to rid the world of such vermin, but we're not thorough enough. We'll ask a question or two. About your dear friend Cheyenne, who left you here alone to do a job too big for you. He didn't go back to the house. Where would he likely be?'

The sulky eyes of Hayes fastened on Gordon. He did not feel that he was out of the woods. After these men had got information from him they might pour bullets into his body and ride away. It was what he would have done if the situation had been reversed.

'How would I know where he went?' he asked thickly. 'The skunk lit out without saying a word to me. When I meet up with him——'

He left the sentence in the air, but the savage tone left no doubt of the meaning.

'You might guess,' Gordon suggested, his voice low but not at all reassuring. 'You don't like him. Nor us. If we should find him somebody will probably get hurt. That would suit you, wouldn't it?'

It would exactly suit him, Hayes thought. Moreover, it would be a very likely result of a meeting between these men and the one they evidently meant to hunt. Cheyenne was a fighter, ready to fight at the drop of a hat. Rather than surrender he would go to smoking as soon as he saw these fellows. Somebody would get killed. Maybe all three of them.

163

'How do I know you'll stick to what you say and not gun me?' the Bar B B man demanded.

'You don't,' Gordon told him. 'But you can use your bean. We've had chances to wipe out eight or ten of your outfit and we haven't done it. We're not killers except in self-defense.'

'Tom Webb,' said Hayes.

'Self-defense. He had his gun out blazing at me. I have no time to waste. Come clean—or don't.'

Hayes did not like the look in Stone's cold, hard eyes. The man was dangerously explosive. Better tell him what he could.

'I wouldn't know for sure,' the prisoner answered morosely. 'It would depend on what Cheyenne has in the back of his crazy nut. He might do anything. I been trying to figure it out. Maybe she hired him to throw down her uncle and take her to town.'

Gordon shook his head. 'That's out. If it had been that way she wouldn't have screamed. Say he was thinking of holding her for a ransom. Where would he hole up?'

'Somewheres around the Stevens Park country, I'd guess. There's a hundred pockets and ravines up thataway where he could hide—if he was outfitted with grub for a stay. But that's the catch. He can't have made any preparations.'

'So he would think of some place where he could buy or forage food. Where would that be?'

'Well, if it was me I'd go to the old Heidemann homestead line camp. He would have to pass somewheres near it, anyhow. Bud Cowell is stationed there. Cheyenne could get grub and blankets there.'

The Heidemann homestead had been taken up by a German of that name. It included two water holes Gilbert had needed. The Bar B B riders had hazed Heidemann plenty, but the old man was stubborn. He would not surrender his claim or sell it for a few dollars. While on his way to Barranca to make final proof he had been shot down by some party unknown. Later, by one of the coincidences not unusual, it had come into possession of Gilbert. Situated as it was in the foothills just above the plains, the Heidemann camp would be a logical place for Cheyenne to stop if he was heading for the Stevens Park country.

'What sort of fellow is Cowell?' Gordon inquired. 'Would he give Cheyenne what he wanted? Wouldn't he interfere to save Miss Gilbert?'

Jack answered. 'He would do whatever Cheyenne told him to do. Bud is weak as skim milk. He would whine some, but that is all. I'd been thinking about the Heidemann camp myself. Looks to me like a good bet. If he has left any grub there we'll have to borrow some ourselves. We're going to

164

have a helluva hunt. You'll think finding a needle in a hay-stack easy compared to digging Cheyenne out of that wild country.'

Gordon frowned, 'Point is whether he's there. There's a chance this is all a mare's nest in our minds. By now Cheyenne may have brought Miss Gilbert in safe to the ranch house. Gilbert wouldn't give him orders to take his niece to town, would he?'

'The girl showed up here unexpected,' Hayes volunteered sourly. 'Darned if I know why she came. But it sure wasn't to meet Cheyenne.'

'No. So Cheyenne couldn't have been deputed to escort her to Barranca. But why should he start to play a lone hand against Gilbert—if he has? Was he sore at the old man about anything?'

'Not far as I know. But Cheyenne lives under his hat mostly. He doesn't talk.'

Gordon slammed a fist into the palm of his other hand. 'Not a thing to go on but guesswork. Not a fact to build on.' Abruptly he flung a question at Hayes. 'Had Cheyenne been drinking?'

'Some, but not much. Curt gave us two drinks apiece.'

'Before he sent you out to ambush Gordon,' flashed Jack.

'If we go to Heidemann's and he hasn't been there we waste hours,' Stone said with angry impatience. 'I wish to God we had some kind of a trail to follow.'

'We'll have to make out with what we have. First, we know the direction they started. If Cheyenne isn't taking her to the ranch house he must have cut a fence at the other end of the pasture. That will do for a beginning.' Jack ticked off the possibilities on the fingers of his hand. 'If he took her to the house she is safe. Same if they went to town, or anywhere else under orders from Gilbert. We don't have to worry unless he's shelling his own corn. That would be a plumb idiotic thing to do, but we've got to remember that Cheyenne is a wild, uncontrolled devil. To hold her for ransom he would have to get her into the hills. So the thing narrows down considerable. Far as we are concerned the hills are our only bet.'

'Looks like,' Gordon agreed. 'Let's get going.' After he was in the saddle he swung round on Hayes. 'Get word to Ford and Gilbert about this quick as you can. Tell them to have Sheriff Scott send out posses. Ford can do that from the ranch too. If we get enough men combing the hills we'll jump up this fellow in some gulch or cañon.'

He spoke swiftly, jerkily. Jack was surprised. Usually Gordon was a cool customer, held a tight reign on his emotions. But something now was moving him profoundly, stirring him out of his customary quiet. It was of course anxiety for Karen. Turnbull was worried himself, but not to the extent that a fire of fear blazed in him and flung him off balance. He knew now that his friend loved Karen, though he had kept all evidence of it under an iron repression.

They rode across the pasture, reached the fence, and rode along it till they came to the cut strands of wire. Here they dismounted, and under what light there was studied the prints of the horses' hoofs.

'Heading toward the Heidemann line camp,' Jack said. 'We'll make time if we take that for granted now and follow a bee line.'

'Yes,' Gordon replied tensely.

He was already off at a gallop.

36. The Shadows of Darkness

As GORDON and Jack rode down the hill just above the line camp a light in the cabin went out.

'Going to bed or saying "*Adios*," ' Turnbull guessed.

They found Bud Cowell just swinging to the saddle. He blurted out the news.

'Miss Gilbert told me to get word to you,' he said to Gordon. 'Your getting here right now saved me a long ride. I'll hump right along to the Bar B B and tell Curt.'

'He knows.' Contempt was in Turnbull's level gaze, and when he spoke irony edged his words. 'The way you're all beat up, looks like you must of put up a terrific fight to save Miss Karen.'

'I'm a man of peace,' Bud said, aggrieved. 'Me, I don't even have a gun. I told Cheyenne folks wouldn't like it.'

Gordon brushed this aside. There was no use wasting time upbraiding a worm for not having a backbone. 'Did Cheyenne give any hint where he was going?' he demanded impatiently.

'No, sir, he didn't. But he wouldn't of took grub and blankets if he hadn't expected to camp in the hills, would he?'

'How long would the food he took last him?'

'Well, I wouldn't know exactly. Lemme see, they took——'

'Two days—three days—four?' Gordon snapped explosively.

'Well—three, say.'

'We'll take what grub you have left,' Jack said. 'How about blankets?'

'Cheyenne cleaned out the camp.'

'Any horse blankets at the barn?'

'Couple of old saddle blankets, I reckon. Kinda ragged.'

'Get them—in a hurry.'

Swiftly they packed what supplies they could find. Not ten minutes after their arrival they were vanishing into the darkness again. Cheyenne was less than twenty minutes ahead of them, Cowell had said in his first excited burst of news. That would give him half an hour now, but Stone realized with a heavy heart that there was practically no chance of finding the fugitives tonight. The tangle of hills into which they were riding was full of bypaths running into obscure ravines, hidden pockets, and wooded parks.

Given plenty of food, a rider like Cheyenne, who knew this district intimately, could keep on the dodge for weeks.

Hunting him was a job that called for patience, and for once Gordon had none of it. The anxiety in him was a consuming fire. He knew nothing about Cheyenne except that he was an unscrupulous villain who would kill for money, a bold and hardy devil not to be deterred by fear from any crime to which his will drove him. He had known scoundrels too clean of fiber to harm a good woman against her wish. If Karen had been kidnapped for ransome Cheyenne must have confederates, which would be a protection to her to a certain extent. A more appalling possibility was that he played a lone hand, driven by an urgent passion for the girl.

Gordon broke a long silence to fling a question at his friend.

'How well do you know Cheyenne?'

'Well enough to shoot at him but not well enough to say "Hello!" when we meet.'

'You wouldn't trust your sister with him!'

'No farther than I could throw a rope.'

His voice rough with disquietude, Gordon said, 'I don't think this is a kidnapping for money.'

'A man who would kill for money would do anything else in the world for it, wouldn't he?'

'He did not know she was coming to the pasture. Some crazy impulse must have led him to take her away.'

'Troubles are never as bad as you figure they're going to be,' Jack said gently, after consideration. 'There won't any harm come to her.'

'I wish I could be sure of that.'

Jack wished he were sure of it himself.

They were in rough country now and could not travel fast. Gordon found it necessary continually to curb his desire to push the horse. He reminded himself that it was of no use to hurry. It was not possible to go fast enough to outride his dread. After a time they would have to tie up until daybreak. It would be better not to be too far up into the hills at dawn. There would then be a chance of picking up the tracks of the two horses.

That love would enter his life was something for which Gordon had not bargained. He had come out of the peni-

167

tentiary an embittered man, with one corroding passion burning in his soul. A woman had given him warm and generous friendship, sweeping aside his surly resentment. She had been like rain and sunshine to parched and arid soil. In him had burgeoned a new spirit, one that had not nourished the noxious weeds of hatred and revenge. Nothing could come of his deep feeling for her except the quickening of his own being. He was a branded felon. That neither of them could ever forget. But at least, if God was good to him, he could pay in part his great debt to her.

Jack pulled up. 'Far enough for tonight. We're still on the trail to the Stevens Park country, but if we go much farther we'll have to begin making choices of which way to go. I say camp here.'

Stone dismounted heavily. He felt old and weary, discouragement weighting his shoulders. 'Might as well,' he agreed.

While Jack gathered wood for a fire Gordon picketed the horses. Sleep he gave no consideration. After Jack had rolled up in two saddle blankets he sat cross-legged, a scowl on his harsh face, staring hungrily into the flames. When his restlessness grew too great he rose and tramped a beat. The night seemed eternal. With the first flicker of gray in the eastern hill crotches he made breakfast and awakened his friend. The horses were saddled and packed while it was still not light enough to pick up a trail.

37. Cheyenne Goes on a Long Journey

THOUGH Cheyenne did not say so, Karen knew he was traveling fast in order to reach the plains before a posse blocked the entrance to the cañon by which they had come up from the foothills. His face was grim and lined. She noticed how warily he watched the trail ahead. Her anxiety was no less than his. That he was endangering his life by bringing her back she was aware, and she had remonstrated with him.

'I'm sure I can find my way back from here. You had better be heading for the border.'

'I brought you up here. I'll take you back.' He added, less harshly: 'I have to reach the desert anyhow. If I'm lucky we'll be in time. Likely we won't meet anyone. If we do, get as far from me as you can right away. I don't want you near when the fireworks begin.'

'If we meet anyone, let me talk to them. When I explain, they can't do anything to you.'

'Except shoot me into rag dolls,' he answered. 'I'm not hiding behind a woman's skirts. Get this right. If we bump into a posse there will be a fight. Yore job is to skedaddle and hunt cover.'

Karen was greatly distressed, not entirely because of her present situation. Always, beneath her surface thoughts, ran the dreadful doubt about Gordon. She could not believe he was dead. Surely God would not let him be killed just as he was beginning to get some joy out of life after all the years when he was buried. That would be too cruel. And yet such things happened. The shots she had heard might have marked his end.

She was thinking of him at the moment when they rounded a bend in the cañon and came face to face with him.

In a queer, shaky voice she cried 'Gordon!' She forgot the enmity between the two men, the fact that one was the hunter and the other the hunted. All she thought of was that he had come back to her out of the valley of the shadow. Arms outstretched, she rode forward to meet him.

Cheyenne swung sharply to the right, so that she would not be between him and his foe. Swiftly he raised his rifle and fired, with no time to take aim.

'Keep away from me!' Gordon cried to Karen, and slipped from the saddle.

She was beside him in a moment, her arms around his neck. 'I thought—I was afraid——' The words ended in a sob.

Gordon caught her wrists and dragged her arms down. 'Get away,' he ordered harshly. 'Can't you see he may kill you too?'

The girl's mind came back to the present danger. She saw that Cheyenne was behind his horse, rifle in hand, watching for another chance to shoot.

'Wait! Wait!' she cried. 'It's all right. Let me explain.' Desperately she clung to her lover.

'Come out and fight, fellow!' Cheyenne cried savagely.

'No, no! He didn't hurt me, Gordon. He was bringing me back. Wait and listen, both of you.'

'What d'you mean, bringing you back?' Stone asked.

'I mean he helped me get away from the ranch—from my uncle and Curt Ford. We hid out in the hills—got food and blankets from a line camp. Now he is taking me to Barranca.'

'That's not true, Karen. You're trying to save him. But Cowell said he was taking you against your will.'

'I didn't understand, Gordon. I thought because he is one of the Bar B B men he meant to harm me. But he has treated me fine. You must believe me. You must.'

From back of his horse Cheyenne flung out a taunt. 'How long you going to hide behind a woman, Stone? Come out from there a-smoking.'

169

'Hold your horses!' Gordon snapped. 'I want to get the truth of this. If you've done no harm to Miss Gilbert any other quarrel I have with you will wait.'

'Make up yore mind,' Cheyenne scoffed. 'Either way will suit me. But don't go to sleep over it.'

While they talked the two men watched each other vigilantly. If Cheyenne fired again Gordon meant to run out into the open where Karen would not be endangered.

'Listen!' the girl cried. 'Both of you. Give me a chance to explain. Please. Please.'

'Say yore piece, lady.' Cheyenne's rifle barrel rested on the saddle. He was ready for any break that might occur. 'But make it kinda brief. I got an engagement for supper tonight a hundred miles from here.'

Karen told her story, giving it a color wholly favorable to Cheyenne. There were joints in it which did not fit, but Gordon did not examine these too closely. Whatever the gunman's original purpose had been, he had apparently voluntarily given it up.

Some questions Gordon asked the other man. 'I don't get this. Is it some of Gilbert's underground work? Or have you split with him?'

'I'm through with the old wolf, but I haven't been fixed so I could tell him yet.'

'He gave you a job to do last night and you ran out on it. Why?' Gordon's voice had the snap of a whiplash.

'Are you complaining because I ran out on it?' Cheyenne drawled.

'I'm asking you why?'

'The young lady butted in, so I took a ride with her. Too bad she didn't arrive ten minutes later. You're a lucky bird. I'll say that.'

Gordon said harshly, after a moment's reflection: 'Your story won't go down with Gilbert. He'll have to hang your hide on the fence because he won't dare to leave you alive. And last night's damn foolishness gives him a chance. His posses will have orders to kill on sight.'

'I'm right at the head of the class with you,' Cheyenne claimed sardonically. 'I had done guessed that too.'

'The odds are you'll never get to the border alive, if that's where you are aiming to go.'

'About ten to one against me,' the cool villain hazarded hardily.

'I'd meant to shoot you down on sight myself.'

'Me, the hero who rescued the lady from the ogre's castle?' Cheyenne said in mock surprise. 'You surprise me, Mr. Stone! But of course if you still feel that way——'

'We'd better get going,' Gordon interrupted. 'Every minute

counts for you. Just below we'll pick up Jack Turnbull. He went up a side ravine, but your shot will bring him back.'

Jack was just emerging from a little gulch into the main cañon when they reached the junction. He gave a whoop of joy at sight of Karen, but it died down into an astonished question when he recognized Cheyenne.

'We're all one nice, happy family,' replied the gunman with ironic derision. 'Traveling through the sand, to the happy land, as the old song goes. With heaps of Christian love in our hearts.'

'If we meet a posse our story is that we've arrested Cheyenne,' explained Gordon.

'When they see this Winchester I'm toting they'll believe that,' Cheyenne mentioned.

'Somebody might wise me to what this is all about,' suggested Turnbull in bewilderment.

Karen told him on the way down the gulch.

It was when they came out into the foothills above the line cabin that they caught sight of the posse bearing down on them not fifty yards distant. Five of the men were Bar B B riders, Curt Ford at their head. The other three were from John Fleming's ranch.

'Give me that Winchester,' Gordon said quickly to the hunted man. 'I'll make it stick that you are my prisoner.'

The eyes of the outlaw had narrowed. There was in them the look of a hunted wild animal who meant to go down fighting.

'Hands off, Stone,' he snarled. 'I wouldn't trust Curt an inch of the road.'

'I'll tell him how it is!' Karen cried.

'Fine,' growled the outlaw. 'But just the same I'm going on a long journey.'

He was at the right of the little party. His foot touched the belly of the horse he was riding and the animal moved a few steps, so that he was about ten yards from the others.

Ford gave a triumphant yell. 'Spread out, boys. We've got him.'

'Don't shoot!' Gordon cried out. 'He didn't hurt Miss Gilbert. He was bringing her back to Barranca. All he did was help her escape from the ranch.'

The only answer Ford gave was a jeering laugh. He and his men continued to encircle their prey.

Little Lincoln Conway shouted a protest. 'Hold on, boys. Let's get the right of this.'

To Ford, closing the trap on him, Cheyenne shouted an order: 'That'll be far enough, Curt.'

'Throw down that rifle, you villain,' the foreman answered.

At the same moment he lifted his own Winchester and fired.

Cheyenne reeled in the saddle, steadied himself, took aim, and pulled the trigger. A moment later the weapon clattered down among the stones, an instant before the body of its owner plunged to the ground.

The foreman too dropped his rifle. With both hands he clung to the horn of his saddle. On his face was a look of agonizing pain.

One of his men ran to help him from the saddle.

'He's killed me,' Ford groaned.

Karen ran to Cheyenne and knelt beside him. She propped his head in her arms.

'Are you badly hurt?' she asked.

He said, grimly, 'Plenty.' Then: 'I've got something to say. Call the boys.'

When they were gathered round, except two of them who were with Ford, he spoke, with growing difficulty.

'I've come to the end of the trail, boys. No complaints. I've been a plumb ornery devil. Listen to me. Gilbert hired me to kill Linc Conway, but he got into the hills before I reached him. Last night Lyn and Curt laid a trap to kill Stone. I was to do the job. It didn't work out on account of this young lady here.... It was Curt Ford bumped off Harrison Brock. I was in it with him to steal the payroll, but not in the killing. Lyn fixed it up to lay the blame on young Stone because the boy was in his way. That's the truth, as sure as that I'm headed for hell. I swear it.' He leaned back, his head sinking lower, his breath short.

'Is there anything we can do to make you more comfortable?' Karen asked gently.

There was a glimmer of an ironic smile on his face. 'Not a thing. I'm ... on my way out.'

Ford too was fatally shot. After Cheyenne had died they carried the foreman into the cabin of the line rider. He asked for a doctor and for Glenna. Before he passed away he confessed the murder of Brock.

38. The End of the Beginning

THE confessions of Cheyenne and the foreman ended the reign of Gilbert in Barranca and the neighboring country. The district attorney, Arthur Driscoll, made a right-about-face and indicted the big man as an accessory after the fact to the murder of Brock. A supple politician, the young lawyer had no intention of being sacrificed to a lost cause. He filled the newspapers with bitter invective against the man who had betrayed his confidence.

Gilbert saw the handwriting on the wall. His world was full of enemies, men whom he had trampled down and ridden over roughshod. Temporarily impotent, their hatred of him had never abated. Now their day had come. Even those who had been his allies were currying favor by turning up evidence against him. He fought with his back to the wall, and knew he was doomed. A long term in the penitentiary awaited him.

The day his trial began he shot himself.

Three days before that time he had made a new will leaving all he owned to the city for the building and maintenance of a hospital. Karen he cut off with a dollar.

She was devoutly glad her uncle had not left his money to her. What she could have done with it she did not know. It would not have been possible for her to have kept it for herself, since she felt that all of it was tainted with injustice and crime.

For three months she had not seen Gordon Stone. He was busy on his uncle's range, rebuilding a property that had been of declining value. He obtained a new government lease of grazing land and made arrangements for a renewal of the mortgage. Not once did he go near Karen.

Before his death, in the hope of placating public opinion so that he might escape without a trial, Gilbert had turned over to Karen her ranch and other interests. She had made Jack Turnbull her manager, and she spent much time on the place renovating the house. It had fallen into bad repair, since her uncle had never spent a dollar keeping up the house and barns. The paper was falling from the discolored walls. A new roof was necessary. Other repairs had to be made.

'Have I done something to offend your friend Mr. Stone?' she asked Jack one day after they had discussed the purchase of some Herefords.

'No. I asked him about that the other night when we met. He's for you both ways from the ace.'

'I can see he must be,' she said dryly. 'The last time I saw him was the day we all came out of the cañon together.'

'He's right busy,' Jack defended.

'Yes. Too busy to waste time on me.' She flushed, and was annoyed at herself for the access of color. 'I suppose he thinks I'm a forward hussy. When I first saw him that day I was so glad to meet someone I knew that I practically threw myself into his arms. You might explain to him that almost anybody would have been the victim. I didn't pick on him personally. It was only that I had been under a great strain and the reaction rather unnerved me.'

'He knows that.'

'From the first time we met he disapproved of me. I was a busybody, he thought.'

'No, he didn't think that, and he doesn't now.' Jack hesitated a moment. 'I tell you what's eating him, if you want to know.'

'Yes, I would.'

'All right, lady. You've asked for it. Understand I'm just guessing, but my guess is one hundred per cent correct. He's in love with you.'

A pulse of happy excitement beat in her throat. 'He shows it in a strange way.'

'He thinks he has no right to show it at all. The way he looks at it his prison record bars him from making a move. It wouldn't be possible for him to marry you, even if you cared for him. So he stays away.'

She said quietly, 'I thought he had been proved innocent.'

'Yes, but he thinks the years in the penitentiary can't be wiped out.'

Karen went to bed that night happier than she had been for months. It was long before she fell asleep, and when she did it was with a definite plan in mind.

She went to see John Fleming at a time when she knew his nephew would not be at home. The old man listened, chuckling, and said, 'You little devil, you mean to get him if you can, don't you?'

'Yes,' she told him. 'You're wishing me luck, aren't you?'

He nodded. 'If I were younger I wouldn't.'

'That's a nice compliment,' she said, dimpling. She rose to go and shook hands. 'You'll be sure to phone me.'

'Yes, I don't like the tarnation things, but Gord had to have one put in. Sure, I'll help you steal a good man's freedom from him.'

'To get him something better, we both hope,' she amended.

The telephone call came next day. Karen got in her car and drove down till she could see the main road. A man on horseback jogged along it. She picked him up with field glasses. The man was Gordon Stone.

Her car passed him five minutes later. Around a bend in the road, three hundred yards in front of him, she stopped, let as much air out of a front tire as she could, and jabbed a knife into the rubber side wall.

When Gordon reached the scene three minutes later she was hauling tools out of the tool box on the running-board. Already she had donned her coveralls.

She said, as once before she had done eons ago: 'Please, I can't seem to manage this. If you wouldn't mind helping me, sir——'

174

Gordon took off the tire and replaced it with a spare.

'Awf'lly good of you to help me,' she said. 'This happened once before, didn't it? I suppose you think I do it on purpose.'

'Not exactly,' he smiled. 'But I'm glad to be of service.'

'My name is Karen Gilbert,' she mentioned.

'Not news,' he said. 'We've met before, you know.'

'So we have, but I thought you had forgotten it.' Her brave eyes stabbed straight at him.

'I've been busy,' he answered awkwardly.

'So I hear.' Straight and slender, she faced him gallantly, chin up. He did not know how her heart was hammering against her ribs. 'I did make this puncture on purpose. With a knife. I wanted to ask you a question. Will you marry me?'

Stuck dumb, he stared at her, a vision of gracious young loveliness, to him the most desirable woman in the world. The blood in his veins pounded. A warm glow flooded his body. He clamped down on desire with an iron will.

'I can't,' he said hoarsely.

'Why can't you?' she demanded, and did not wait for an answer. 'If I'm wrong—if you don't love me—it will be kind of you to get on your horse and ride away . . . for always. But if you do care for me . . . Oh, please stay.'

Her voice was so low it was almost a murmur. Every fiber in him yearned for her. She had torn down his defenses. It would be cruelly humiliating to leave her now without telling the truth.

'God knows I love you!' he cried, his voice rough with feeling. 'But I can't marry you because I have been a branded felon. Your friends——'

She interrupted, her whole being quick with vibrant life. 'My friends! They would like you as they do me, and if they didn't they would not be my friends. All my life I shall be an unhappy woman if I am not your wife. I have never loved a man before. I'll never love another. Don't let silly pride stand between us, if you do love me. Everybody knows you were innocent. Isn't that enough?'

He said, 'Our children, if we had any, would know their father had been a convict. Wouldn't that make you unhappy?'

'They would know their father was a strong man who had fought a good fight against a terrible injustice. They would be proud of him, as I am.' She held out her hands, in a gesture tender and giving. 'Oh, Gordon, you mustn't fight against fate. You are my mate. We both know it. I'll never let you go.'

Into his harsh face came an expression she had never seen before. Love broke the lines as a spring thaw does the river ice.

'I give up!' he cried. 'We'll belong to each other forever and ever.'

And so at last they came after trouble and heartache to each other's arms.